White Light

Praise for *White Light*

"This first novel by Vanessa Garcia, the 2009 runner-up for the Rolex Mentor/Protege Initiative for Literature, has indirectly rewarded that project in its world-wide search for fresh talent in the arts. A subtly woven network of relationships, it seduces with its lyrical pace and texture, tender and poignant, yet unsentimental. An artiste's 'walk in the woods' that gently takes the reader by the hand."

—Wole Soyinka, Nobel Laureate,
author of *You Must Set Forth at Dawn* and *Outsiders*

"A relentless engine, told in rich, smart prose and lucid detail—equal parts elegy and portrait of an artist. A lush, vibrant portrayal of the creative process, a daughter's love, and the unstoppable maelstrom of grief."

—*Kirkus* (starred review)

"*White Light* is a wonderfully generous creation, including a myriad of worlds while never blurring the firm line with which the author is always in control. The world of visual arts, of a Cuban-American daughter and her difficult father, of food—its joys and terrors—of a young woman's trying to navigate her way in a world that offers her simultaneously too few and too many possibilities. It is a throbbingly original achievement."

—Mary Gordon, author of *The Love of My Youth* and *Spending*

"Vanessa Garcia's brilliant first novel is a fresh contribution to the American portrait of an artist, following a young Cuban-American woman through a journey of personal disaster juxtaposed against professional success. *White Light* illuminates the complex assimilation of past into present, of heritage into culture, of life into the sort of art that is lasting, meaningful, and necessary."

—A. Manette Ansay, author of *Vinegar Hill* and *Blue Water*

"Many-tongued and of mixed-media, *White Light* is a novel as much about losing a father as about constructing a self through art—and as vibrant for its intelligence as for its emotions, colors, and pure passion."

—Jane Alison, author of *The Sisters Antipodes*

White Light

Vanessa Garcia

Shade Mountain Press
Albany, New York

Shade Mountain Press
P.O. Box 11393
Albany, NY 12211
www.shademountainpress.com

Garcia, Vanessa.
White light / Vanessa Garcia
ISBN 978–0–9913555–4–9 (pbk. : alk. paper)
1. Women painters — Fiction. 2. Cuban American families — Fiction. 3. Children
of immigrants — Family relationships — United States — Fiction. 4. Miami (Fla.) —
Fiction.

Printed in the United States of America by McNaughton & Gunn, Inc.
17 16 15 14   4 3 2 1

Illustration Credits:
Cover art: Detail from *Mariel*, © 2011 by Vanessa Garcia.
Icarus: © 2015 Succession H. Matisse/Artists Rights Society (ARS), New York.
Guernica: © 2015 Estate of Pablo Picasso/Artists Rights Society (ARS), New York.
Photographic Archives Museo Nacional Centro de Arte Reina Sofia.
Cathedral: © 2001–2003 by Vanessa Garcia.

Author photo: Ozzie Rodriguez

Shade Mountain Press is committed to publishing literature by women.

For my father

Painting Is (Not) Dead

Panel 1

Harry Rand: Why do people become painters?
Friedensreich Hundertwasser: For different reasons. True painters because they want to be priests, because it is a kind of religious activity.

Sometimes you wake up with a hole in your heart and you're not sure why. It's a circle, carved by something you can't touch, something that opens up in your sleep and wakes you up, hungry. This morning, before I got on the plane, it was like that, like those lagoons left by old, erupted volcanoes. They pull things and people into them because the core of the earth, after it shoots out its molten lava, is as hungry as I am.

My nerves are shot, as if the ends of them have brushed up against coca leaves and are standing on edge now, porcupine-like, pricking me under my skin. Must be why I've had on-again, off-again goose bumps since last night.

I can't come back with nothing.

If something big doesn't happen on this trip, I'll have to leave Tony, leave town, go back to school. Teach.

God, please don't make me a high school art teacher.

My poor mother doesn't even know where I am. My sister either. I'm sick of bringing them down from all the "almosts" and "maybes," the *nearly* solo shows, the hairline fractures between me and success, that line between being a total loser and being a successful artist. I'm starting to hate that word: artist. It's embarrassing.

Only Tony knows where I am, dropped me off at the airport. And Lee. This is all Lee's doing to begin with. She said we could settle it over the phone, if I "really couldn't make it." But I knew what that meant: another artist would eat smashed, stepped-on, black gum off the subway platform for the chance. Chew and swallow and smile. That's how Lee is—she always makes sure her subliminals are obvious. She's also totally old-school. Been like that from the start. There are dealers you never talk to, hardly ever see, some you never even meet; do it all over email. But Lee's different. She likes setting up coffees and cocktails and power brunches. All of which is why I said I'd go, come up to New York, see what she wanted. That, and she was paying for my ticket. I didn't want to risk it, didn't want me not flying up to be the reason why it didn't happen. Whatever "it" was. She wasn't very clear. All she said was, "If you get your painter ass up here, it could change your life." And my life needs some change, in every sense of the word. In my pockets, definitely.

So here I am, pulling my orange backpack from my shoulders, up and into the overhead bin. I got the backpack in Amsterdam a while ago. It gives me a feeling of satisfaction and loserhood at the same time. Satisfaction because it's been so many places with me, makes me feel like I know something about the world. Loserhood because it's also the backpack that served to bring home every painting I failed to sell.

A few years ago I'd decided to submit work to a bunch of group shows outside Miami and New York, because Miami and New York kept shafting me. And one after another, galleries in Barcelona, Amsterdam, Santo Domingo, and San Francisco chose me for their "juried group shows." The elation at any kind of invitation covered up the fact that I had to hit each country on my own dime and lug back out whatever I didn't sell—which was everything. Which equals: Loserhood.

I was trying to convince Tony it was an "investment," a building of my CV, but I could tell what he was thinking: *She's never gonna make it. She's being irresponsible, not saving any money. She's too old for this. I can never marry her.*

And then Lee came along, and the possibility of a contract with a real New York gallery, a respected one.

Lee had the potential to transform my life—Oprah makeover-style—with a snap of her finely manicured fingers. Get me and my work in front of collectors who drop twenty grand if their interior designer tells them it goes with their rug. Or the snootier collectors, the best kind, searching for someone to "discover." For now, though, there's just this, a nervous curiosity about what she wants and stale airplane oxygen clinging to my lungs. Looking through my wallet, I realize I don't even have enough dough to buy a morning-glory Bloody Mary. At least I have an aisle seat. Time to sit here and pretend to read as everyone trickles into their seats, squirming by me.

The guy sitting across the aisle in the row in front of me seems even more antsy than I probably do. He's wearing an olive-green jacket that keeps catching my eye with peripheral movement. The guy's really young, maybe twenty, twenty-two. Bearded. Black, Middle Eastern watery eyes that look a little like the night sky after it rains. Sparkles here and there when his dark pupils catch glints of his reading light. If he weren't such a live wire, he'd be kind of handsome.

I look down at my *Art in America*, ignore him—try to, anyway. Except that his green jacket keeps whaling around and flinching. He's looking up and down the aisle now. Up and down, up and down. Rubbernecking. The kid has a massive book in his lap I can't quite catch the title of. The thing is a tome, could knock someone out flat with that brick. Jesus, I hope it's not the Koran.

He gets up and goes to the bathroom at the front of the plane. Sits down. Then goes to the bathroom again, this time at the back of the plane. We're about to take off. The flight attendant leads him back to his seat. I put away my magazine, and I realize that, all of a sudden, I'm nervous about this guy. Maybe it's because he's wearing that jacket and I'm Cuban-American, and anything that resembles green fatigues does something to my psyche. Maybe it's something else, the slant of his eyes. What's he doing? He sits down again. Gets back up. The flight attendant comes by and asks him to sit still, to please buckle up. We're reminded, over the loudspeaker, to please make sure all electronic devices are turned off. I check my phone. The kid's leg starts to shake. The guy next to me taps me on my knee—a suit, *Wall Street Journal* in hand. "What's wrong with that guy?" he asks. I have no idea, I tell him. We're trying not to stare at the kid. The suit folds his *Wall Street Journal* until it crumples into a pocket of news that's already old and expired, gaining obsolescence by the half-second.

"Should I say something?" I ask him quietly, trying not to make a fuss.

"Somebody has to, I think," the suit says.

Which is when my heart starts to beat like an enormous, swelling, red balloon inside my chest. Ba-boom, ba-boom. I'm being racist. I'm a jackass. You'd think an "artist" would be more enlightened. What a stupid word. I'm an educated person, right, I shouldn't think that just because the guy looks like he's from… Maybe he's just—

The kid gets up again, stands in the middle of the aisle. Sits back down.

Ba-boom. Ba-boom.

"We have to do something," says the suit. He's growing agitated, his freckled face turning paler than it already was to begin with.

Why didn't I tell my mother where I was going? I don't even think she knows Tony's number, and Tony won't know anything's happened until he sees it all over the news. And Lee. Lee's going to think I stood her up. And Leo, who I haven't seen in forever, is going to wonder why I never got in touch, to meet up after my meeting, like I'd promised over email. I should've at least told Nina I was going to New York, maybe she'd have come along, had a sister-trip with me or something. But no, because then she'd be here right now, in danger. And Dad, when was the last time I saw Dad? Even talked to him? I'm a shit daughter, we have a shit relationship. We have a *shit* relationship—

"I'm going to tell the flight attendant something," I tell the suit.

"I think you should," he says. He looks like he's about to throw up.

Ba-boom. Ba-boom. Ba-boom. All the way down the aisle.

"See that man over there?" I tell the flight attendant, trying to keep my voice calm. "The guy with the green jacket?"

The flight attendant looks at me like I'm annoying him.

"Listen, he's been acting really weird, he's freaking everybody out. He keeps getting up and sitting down and he's, I don't know, please, just go over and look and see, you'll see he's acting very strangely—"

"Well, he's definitely freaking *you* out, miss," he says, continuing to prep the drink cart. "We'll see what we can do."

The flight attendant stays very cool, practically rolling his eyes at me. This must happen to him a million times a day, I get it. But what if this is the real thing? I don't know what else to do and I don't want to make a show, so I go back to my seat.

When I reach my aisle, the suit's eyes question me.

"I told them," I say.

"You don't think they'd do the same thing all over again, do you? Same tactic. That'd be stupid, right?"

I guess it would be stupid. They wouldn't ram another plane into—

The flight attendant is standing in front of the kid, with the drink cart now. The kid orders something, but I can't hear his voice. Then I see the flight attendant is reaching for a Budweiser.

"The kid ordered a beer," I say to the suit. "That's a good sign."

"Yeah, that's true, they don't drink, right?" he whispers.

"Can I see your passport, sir?" The flight attendant asks the kid, before handing over the beer.

"Good, good. They're taking precaution," says the suit.

Then the flight attendant hands the kid his beer and it's our turn to order our beverages. Suit and I remain vigilant. We order ginger ale.

An hour goes by quicker than I realize, and half of one of those stupid romantic comedies they play has taken its course, when the kid, who's been staring straight ahead for a while, starts to look back and forth again. And then because I'm looking straight at him, he gives me a big smile. "I kind of love Jennifer Aniston," he says, pointing at the screen. "She's hot. Plus, you know, I think she's a good actress. I know that sounds stupid, but it's true, man. Rachel was a great character. She was hilarious."

He says all of this with a perfect American accent. The kid is American. He's talking about *Friends*, for God's sake. The suit next to me starts cracking up and the kid thinks it's because he agrees with the Jennifer Aniston thing. "Right? Am I right?" says the kid with frat boy intonation.

I feel deflated, like a complete and total fool. The kid's just nervous. Maybe he just doesn't like flying. Maybe he's got a big meeting, like me. Wait till I tell Leo. What a ridiculous misunderstanding, what a ridiculous person I am. I'm laughing a little too, now. Nervous laughter.

"I like Ross," I say. "He was the best character on *Friends*."

"David Schwimmer," says the kid, nodding. "Yeah, he was good too."

I flush pink with shame. The suit and I are embarrassed to look at each other. The suit stretches his hands in front of him, grabbing for the news again, shutting himself off to further conversation. So the kid talks to me instead.

"Did you watch the movie?" asks the kid.

"No, I've been trying to avoid them lately because I overreact," I say, fumbling through the words a little, but trying to be cool. "You know what they say about planes, that, um, that you cry more and laugh more. I get hysterical. Especially if I drink wine, then I know it's the end. Something to do with, I can't remember totally, but something about the oxygen level, or disorientation—"

"Or just plain plane nerves, man," he says, chortling. "Ha. I punned."

A statement that makes me realize the kid's in college, probably a freshman, and that the book he had on his lap earlier was probably some Russian novel he's been assigned, or a massive chemistry textbook.

"No, seriously," he continues, "it's scary to fly now. I spaz out. And it's not like the stewardesses are hot anymore either. The one that came by earlier hasn't shaved her legs in, like, months. Scruffy. Girls at school are like that too. I don't get it."

"Feminism," I say, "I guess." I smile and, not sure what to follow with, I start to stand, deciding I should pretend to go to the bathroom, even though I could've probably waited until we landed.

I kick myself all the way to the bathroom, feeling dumb for my fear, sad about it even, regretting all those hours of CNN and, just to get the other side of things, Fox. All those traffic jams filled with NPR streaming on the car radio reminding us that there are still terrorist operatives living and learning inside and outside the country. Red alerts, orange alerts, yellow alerts. Take off your shoes, lift up your hands, x-ray, scan, search. Bend over. "Better safe than sorry" robotically looping in everyone's mind like neon ticker-tape flashing headline news.

By the time I get back from the bathroom, after standing in line fifteen minutes, the kid is fast asleep, mouth wide open, hands folded on his lap. The suit is too. Both of them sound asleep. Suit's even snoring a little.

Soon enough, we're zooming in on the city from ten thousand feet in the air. Looking down at all those street grids, I feel calmer, less heart-punching ba-boom, but I still feel the hole in my heart from this morning. That hasn't changed. An hour ago I thought I was going to die, and now I'm pretty sure I'm going to live to see another day. But the hole's still there. There's no sense of real relief in that department, which is desperately unsettling. What's wrong with me?

There it is, spread out before me—the freefall between me and the messy muck of being in the city again. I hate New York. Because when you're there, inside the grid, you can't see the whole picture, just what lies in front of you. You can get lost. Not like painting, where whether you're inspired to the point of bliss or you think you're losing control, the canvas is always there—whole in front of you like a map—and you're the one drawing lines of perspective. You can always find your way out. That's the power of painting.

Landing in LaGuardia all alone, it's cold for September. I try not to look at the suit or the kid I took for a terrorist as I brush by everyone on my way out of the plane. I go straight, follow the signs to the exit, out the door, onto the glittery sidewalk. I forgot what this felt like, the sharp invisible burn through your clothes, going straight for the bone. I zip my jacket, wrap my scarf, and off I go onto the M60 into Manhattan. Every once in a while a blush rushes through me when I flash back to telling the flight attendant he had to watch out for the kid. I can't help but feel like an idiot, like I swallowed the same pill everyone else did.

Forget being independent, individualistic, all those "American" things that used to be strong and good, where the "American" and "Artist" in me melded together—at those traits, those words. I knew I'd have to respond to the attack as an artist, I knew that right away, that would come eventually. But what I'm finding is that responding to what happened to me as a person is harder, harder personally than professionally, because when I think about being in New York that day, not that long ago, and I remember the immobility of it all, how time froze over like in some superhero movie where Gotham stops in its tracks, when I remember that—the virtually impossible made real—it's almost okay to be irrational about the whole thing.

Regardless, I've got to stop hashing this over in my head, put some sort of clarity in my stride, start concentrating on the meeting now. That's why I'm here, isn't it? Not to go backwards in time, not to revisit the past but to move toward the future.

We ride straight through Queens. The houses with Christmas lights still on, even in September; nothing's changed. Strolling through Harlem—an Old Navy now near the Apollo—and then there I am on 110th Street, getting on the subway, on my way to Chelsea to see Lee.

On the subway, I recognize the same homeless people from when I used to live here, mad with the loneliness of this jam-packed, city-slicked, Manhattan freak show. Here, nobody cares if your mind's cohesion is coming apart like the spine-glue of an old book. Now I remember why I left on that "six-month break" three years ago and never came back. You know you have to leave when the bums start talking to you. Usually they talk to themselves, and occasionally to each other, but sometimes they find a twin soul on the subway, and when that soul started to be mine, that scared me more than anything in the world.

In the early days, it was okay. I was a wanderer and the Village was the shell I could bring to my ear—listening there to the whole of the ocean. But all that changed. Soon it was 2000 and I was living in Washington Heights and then it was 2001. Seven years in New York had taken the wind out of me. I was sandwiched between drunks and immigrants without hope, people who had all sorts of things wrong with them from the rich to the ditch of poverty, and suddenly the idyllic landscape of bohemia turned to Gotham, as the world went up in smoke and buildings got blown down like they were paper models in a college architecture class. Shock. And all I wanted was some fruit—some hope—the sweet juice of paradise trickling down my chin, but nowhere in this whole damned wasteland could I find an orange. And soon September turned to winter and the world collected more disorder, and though the broken glass and paper eventually got picked up, the blizzards blew and I couldn't take it anymore.

Funny how the past rushes by you while you're on the train. 23rd Street stop now. Chelsea. Out of the subway. And, air. My phone ringing three paces into the cold.

"*Gordita.*"

It's Tony. He's calling, I can't believe it. He's never done this before while I'm away. It's like he prefers to completely disconnect, which always makes me feel abandoned. We had a big fight about it before I left. I brought up marriage, how much I wanted it, and he brought up how much he "just didn't feel it," wasn't sure it was "in the cards" for him. He thinks it's because I'm jealous or insecure that I want him to call me while I'm away, but it's not that. I just like to know I have roots in people.

Lately, I've been feeling like Tony could just disappear one day. He doesn't kiss me the same way he used to and I'm scared he doesn't get the ups and downs that go with real growth. That he'll just leave on a down, in search of another up with somebody else.

"*Hola, mi amor,*" I say.

"*Cómo estás?* Are you going to the meeting now?"

"Yes. Right now." My voice is breathy as I walk briskly toward the gallery, which is almost in sight. I think about telling him about the plane incident, but I decide not to, better to just keep moving.

"*Suerte, gordita.*"

"Thanks, *mi amor.* And you? How's everything down there?"

"Good, good. Everything is good. Same ol' same ol'—making money." And then, as if to add a little spice: "I'm going sailing later."

"I'm jealous. Tell the Captain I send my love."

The Captain, who introduced us: a seventy-year-old Egyptian with a PhD in some kind of plant study or another, and a love for the sea. One day, at an opening, that was it: "Veronica, this is Tony. Tony, Veronica."

"He asked me about you, but I told him that you were away."

"I'm sure he likes it this way better anyway, just the boys."

"Maybe, but when you come back we should go together."

"That would be nice, it's been a while."

I think of Tony on the sea, how he loves it. It's a false sense of freedom he has on that boat. And really that's the big difference between us—my freedom is real, somewhere inside me, not linked to motion or to a boat, or some pretend adventure. Or maybe I'm just kidding myself. Tony doesn't like roots, doesn't think he needs to be watered. In fact, I don't think he thinks of himself as a plant at all.

"I'm sort of nervous," I tell him.

"*Dale,* you're going to be great *gordita, dale.*" Tony's trying to be supportive, I can tell. Usually he thinks these trips are nonsense, but this one's different and he knows it. His voice is calm and confident, the soothing voice of peace and reason to my high-pitched, passionate, outward driving, inner-sounding yawp. Even though we've only been together about three years, sometimes I wonder how I got along without him.

"Okay, *besitos*," I say, blowing him a kiss over the sound waves. "*Nos vemos mañana.*" I don't wait for an "I love you." Those are as rare as ripe dragon fruit, but when they come, they're extraordinary. I'll have to do without one today.

By the time I click the phone off, I've already walked two quick blocks. I cross my fingers so hard they go white at the knuckles. A wave rises from my belly and I feel like throwing up. My breath begins to shorten. And there are the goose bumps again. What if I fail? What if I go in there and talk to Lee and whatever it is she wants, I fail at? What if it's how it always is — close, but no cigar. What about Plan B?

There is no Plan B.

There has never really been a Plan B. How to go about being a graphic artist, or making billboards or magazine covers, or becoming a high school art teacher. I don't have the map for that kind of thing. The only grid I know is on the canvas, or in the plans for an installation.

Echoing in my ears like the aftermath of bells, following the beat of my footsteps: *You will make it, Veronica.* The voice of a thousand teachers, all telling me, *You can really paint. Keep painting. No matter what you do, keep painting.* Tony's voice, on the other hand: *We agree it's very unlikely, right? That it's one in a million, the ones who actually make it.* My father: *What about company logos? You can make a living off of making logos.* Logos — the logic of capitalism. Branding. My father would love it if my work was on the side of a bottle of detergent. He'd probably stand in the aisle at the supermarket and announce to people that his daughter had designed the package for the newest Clorox cleaner.

What about me? Can Lee brand me? And all of this, for what? What if nothing comes of it except a couple of dirty marks on canvas? What does it *really* matter anyway — did it matter on the plane just now, when I thought it might all be over? What if canvas is supposed to remain white? What if I'm just dirtying everything?

Shit. The shortness of breath hasn't been this bad since the fourth grade, when I ran out of the linen closet I used to hide in to ask Mom for help. My first panic attack. This feeling right now, walking to the gallery, and the childhood feeling are almost exactly the same. Except I have more control now; I know it won't kill me. Could the hole in the heart be from then? Could it be that old?

Fourth grade. I don't know where my father is. I know my mother is in the kitchen, watching Oprah on the tiny kitchen TV, staple of the '80s. It's the same TV we watched the *Challenger* go up on, only to explode into a thousand pieces, that schoolteacher gone. I remember the teacher's curly hair, hanging over her shoulder, a smile from ear to ear. *What an opportunity*, she must have thought. *All these years I've spent with four walls surrounding me, trying to teach kids civics, government, history, all about the American woman*—she was a feminist—and she explodes. Which was her Plan A, which her Plan B? Schoolteacher or astronaut? Which one failed? I can't breathe.

A taxi's exhaust pipe booms loudly into the city's grumble, unsettling the regular patterns of sound, placing me back on the corner of 18th Street, fully in the present, neon red hand lit up across the street from me: *Stop*. The gallery is only four doors away, but I'm slightly early and decide it's just as bad to be *too* early than late, so I make a right turn. I'll circle the block, take the long way, make some time.

Mom takes me straight to the doctor when I tell her I can't breathe. The doctor tells Mom there's nothing physically wrong with me. I don't have allergies. I don't need an inhaler. What I need is a "worry doctor," he says, while I'm sitting in his office, on the crinkly white paper that's almost exactly like tracing paper.

Dr. Damien, the worry doctor, as Mom called him, said I had "anxiety attacks."

What if I fail? What if I walk into that gallery now and nothing happens? Or more of the same? What if I come back with another group show, and that's it? There will only be two options left at this point: keep wading through this milky feeling until something happens. Or change my life, stop being an "artist." Is that even possible?

My head feels like a tank, swimming with a million minnows that don't know where to go. What if I forget how to use a brush? What if Lee dumps me? What if I go back and Tony dumps me too? Then what? It feels like I'm floating in a hot-air balloon where the flame in the middle is so hot and so big that if I move I'll get burned.

It's time.

There's nowhere else to go but in. So I walk right up to the gallery and open the frosty-white glass door, UV-protected glass, and a cold rush of air conditioning blows over me. The same air conditioning that protects the works on paper, keeps the paint intact, prevents Dali's clocks, so to speak, from melting further into sand.

The gallery is as it always is. White. Very white. Lee's showing a collage artist, a woman who's mixing Indian miniatures with cartoons. Lee's got "the eye" for the good stuff. That's what she calls it anyway. I always imagine a periscope coming out of the ocean when she says that. Sometimes I can see it coming out of her skull in old Technicolor.

She's giving orders in the back room, you can hear her all the way from the entrance. As I get closer to the reception area, the echo of my footsteps announces my visit. Marge, Lee's assistant, looks up from her desk. Her big eyes and sinewy arms make her look like a perched bug poking her head from behind the high wall of the counter right in front of her desk. I lean onto the counter, near the press material for the Indian-miniature-meets-cartoon collages, waiting for rich fingers to strum its pages.

"Hi," I say to Marge.

"Oh, hello there, Veronica," she says, opening her fingers like a fan, the rest of her still rigid behind her desk.

"Is Lee around?" I ask politely, already knowing the answer.

"Yes, Ms. Strauss is expecting you. You're right on time."

"You know me, the only anal painter you've got in this place."
I laugh. She doesn't. We're always awkward like this. It's a game by
now.

"Yes. You are always punctual," she says matter-of-factly, nervously, getting up to lead me to Lee. Ironing the pleats of her skirt,
the old-pilgrim-looking hot-pink buckles of her shoes catch my eye.
They're lovely in their patent leather glint. I know they cost a fortune.
I don't say anything because I know she wants me to. She wants to
get "in" with the painters, but she never will. She's an art dealer's
assistant. And one day she'll be an art dealer. No, the painters will
never really care about her, but she might be rich, with a Carrie
Bradshaw closet to boot.

I want to be rich too. Rich and Famous. I want people to see
one of my paintings and say, "That's a Veronica Gonzalez," as if that
encapsulated everything.

Marge leads me to the back room and stands like a caryatid
behind Lee, waiting for Lee's next command, which never comes, so
Marge just stays there. Lee is sitting at her crowded desk. Catalogues
and catalogues of every show in Manhattan, London, Miami, and
Beijing. "China is hot," she'd told me last week, right before she'd
called to say, "Miami is hot."

Taking a drag from her cigarette, she looks up at me over the
top of thick white plastic Chanel frames. Her hair is slicked back
in a low bun, black with a streak of white hair running down the
center-left side of her head, a birthmark. She stands up, excited but
languid. She's on something, I know it. I'll be able to tell once she
starts talking. For some reason, Xanax and Valium have very different
effects on the woman.

"Veronica, darling, how are you?" She leans over her desk and
hugs me, the cigarette smoke wafting in my hair, which is so wild
and loose, I realize now, compared to hers. I'm a mess. I should have
come better dressed.

"Hi, Lee."

"Sit, sit." She takes another drag, not caring in the least that she's breaking the law by smoking inside her gallery.

I sit.

"So tell me, darling. Tell me why you should be my pepper shaker among pillars of salt, my macadamia nut among peanuts."

It's the Valium. The Valium makes her calm and funny, inspires weird analogies and metaphors. The Xanax makes her dry, kind of British. She's not British today; she's totally black-chic-New-York-strange-metaphor Lee today. I might know what she's on, but I don't know what she's talking about—I'm lost and it must be showing.

"How much have I told you?" Lee continues, cocking her head and ashing her cigarette into a vintage ashtray from the '50s shaped like a cupped, red-nail-polished hand, the kind on old TV ads for dishwashing liquid.

"You told me to bring my most recent work and that it would be worth my while. 'Big career move,' you said. And then you said, 'Maybe.'"

"Righty-o, because that all depends."

"On what?"

Righty-o? I'm not sure I believe her. It was a big deal to get her to sign me on. She'd been selling my work on consignment for a year, but without anything in writing—no commitment. She sold my stuff pretty well when she tried. It made me happy, brought in money, helped me take less hours at work, but I wanted the real deal, the ring on the finger. When she finally did officially take me on, on paper, I thought, Finally, a dealer, the New York gallery contract I'd been waiting for. The world and my life are going to change. But nothing big has happened since the contract, not even a group show. And that was already six months ago. The honeymoon is coming to a close.

"We're opening up a gallery in your neck of the woods. Miami. Wynwood."

"You are? But that makes no sense. You're, you're so New York. Strauss, Kay & Jones is so New York. You guys are never going to make it down there." I take a quick look up at Marge, who's still standing motionless behind Lee, hands behind her back now, legs crossed at the knee.

"Don't be daft. Of course we are. Plus it's just temporary. For Basel only."

Daft. Huh. Maybe I'm wrong. Maybe I don't know anything. Maybe it *is* Xanax. Or a nice little cocktail of both.

"And what does any of this have to do with me, exactly?" I ask, still semi-confused.

"Point is we need to do a solo of one of our artists. I need to make somebody pop. Introduce someone to the art world, make a splash. You know how it goes. I've picked three of you and now I need to chisel it down to one. So, what did you bring me?"

"Wait, you want to give me a solo show during Basel?"

Only the most important international art fair in the U.S. My heart feels like a butterfly, the loaves of bread in *Alice in Wonderland*, animating, fluttering to life. Hello second honeymoon. This would be an enormous jump from group shows only.

"No, I didn't say that. I said you are one of three possibilities. Now show me what you've got, sweetpea."

"Some JPGs of what I'm working on." Now I'm getting even more nervous. I thought when she called that she might be thinking of planning on having me join in on a show in New York. During the summer or sometime lame like that. But Basel! My God, this is a whole other ballgame, this is huge, this is—. Okay, I have to calm down. Collect myself, and be articulate.

"Do you have a link, teacup, or have you brought your darling dealer a CD?"

"It's all on my website."

"Good girl. Let us have a look-see, then."

I move over to her side of the desk, lean over, try to contain the shakes and steady my hand. She pushes the slick white Mac keyboard toward me, and there we have it: "New Work."

"I'm not sure where it's going yet, but I know it has something to do with a made-up religion. Maybe. You know things change. Process and all that, but I think that's what it is for now. A religion."

"You're making up a religion?"

"Sort of. I started with an altarpiece, that's not finished. It's all going to be bigger, transferred onto three wooden panels."

"It's quite stunning."

"It's not finished. Don't say anything. I've only gridded the pieces of the first panel so far."

"I won't say a word," says Lee. "What about that one?" Pointing to another piece.

"That one's older."

"Is that a penis?"

"Yes. It's called *Annunciation*."

She laughs.

"It's Gabriel fucking Mary," I tell her. I can tell she wanted me to say it, so I whore myself out. She enjoys that artists can "say it."

"Oh my God, sacrilegious. I love it." Again, another laugh, almost a guffaw.

"And then that one there, that's the God of the religion. It's pretty big, 108 by 98. Not sure what I'll do with that yet, or if that one will even make it into the series as a whole, because I think I'm envisioning some kind of installation with all of this. The whole thing might be like some kind of cathedral, where all these paintings play a part. That's what I would call the whole series, I think: *Cathedral*. Yeah. I was thinking of toying a little with Flash and video, but I'm not sure. I might only do that in the other series. Because I also have another series I started, but that's more about urban development and globalization. *Cathedral*'s also about globalization in a way, but in a different way. The other one, not *Cathedral*, the other one, is called *Model City*—"

"Okay, I get the gist," Lee says. "Stick to *Cathedral*, and I'll let you know if you're the one I've picked of my painterly buds."

"When do I know?"

"Soon."

"It *has* to be soon. Because I have to know when to finish by, if it's me. You know I need deadlines, Lee. I don't do that 'jam things together at the last minute' thing some of your other artists do."

"Something I am well aware of, darling, and most of the reason why I love your dear self. You're almost an outsider artist, with a keen sense of how to stay just inside the lines."

"So?"

"I like it, but I can't give you an answer today. I still have two more painters coming between today and tomorrow."

"So can you tell me by Monday?"

"You'll be in Miami by Monday?"

"I'll be there Sunday night, tomorrow." You bought the fucking ticket, Lee, can't you remember?

"Fine. That's fine. That's what we'll do then. On Monday, go to the gallery down there. Well, the space. We can hardly call it a gallery yet." She scribbles an address on the back of one of her business cards and gives it to me. "I've hired someone to watch the work that's being done down there. She's just graduated NYU, curatorial studies, and she'll be my assistant during Basel." Marge, still standing there, gives Lee a pissy look behind her back, like it's a job she wanted. Drama. Bullshit. Same ol' same ol,' as Tony would say. "Go by, see the space. I'll have told her who it will be by then. She'll let you know if you're it."

This setup has to be some kind of joke, like we're pawns in her little game. But I don't complain. I just nod, and I go. Not much else I can do.

BY THE TIME I get out of the gallery, I realize I have four hours to kill before I meet Leo this afternoon—haven't decided where yet, just somewhere near my hotel. Haven't seen the kid in so long, I'm excited, but I've got time, lots of it. So I walk. It's what I always do in New York, one foot in front of the other. The rush of possibility runs through me with every step and I drift into color and *Cathedral,* wandering what it will turn out to look like. What possibilities, what forms, what will happen to me, or in the world, that will morph into brushstrokes. It's always the same—that element of surprise that makes it all worthwhile, despite the planning, something to do with all those things that are bigger than you. I'm trying not to get revved up, because there have been close calls in the past that have fallen through. Maybe she'll pick someone else. Maybe she'll pick me. Maybe she'll pick someone else. She loves me, she loves me not.

Before I know it, I'm a long way uptown, right in front of St. John the Divine, stone gray and tall as heaven. I've walked from Chelsea to 112th Street, which is sort of stupid since I have to go back downtown later. But my body's done it without much of my brain's say. The exercise warms me. Here it is, the oldest cathedral in the city, where slabs of cement are dedicated to those who loved words in the Poet's Corner, a spot where the names of poets are inscribed on the ground of a small altar, along with lines of their poems, like graves. I used to come here all the time, sit and ask the dead poets to help me. Maybe I was wrong to do that, because Emily Dickinson was a hermit and the rest of them died off too, one by one, from some lonely malady or another. What is it about poets and painters? There's a theory, in psychology, that they feel the world on them more than other people. Other people can handle the pressure, the elephant on the chest.

For all my self-proclaimed agnosticism, churches and cathedrals are still the places I go to when the world seems too much to hold inside the thin walls of my skin. Sitting in the center of St. John's, I think about Lee, and the possibilities ahead, and of Sainte-Chapelle, the first of all my holy places.

It was on a trip with my parents when I was about twelve, not long before the divorce. My father had wanted me and Nina to know the Spanish side of the family (my grandfather on my mom's side has sisters and brothers there and in France). Dad said it was important to know where we came from. And that we would go to Cuba if we could, but we couldn't, so Spain and France were the closest thing.

One day, in Paris, Dad said that the concierge told him about a special place that he loved called La Sainte-Chapelle, one of Paris's hidden treasures. Nina and Mom wanted to go to the Champs-Élysées, but I didn't care about shopping, especially the kind we couldn't afford. Dad looked at me and said, "*Freakia*, want to go with me?" And so I did.

When we got to the Palais de la Cité and made it inside Sainte-Chapelle, we realized we would have to walk up a set of narrow, spiral stairs to get to the main attraction. The bottom, first floor, was bigger, but the top floor was supposed to be a gem. The bottom floor, plain and austere, was made for servants and soldiers, while the top floor catered to royalty and clergy. I remember Dad was adamant about going as early as possible, right when it opened. I didn't understand why until we reached the narrow steps. As soon as he saw them he told me to go ahead in front of him.

I took two steps at a time and by the time I was almost at the top, I realized he was lagging way behind. I looked down and saw that he was as wide as the stairwell, and that he was making his way up the steps the way you try and take a tight ring off your finger, slowly and with a lot of nudging and force. He was breathing so hard I could hear him all the way from where I was, far ahead of him, and by the time he got to me, he was sweating like he'd just run a marathon. He looked at me with his droopy, Chinese-looking eyes and tried to smile. My breakfast swam in my stomach and I wanted to hit him. I was filled with overwhelming anger, a heavy pressure on my chest, that ever-deepening hole I've felt so many times since. I wanted him not to be my father. I was embarrassed and, I realized, so was he. That was the first time I ever saw my father as what he was: morbidly obese.

When we finally reached the top of the stairs and I turned from my father to step inside the chapel, I let out a small yelp that squeaked at the edges. I was struck. *Struck* is the right word, the perfect word, because I felt like I'd been hit and the mark remained for a while, like the fingers on a silver-screen Hollywood face after a fiery slap. I used over a roll of film up there, because I wanted to catch this place, be able to hold it somehow, like a bird in a cage. There seemed to be no walls here—they'd been displaced by glass, by hymns made of stained, solid liquid. I was just a kid feeling her way around in the world, navigating through the monuments people build, foolish enough to think I could trap divinity—that illusive strain of holy hope.

And all that time my father just sat there, pouring out of one of the small wooden seats, sweating and panting less and less until his breathing got back to normal. I decided I needed to lose the extra pounds I was already starting to carry around, I would fast for the rest of the trip, starve if I had to. Anything but what he was doing. That's how mad I was at him, how pissed off I was that he was sweating too much to care about the beauty around him. It had been his idea to come here in the first place, and he wasn't even trying to walk around or get a closer look at it all.

But what did I know of the effort it took him to carry his body? And what if that effort was all for me?

The first time Tony met my father he said, "*Tu padre es un artista frustrado.*"

"My father's not an artist," I'd snapped back. "What are you talking about? He's a salesman."

But maybe Tony's right, maybe Dad was supposed to be a musician, an artist. He loves music, really, deep down loves it. How many times had I heard him asking the music gods to free his soul as he belted out Dobie Gray's version of "Drift Away"? But no one ever took him to his Sainte-Chapelle when he was twelve, nobody made the sweaty effort to take him to a symphony or buy him a guitar.

This morning on the flight to New York, when I thought I'd die, stupidly, like a moron, thinking about him was the biggest sting. Mom and Nina—I'm okay with them, if something happened to me, they'd know I loved them, we've done so much together. With Tony it gets a little messy sometimes, yes, but it's fixable. But Dad—I just don't know about Dad.

I think about that day in Paris all the time and I'm still not sure why. It drives me crazy actually. I can never quite figure out if it's a blissful memory or one so sad I can't ever really touch, just like I could never touch Sainte-Chapelle.

As I STEP outside, the crisp air of fall hits me, even though it's only the first day of September. Down the stone cathedral steps, onto the sidewalk. I cross Amsterdam, and then Broadway, down to Riverside, taking the path along the Hudson back downtown. Kids are out with their parents all along the river. There are single joggers and bikers and new lovers embracing too, but the ones who catch my eye are the families. Little girls holding on to their fathers' hands. I'd forgotten this about New York, how all the young hipster dads are uber-involved with their kids. Dads with slings and pouches, like kangaroos, holding their little ones tight, hair disheveled from helping their wives with middle-of-the-night feedings, with diapers, cooing and rocking and worrying. One dad is helping his son with a flat tire on his new two-wheeler. The whole scene is all very *Mary Poppins* and "Let's Go Fly a Kite." I remember after seeing that movie how I wanted a purse you could pull the world out of, like magic, but how I also wanted, so bad, to go to Tamiami Park with Dad.

The moms all seem to be in different phases of elation or frustration, but all of them look exhausted and somewhat rumpled. There's one standing semi-dazed, watching her daughter pluck strands of grass from the ground. "Don't do that, honey, the grass has feelings too," she says, as she herself bites hard into a sandwich and scarfs it down with a succession of juice box squeezes and gulps. Thank God her sandwich doesn't have feelings. I can almost taste the high-fructose grape syrup washing everything down, making her thirstier. It depresses me.

Some of the moms have hints of their own lives showing through. Looking at these women is like looking at a winter landscape right when the snow that's covering everything is starting to melt in places, giving way to what lies beneath, sneak peeks of color. A journalist, a banker, a lawyer, an interior designer. The biggest differences between the moms, though, is not in the hints of their vocations taking backburner status to motherhood, the biggest difference is in how ready or not they are for this, for the kids sitting in front of them, pulling grass from the ground, eating dirt, the kids jumping, pulling at their jeans. I'm not ready.

A text from Leo: *Hey, where we meeting? Can't wait to see you.*

How bout the Hungarian place dwn near Chelsea?, I text back. *You know the 1?*

Yeah. C u there.

:)

NATURALLY, I'm early again so I get a cup of coffee to wait with—the strongest, blackest blend I can. It steams up like a dark, miniature bath in my hands. If I look straight down at it, the rim of the glass is like the event horizon of a black hole. Yet it's soothing. Black holes are supposed to make you nervous. Imply the end of the world as we know it, like that old R.E.M. song. But just like that great big cave in my chest, black holes are magnetic too, they force you to think about them, wonder—suck you all the way in until you've got no choice but to look at what's inside, straight in the eye.

Sound bites of other people's coffee orders and the noise of *New York Times* pages turning rush through the air. Bits and pieces of headlines flash before me: The true founder of Facebook is brought further into question. Harvard classmates vie for founder status. Palestinian children dig through dumpsters for toys. A kid with Halloween-costume-fairy wings pretends to fly over sand and landmines. Iowa allows for same-sex marriage—for four hours. "Pay at Investment Banks Eclipses All Private Jobs"—$8,367 a week, it says. Must be nice. Mohsen Namjoo is Iran's new Bob Dylan—listen up.

"*Profe!*"

My head pops up to find Leo half a block away, yelling. His Dominican fro is bopping up and down as he speed-walks toward me. We hug.

"It's been so long!" I scream out, smiling like a nut. I haven't seen him for at least four years. And even though we email all the time, it's something else seeing him in person again. It feels good. He's all grown up.

"Tell me about it, *Profe!* You're looking good. Sorry I'm so sweaty, it's been a crazy day. I'll tell you all about it later. Immigration's on my ass again. Have to fix this resident thing, but whatever, that's not important now. Wow, I can't believe I'm seeing you!"

Leo is jittery, but he looks happy, even if it's just right now, right this instant. I try not to do the old-lady thing as he talks, try not to actually tell him how he looks like a man now, not a boy anymore. Hell, I'm only five years older than him anyway. That's less than me and Tony, just the other way around. I'm surprised at how at peace I feel all of a sudden. He feels like home, like a little brother or something.

"Why?" I ask. "Don't they extend your visa as long as you're a student? Why aren't you a citizen by now, anyway, you've been here forever and a day?" I'm surprised this hasn't been solved by now.

"It's complicated. *Nueve Once* didn't help none, son. But naw, listen, it's a long story. Seriously, 'nough about me. How come you're here, *pintora?* I'm so happy to see you, you don't understand. How you doin', how was your day *en la ciudad?* What you done, see any good art? I bet you miss that about the city, there always being art around. How was your flight?"

Twenty questions spew out from Leo. I don't know which to answer first, but when I hear "How was your flight?" I think back to this morning and my face flushes again. He's also done something I'd forgotten about. He never says "9/11" or "September 11," he always has some other name for it, like its Spanish translation: *Nueve Once.* I think of his big brother, Shell.

"Hey," says Leo, "you're turning pink."

"It's the coffee. I've been gulping hot Hungarian."

"Wanna walk? I don't feel like sitting still, you know what I mean?"

"Yeah, that's cool," I say as I pull my backpack over my shoulders. I look nerdy, I know it, but it's okay.

It feels like just the other day he was hanging out in my apartment, checking out books from my "library," as he called it, me trying to get him to stop skipping school, him bringing me mangos on sticks from his friend who sold them on the corner of our street, offering them to me. Those mangos were probably the only good thing about Washington Heights at the time. Those, and the popsicles. He used to extend his hand to me with them and say, "m'lady," which he always sounded hilarious saying and it always made me crack up, which is why he did it.

"So how come you're up here, *Profe*, all of a sudden?" Leo says, nudging my shoulder. "Thought you hated it here now."

"I came to see my dealer."

He laughs. "That doesn't sound good."

"Not that kind of dealer."

"I'm just playin', *Profe*, I know what you meant."

I tell him I might have a solo show, and Leo is thrilled, but I calm him down because it's not for sure yet, no matter how much I want it to be. When he hugs me again (he does this a lot), I realize how muscled he's gotten because this time he squeezes me harder. He's way over my head in height, and when he holds me it's like he folds over me, like some kind of big bird, which is funny because he used to always tell me, "You got my back, *Profe*," and now it feels like I could never have his back, not really. Like maybe I never really did. He'd have to have mine now, he's learned to stand up for himself. It happens when your big brother dies, I guess. That fast shift.

Although that's never what he meant when he said I had his back, it wasn't ever about the physical, it was more about him being without anyone to talk with about poetry and books, which he was starting to realize, at the time, that he loved; without anywhere to go that he wanted to be, until he found my apartment.

"How's your Mom?" I ask him.

"You know how she gets when the anniversary gets close, it's 'round the damn crooked corner, *Profe*, *y ya* Ma is gettin' antsy and weird, kind of like, you know, stoic and shit. She gets like in a coma when the day comes close."

Leo says this without looking at me, looking down at his neat, white sneaks, his baggy yellow jacket hanging loose around him.

"She going to the DR?"

"Like always. Leaves tomorrow, but I'm stayin'—it's gonna be the first time since Shell died that she goes by herself. But I know how it's gonna be, son. She steps foot in DR and she lets it all out and the tears start coming out like nothin' can stop her. But it's better than the mummy-ass shit she pulls here, though. Breaks my fuckin' heart."

"If she didn't hate me so much I'd tell you to give her a kiss from me." I say it jokingly, but I can feel my eyes are watery.

"Yeah, I better not say anything," he says, laughing. "She might curse your show."

I change the subject. "So how's City College? You liking it?"

"Naw, *Profe*, let's not talk about that, tell me more about the show that's gonna make you famous."

That's when I know.

"You dropped out, didn't you?" I ask.

"I don't know, *Profe*, you know? It's just not worth it anymore."

"What's not worth it?"

"School, poetry, none of it."

"Wait, what? You're not writing anymore?"

"What for, son? It ain't payin' the bills. I mean shit, ma had to go to La Dominicana and she almost didn't even have the money to get on that damn plane. I'm just sick of it. So I got another job and I couldn't have the two jobs and go to school at the same time, it started to be too much—"

"And that's why you're having trouble with immigration, because you stopped going to school."

"Exactly," he says, dejected. "I'm sort of fucked unless I get married." And then, abruptly: "Wanna marry me?"

"Shut up!"

"I'm sort of serious. I mean I was thinking about it, when I was coming over here, I mean we've been friends forever, *Profe*, and we could pass the test, you know, the green card interview, like in that movie with the French dude. It could work."

"You can't be serious."

"Why not? You want me to get down on one knee? We could talk about me paying you too, I could figure that out. I mean you could just paint and not have to take on the day jobs if I gave you a chunk of cash. Or who knows, I mean, I don't know, maybe it'd even work out." He says this last part shyly, almost under his breath.

"No, definitely not," I say. "That's a pipe dream, Leo. I mean seriously. Jesus." I have to look away from him again because I'm losing my balance a bit. There must be something in the stars today. First the kid on the plane, and now this. Not to mention the possibility of Lee and—

I can't stop the millisecond-lasting flash of what life could look like if I said yes to Leo, what could happen if I took him up on the offer. But I force myself to erase it. I just don't have those kinds of feelings for this kid.

"Leo, I love you man, but that could never happen."

"I know, *Profe*, I know. It's just—"

"It's just you have to go back to school, that's what, that's the only thing that's going to help you stay a resident and become a citizen and move on and up and—"

"And what? Do what? What the fuck am I gonna do with a degree in poetry? In fucking creative writing, *Profe*? Starve like you? Sometimes I wish I never got into the damn shit."

This makes me feel bad. Like it's all my fault. Like he might be right.

"Leo, c'mon, you love it. I'd never seen anyone so hungry when I met you. Please keep writing, Leo, you're so good. It's just a matter of time." As I say this I feel a slight doubt. What if it doesn't happen? This is exactly what I was feeling this morning. What if I say all of this and he fails?

He won't.

And if he does?

Tony deep inside me says on repeat that making it as an artist is really very "unlikely" — and as a poet? Please. Compare the number of books that make it into the *New York Times Book Review* to the number of waiter/writers serving up mimosas on any given Sunday. Why would I want to bring him into the quicksand with me when there are a limited number of ropes we can use to climb out?

Then again, there's a real rush to it — more than a rush — to moving people with your mind. Emotional telekinesis. A responsibility. Is that dramatic? I don't care, it's true. Making something that gets inside a person's skin, it's a virus without a cure, contagious and delicious at the same time. Something you have to learn to live with, like Clark Kent's x-ray vision, a blessing and a curse. Plus he's already come this far. What a waste to let it all go.

"Listen," I say, "I'm the first to know how hard it is."

Leo doesn't say anything.

I keep at it. "But you can't just quit."

He stays quiet for a while and I stop pursuing his half of the dialogue. Then he makes a quick turn into a flea market.

"Oh, no, we can't go in here," I tell him, pulling him back by the elbow. "You know I can't go into flea markets, you *know* that!"

After giving away all my clutter (half of it to Leo himself) when I moved from New York, I'd promised myself never to buy or take home any junk from the streets again. I'd vowed, in front of Leo, to live as simply as a Mondrian, never even go into one of my beloved flea markets again. Ever. Not even to look.

"Sure you can," he says, pulling me in. "Use your self-restraint." He's doing this on purpose. He's got a lopsided smirk that's cute and infuriating at the same time.

Immediately I start to get sucked in. It's like an addiction. Except this time, it's not so much the stimulation of the regular flea market mélange that beckons me — those bits and pieces of color everywhere, teacups with grapevines inscribed, antique jewelry, nude statuettes,

1970s yellow and orange vases with imprinted flowers, tall white book casings, an old French bidet, rings and brooches that look like snowflakes. That's all appealing, always is, but more than that it's Old Matisse who calls me. Not a painting, but a man.

"See that old man over there?" Leo says.

"I was just looking at him," I say, whispering, as if conspiring.

"Let's go."

We move toward a stall where an old vendor with a white beard and straw hat stands by his tent, selling boxes of old postcards and old photographs. He looks *exactly* like Matisse, quiet, thinking of light and bathed in it and looking like he loves to eat good cheese. Matisse's *Icarus* flashes across my brain-screen as I walk toward his booth.

Icarus, plate VIII of the illustrated book *Jazz* by Henri Matisse, 1947.
© 2015 Succession H. Matisse / Artists Rights Society (ARS), New York.

And there it is again: the hole in the heart.

I half expect to see reproductions of the painting everywhere inside the booth. I even fantasize about finding an original, unknown Matisse. But there are no paintings anywhere, just a lot of old snapshots from the 1920s to the 1950s.

"The photographs are only a quarter each today," says Old Matisse, leaning on a flimsy folding table as we enter his tent.

I thank him and look inside his boxes.

"Where are those from?" Leo asks, pointing to the pictures that are now in my hands. People and their stories, captured and muted.

"I find them in albums at estate sales mostly," he says. He walks toward me, and I feel like it's just me and Matisse in a tent in a cool African desert at night, looking at archives and old bones. "It's always so fascinating," he says, "how in old photographs you can see how shadowy life really is."

I pick one out and look at it for a while, a group of kids sitting on what looks like a country stoop. What were these people doing in New York? And if it's from an estate sale, who's dead? Was it whoever was supposed to be sitting in that empty chair in the background? Or was it one of these kids—all grown up and dead? They pull me in and Old Matisse pulls me out: "Take it," he says.

"I got it, I'll get it for you," says Leo, jumping in, pulling out his wallet.

"Oh, no. It's not the money," I say, putting the photograph back in the ash-gray shoe box it came from. I give Leo a sideways look, as in: *Stop encouraging old, bad habits.* "I know it's just a quarter. It's just I promised myself I wouldn't buy things I don't need."

Old Matisse swings his hands in his pockets and smiles at us. "Need is relative, I guess," he says. And then he takes out a cigarette, which ruins my moment with Old Matisse in the African tent. Maybe if it would've been a pipe?

"You can have it," says Matisse. "You should have it."

I refuse for a while, but then he takes it out of the box, along with another one I can't see, and wraps them in tissue paper like they're gems, and then places them in a thin, brown paper bag. Leo stares at him as he does this. Then Matisse hands the package to me, and refuses to let either Leo or me pay for it, and I wonder why. Why in the world Matisse is giving me a pair of black and white photographs.

We walk away, almost skipping, like in an old movie.

"That was awesome," Leo says.

"Yeah," I say. "Hey, wanna go on the ferry?"

Riding the Staten Island Ferry is the last thing we do for the day. We walk down there, the air around us getting crisper. Then we wait for the ferry and I think of Edna St. Vincent Millay and her poem "Recuerdo." I know this moment will fold itself into memory, waiting to be pulled out later, like the lyrics of a song. In the terminal the pigeons coo, their wings flapping from one end of the room to the other. Clocks tick steadily. Leo buys a bright pink Now and Later candy. I love the Staten Island Ferry—New York isn't *all* bad. When it's finally time, we get on and wait for the horn to sound, walking all the way up to the front of the boat, taking in the wind whipping all around us, lashing through our hair.

There's something sad about the ferry that I can't quite grip. It's not a squeeze like what I felt this morning, not a compression of breath, or suspension of it. It's something else, like a picture full of fog, even though there's no fog here, just the same sense of nostalgia. Like the beginning of some kind of melancholic journey I can't understand yet.

Leo's looking straight out at the water; we're not talking much. When we pass Liberty, I think about the elements and things we have all around us. How we're smack in the middle of water, and memory, and ruin. How to the right we have Lady Liberty, massive and beautiful as she is. She's not cheesy when you really think about her, not when you really look at her. That's just the fault of too many postcards. It's the same with places like the Grand Canyon. And then right behind us, the space where the towers were. On Ellis Island, my grandfather's name, etched in stone. And here's Leo, sandwiched between the statue, the possibility of claiming this country as his own, and the invisible towers, where he lost his brother, where his life as he knew it came apart. Drifting somewhere between the present and the past, Leo too has a hole in the heart.

It's almost impossible to grid this kind of map, unless you abstract it, transcribe it, translate it into a different language. Which is maybe why Leo says *Nueve Once*, which is maybe why painters paint. It's important to record moments like this, when a flash of something opens up, it's important to keep these as a *recuerdo*, for later, for when the reel unfolds and you start putting things together. If there's one thing I know, it's to always take notes. They come in handy later, when you're standing in front of the blank, white canvas, when you're trying to pull many things into one, charting. Suddenly, I know I was wrong to think I wasn't going to revisit the past on this trip. You can't make it to the future without taking a few steps back, to build up speed.

THE NEXT day, Leo rides the bus with me all the way to the airport. When I argue, tell him it's a waste of time to come all the way over to Queens and all the way back by himself for nothing, he insists.

"Don't be such an *americana*. I always bring Ma to the airport. I hate how people here don't do that. How the only people standing inside the terminals are drivers with company signs. What happened to the big hugs you used to get from family and best friends and girlfriends?"

When Leo says this, I remember how Mom, Nina, and I used to wait for Dad inside the terminal when he went on a business trip, how we'd park and come in when we dropped him off. How Nina would jump on him when she saw him come through the electronic doors on his return. We've lost that somehow, that warm, Cuban part of ourselves. Leo still has it. DR wasn't so far away for him.

So I let him ride with me, all the way to the airport, even if it's silly. And the ride is kind of nice. We buy a fashion magazine and spend the whole time talking Hollywood and NYC cheese, which we both pretend is not our style, totally superficial and ridiculous, and just plain wrong, but which is fun. Somewhere inside each of us, the song of celebrity sings out, a persistent and fluttering little bird.

"You know, *pintora*, I think you're right. It's all or nothing," Leo says when we hit the sparkled airport pavement.

"What do you mean? When did I say 'all or nothing'?"

I'm a bit flustered looking through my bag, making sure I have my license, which I'll need over and over again as I make my way through security. Then I search for my phone. I feel like I'm forgetting something, feeling uneasy again.

"I mean about what we do—art. It has to be all or nothing. It has to be something big. Something really big, something that makes us known, something that makes people stop and say *Holy...*" As he says this, he's got a menacing look in his eye that worries me.

I've found my ID and my phone finally, I'm looking straight at him, and a flash of concern splinters around me. Of panic, actually. What does he mean? I can't quite read his expression anymore, but it looks more intense than anything I've ever seen on that mug since Shell.

"Well, I don't mean kill anybody," I say jokingly. "Jesus, Leo, what's that face?"

"It's the face of action, *Profe.* The face of action."

I look at my watch and know if I don't get inside and check in, I'll be running too late for comfort.

"Anyway, you'll see," he says. "Get on that plane and get home safe, and give that Argentino of yours a hug for me, even if he doesn't know me, who cares, right?"

"Thanks, Leo." I give him a big hug. "Don't do anything crazy, though. Nothing you're going to regret later."

"No regrets. Never regrets."

"*Cuídate,*" I say. "You hear? *Cuídate.*" As I turn toward the revolving door, I'm wishing and hoping that everything goes well for Leo, and that I haven't fucked anything up for him, that he's got some kind of angel following him around, watching his steps, holding him back from anything stupid.

On the plane, it feels like the near future is spread before me, but I don't know what the route is exactly, or the destination, not yet. It's an unarticulated feeling. Like something has opened up but I don't know what it is yet. And like something else has closed. And still, somewhere inside me, the pressure of yesterday remains somewhere toward the base of my chest, lingering.

I pull out the pictures Old Matisse gave me, pick the one I'd been looking at in his stall and put away the other one, not looking at his gift yet, keeping it a surprise for later. I think that if I keep the other one for later, nothing will happen on this plane—it will be a safe, smooth flight toward the eventual uncovering of the second photo, which I'm obviously fated to see. It's specious reasoning that makes no sense at all, and it's also really annoying how scared I've gotten, of flying. I was never scared of flying before. It was always Nina who was scared, not me.

My eye keeps going to the empty chair forever and always imprinted in the photograph—somebody missing. You could argue the person missing is taking the picture, but I know that's not true because of the expression on the younger woman's face in the background. The way she looks away from the chair, missing the person who's supposed to be there, right in front of her. Where are the men in this picture? Just women and children, and the seeds of what will be.

Everybody's got one, don't they? Someone who was there once and isn't, or someone who was never there, someone you wish were there, should be there more. An empty chair is two things: a place you always want filled and a place you get used to empty. Running deeper than a delta and further than the Seine, like the muscular roots in the ground that help you grow. So many paradoxes everywhere. Like Shell for Leo. Like why Dad took me to Sainte-Chapelle and then stopped trying. Let go of me when I was in high school, then more in college. Started loving Nina more. And me, out there by myself, without male strength. No one to hold me, not strong and hard.

Even though he had planted that oak, just days before I was born. In our room, where everything was pink, Nina and I would stay up late and watch TV—even our TV was pink. Outside, the oak and its year-round bright green leaves soaked in chlorophyll. Even though the windows were never open, I always thought I heard the wind through the green singing just for me, like slippers shuffling. In the distance Mom and Dad's voices buzzing in their room.

"I planted that oak for you," Dad liked to tell me. He stopped saying it after the house got taken away. The last time I heard that I was ten, when one day Mom told us, "We're selling the house, girls, and going to live at Maman and Papan's for a little while." That was right after the anxiety attacks started. We believed her and didn't understand until much later that Dad had gone bankrupt, but we must have felt something was wrong. He'd lost everything, which meant we'd lost everything, which meant I'd lost my oak. Maybe that's why in New York I became a wanderer, longing for the day I'd be able to, once again, sink my feet in the ground, and have my toes grow deep down into the dirt, making me immobile aboveground, but tall and strong and ever-growing underneath the surface.

When was the last time I saw Dad? Smith & Wollensky? Two Saturdays ago. I'll have to call him, I'll call him tomorrow. I don't want that feeling I had on the plane yesterday, when suddenly everything was about to go up in vapor and… No. I bet Nina's talked to him. He and Nina talk, they're friends. They went to Vegas together and he bought her things and I wasn't even invited. He doesn't buy me things. If this were Nina, on this plane, he would have bought her the ticket. It's my fault. I turned him down once too often; he got tired of offering, I guess. Mixed feelings: Love shouldn't be bought, but he should never have stopped trying. And I shouldn't have either.

When the plane finally lands, I'm grateful. A swift landing and quick exit from the plane—just me, my orange backpack, and the photographs stuffed into my pocket. I think about taking a quick look at the other one, but I decide to keep moving for now, straight toward Tony. Soon I'm rolling through the terminals, straight out the doors, the smell of exhaust from the shuttles and taxis steaming up, and the clingy, humid heat making my face fume lobster-red in three seconds flat. A text message from Nina: *Hey, where are you, I've been trying to call you. Call me. Love you tons, N.*

"*Gordita*," Tony calls out from his Porsche, "over here!" I run over, sliding the phone into my pocket.

Tony gets out of the car, comes to help me with my bag and gives me a big kiss.

It's good to see him. "How are you, monkey?" I say.

"Excellent. $80,000 just now." Tony's smiling big. He loves it: the game, the hunt. Money.

"Jesus, on what?" I ask. "Let's put the roof down."

"An insurance website," he says opening up the roof and zooming off, wind in our hair, life without care. Nice little buzz. Nice to be back. Yesterday begins to disappear and today begins to form, though Leo and the ferry still linger, Lee echoes too. All of it mixing around inside me.

"That's amazing," I say. I'm always impressed with how much money he can make designing a website. Funny how I ended up with a graphic designer, even though I refused to be one.

Insurance website. I guess everybody needs insurance, or at least they think they do. And everybody needs a web designer like Tony, until they figure out how to make websites themselves. I've told him before: *There will come a time when the roles will change between me and you. When everything I've worked for will come to fruition, and I'll be making more dough than you. I hope you'll be around, I won't mind sharing. But what will you do when web design isn't as popular? What will drive you? If it's just about money, what will keep you going during the downs?*

For a second a trace of anger returns, remembering our first big fight, over a year ago, when I was really struggling, not selling any work at all, right before I'd signed on with Lee, around the time of the group shows I charted all over the place. Lee had been "following me," she said, and she'd asked to see a body of work. I asked Tony if he could spot me on rent for a while so that I could make a new body of work, a new solid series, with full force, so I could go for it. He said no, everything 50/50 or we split. There was too much money in this country, he said, for me to be begging. I wasn't special. I would have to get another day job like everyone else. So I had to start tutoring kids, teaching them how to paint, picking up odd jobs, this all apart from my regular gigs as a freelance translator. I was working nonstop so I could buy my paint and pay his rent and work on the "body of work" Lee kept asking to see.

Tony got mad when I called it "his" rent. "It's your rent too," he'd say. But it never felt like home, not after he did that. I would have done it for him, would have supported him for a bit if he really needed it, backed him financially if I had the dough, in a heartbeat. <3, <3, <3. Fuck him. I still painted and did it all. And now here I am: Possibility. A glimpse at the green, the iron-oxide idea of it—money, my own, in exchange for my art. Any way you want to look at it, it's what we both need. He'll see I can make it on my own, be his equal. And I feel it, the growing respect, the kind that leads to a possible life together, for the long run. The specter of being able to be the half of a whole, hold that up, not just the artist who needs a hand, but the one who can make her own way, and making her own way, can join paths and make a stronger one, with Tony.

BEFORE I know it, it's Monday and it's time to head on over to Wynwood, to learn my fate. The anxiety returns. The gallery in Miami is totally different than New York's. It's a raw space, huge, still its original concrete gray. Floors unsmoothed, unvarnished, cement dust floating through the air, full of nothing, except imagination. No crates, no art on the walls, no whiteness, no prior show, no future exhibition set quite yet. Tabula rasa. Well, if there ever was such a thing as a blank slate. Proof that there isn't such a thing is the set of enormous trash bags in the corner, black and full of whatever had been in this place before. The refuse and ruin of someone else's endeavor.

"Helloo," I call from the door, the space still dark.

"Hellooo," a voice calls back. "Veronica, is that you? I'll be right out." This voice has singsong to it, not the harsh notes of Marge's consonants. With fewer walls to hit, our echoes spread out further and farther here than in the New York gallery. All the doors are open at the front and back, letting in geometric slits of sun.

Neatly placed against the wall, the trash bags bring back a vivid image, of moving out of my apartment in New York, as if it had happened yesterday. When I'd decided to get rid of everything. When the last thing to go were the piles, literally piles, of rejection letters from galleries, which I stuffed into plastic bags and stared at before I tossed them straight from my fourth-floor window into the dumpster beneath. *Dear Veronica, Your work seems interesting, it's just not the right fit for our gallery* (hundreds of these). *Dear Veronica, You seem to be working out of a particular dialectic that doesn't sync with our space* (what dialectic?). *Dear Veronica, Have you ever tried galleries that deal in Outsider Art* (huh?). *Dear Veronica, We are not taking on any new artists, it is hard enough to sell the ones we already have, good luck finding a space elsewhere* (nice). *Dear Veronica, Your work just didn't speak to me* (it doesn't talk, fool, it doesn't have a mouth and if it did, it wouldn't speak English). *Dear Artist, Thank you for your submission, unfortunately we cannot offer you a spot in our upcoming exhibition* (not even a name).

At least ten bags of these, full of crushed paper rejections, before galleries went totally electronic; those would come later, digital dust. I'd decided to send at least one submission out a day, and these garbage bags had been the result. Until one day, when I was already back in Miami, an email came from Lee: *Dear Veronica, I'm interested in your work. When can we talk?*

The space's lights turn on in sections, all of a sudden, as if to announce a visitor. And then there she is, a tiny speck at the back of the gallery growing bigger as she walks toward me.

"*Hola*, Veronica, so good to finally meet you. I'm Dia," says a petite Latina woman who I soon find out is Colombian. Straight, long black hair like the belly of a sparrow and just as shiny. "So, this is your space," she says with a smile. "I know it doesn't look like much yet, but don't worry, we'll have it up and running in no time." She laughs. "You know how it is, these contractors in Miami, they are all running on Cuban time."

"My space?" I ask. Wondering if that's just a mistake in her language, if she just means, my "potential" space.

"Oh, you don't know," she says, smiling. "I forgot, I'm the bearer of good news! Congratulations, Veronica! Yes, it is your space."

Dia moves eloquently through a speech about how and why they chose me, alongside some logistics. Her English is careful and balanced, learned and peppered with slang that says: this here language, this is home, just in case you were wondering. She said "your space" because she meant it. My own space in which to play, add a jungle gym and swing. I like Dia.

"I'll send you dimensions and charts all through email. Don't worry, you'll have everything in your inbox by tomorrow. Lee told me you're a planner. Me too." She's smiling again, threading connections.

I'm in a sort of daze when I walk out of the gallery. I've been picked. Plucked. I march out of the space in Wynwood with a spring in my step, the news—*I have a show during Basel*—running on repeat, the desire to dart straight to the canvas and work.

Back in my studio, not knowing quite how I got there, I stare at my painting and wonder, Could this really be happening? Is this what it feels like, this peaceful rush: success? The tendril beginnings of it wrapping around me. Finally. A little pressure, right at the nape of my neck. But more than anything, it's relief. A surge of relief and gratefulness. Looking around at the end-bits of paint tubes everywhere, I know I have to go buy more paint, get started. Urgency and purpose. Who said painting was dead? Who needs a Plan B?

Pieces of a Man

Panel 2

What a piece of work is man… And yet, to me, what is this quintessence of dust?

—Hamlet

1.

Sometimes the sky in Miami makes you want to believe in God. That's what it's like on this Monday afternoon, ordinary, and anything but. Blue, so bright blue — cobalt in places, dashing with alizarin, washed out in spots — clouds of titanium white. Driving home now, bags full of paint in the back seat, I have the windows down, and am sketching the show in my mind, while re-running the meeting with Dia earlier today, on a loop. An installation in addition to the paintings, just as I've always imagined for this series. A few large, luminous pieces instead of a million little ones. Space to think and process for the viewer. I don't know. Maybe.

Basel.

Miami during Basel. My ticket.

Get a grip. Must plan.

Okay, today is September 3rd, so I've got four months to put this thing on — September, October, November — no, *three* months. Shit. Basel starts on December 5, my show has to be done and up by then. That's okay, I'll get it together, all I need is structure. A schedule. This time the work's going to have everything, it's going be the world on a flat canvas —

The phone.

Dig in the purse. It's Nina. Oh shit, she phoned Saturday and I forgot to call her back — watch the road — wait till I tell Nina about the show. I haven't told Nina or Mom anything at all, hadn't wanted to get their hopes up. Then I got caught in the rush of it, getting supplies, daydreaming.

"Hey Ni—"

She cuts me off. "Have you talked to Dad?" Her voice is anxious. Tight. I imagine her left fist closed at her side, thudding against her leg.

"No, I'm driving home, I just went to—"

"Dad didn't go to work. Louisa tried calling him, she couldn't reach him. He won't pick up and he didn't go to work, and Sonny is worried because you know Dad doesn't miss work—"

My pinwheel heart jumps up to my mouth and saunters to a halt, my stomach sinks to my feet. My father doesn't miss work. Not for headache, fever, polio, or TB. Not ever in all his life has the man missed a day.

I spot the chance for a U-turn just seconds away and take it. Dad's condo is on the other side of the bridge from me.

"I'm going over there," I tell Nina.

"Be careful. Sonny said he was going over too. Said he was going to call the police to break down the door. Don't go in by yourself."

We're both imagining the body of my father on the floor of his apartment, beneath his framed *Godfather* and Beatles collectors' posters, the biggest one reading LET IT BE, like some kind of reminder for his volcanic mood swings.

"Don't worry," says Nina. "It's nothing, maybe it's nothing, maybe he's just sleeping in."

Dad doesn't sleep in. He can't sleep. He wakes up at five every morning and goes to sleep past midnight.

"I'm on my way." It's all I can think to say, all that comes out.

"Me too. Mom's coming too."

When was the last time Mom saw Dad? It's the first thing I think when she says Mom's coming. I know I'll get there first, before any of them. Except Sonny, Sonny might be there already. Already I'm only minutes away. Speeding. If a cop stops me, I'll ignore him. There's a valet at Dad's, I'll park valet, that's the fastest thing. But first, the traffic.

The bridge empties me into downtown, which rumbles in construction and congestion and dust, and I zigzag through the debris of high-rise condos in the making. The arena sweeps by. Curve, curve. Red light. Stop. Count. Think: Dad's okay, this is nothing. Just a warning, just a warning. I'll tell him to lose weight, he can't do this to us. How can he do this to us? He has to lose weight, stop drinking. I'll give him an ultimatum. He's fine. He's lying on the ground. He's dead. Oh my God. Why didn't he call *me*? Red light, goddammit, turn green. Green. Go. Up and over, the smaller bridge, Brickell Bridge, I'm emptied out into the financial center. Banks, so many windows blocking the sky. My head is a piece of driftwood. I can see his apartment building, teasing me from behind the Four Seasons Hotel. Summer, Winter, Spring, and Fall blaring at me. Wind gusts in my mind, leaves scatter in 80-degree weather and still some sort of sprouting hope. I can see the turn. I ride up into the driveway.

There's an ambulance.

My body starts to slow like it's in water.

I park on the curb, hand the keys to the valet.

"Is that for 2022? Is that ambulance for 2022?" I ask the valet.

"You want go 2022?" he says in a thick Cuban accent. He doesn't understand, looks at me puzzled. Why doesn't anyone speak English in this city?

I don't have time to translate. I run to the elevator, upstairs, twentieth floor. And there's his door, torn down. And his body on a stretcher and Sonny and—my eyes well. The world goes white. Like it's gone from under my feet. All the centripetal force gone missing, slow and fast motion colliding.

"I'm his daughter!" I yell.

Sonny tells the paramedics, "Let her ride, she's his daughter. I'm just his business partner."

I hug Sonny. For getting them to knock down the door, I say, "Thank you."

I ride the elevator down with my dad, the paramedics.

"You're the daughter?"

I nod.

"What kind of medications is he on? Any conditions? When was the last time anyone saw him? We need to know everything he took. Is he allergic to anything? Did he do drugs? We found an empty bottle of anti-anxiety meds."

The words clutter in a cloud above me, then sink into my head. I look down at my father's body, sprawled, pieces of flesh and fat hanging over the stretcher, his white chest, his silver hair. What great hair. I want to stroke his belly and tell him I'm here. I need to tell him I'm here.

The paramedics need to know. "Did he have any conditions?"

"He had a heart problem, but not a serious one, I don't think. He said it wasn't serious. I forgot what it's called, he took medicine for it. I don't know what he took."

"You don't know what kind of heart condition your father had?"

I'm a bad daughter. It's a shit relationship. I'd been going over it in my head on the plane and now—

"He didn't talk about it. He brushed it off, said it was nothing— an irregular heartbeat. He took something that makes your blood thinner, I can't remember what it's called."

"Afib," one of the medics calls out.

I look at him blankly.

"He had atrial fibrillation?" another medic asks.

"Yes, yes, that's it." I recognize it as soon as he says it.

Downstairs, rolling him out. Nina appears in the background, and my mother. My sister calls out for me and bursts out in a loud cry. I had forgotten to call her back, no one knew where I'd been. Had Dad tried to call me? How could I be so self-consumed? I keep up with the stretcher. I run by my father's side, trying to see his face again, before they put him in the ambulance. His eyes are closed and crusty.

"Dad, Dad," I call out softly. He has an oxygen mask on. He opens his eyes, slightly. He looks at me and I can't tell if he can tell it's me or if the web of his thoughts is thick as milk—thicker than mine. "It's Vero, I'm here," I tell him. He stares at me and then he closes his eyes. The paramedic touches my back and lightly leads me to the front of the ambulance. He sits me down, he buckles me in. My sister is running up to the window. My mother running behind her.

"Tell them we're going to Mercy. Not to follow us. Meet us there," says the medic.

I lower the window. "Mercy. Meet us at Mercy. Don't follow."

They run off. My sister gets in her car, throws her keys to her boyfriend, yells at him to drive. "I can't drive, I can't drive," she says. I hadn't seen D before, but now I can see his dreadlocks from my height, the back of his head in Nina's gold Hyundai. My mother runs in the other direction to her car. They set off. What are we waiting for? Step on it, ambulance driver, c'mon.

"Your dad's gotta change his lifestyle," says the medic. I don't even know this guy's name. I don't care what he's called. It's a stupid thing to say what he just said. Just turn on the fucking car and drive, fucker. Turn it on and put the siren on and get a fucking move on. Can't you see what's happening?

But I don't tell him any of that. I just look back. My father's chest is rising and falling, he's snoring now. His breathing is hard and loud. I should be back there with him. Why didn't I fight for that? I want to breathe for him. I look up at that big blue sky and think, Dear God, if that whole lot of blue is you, let him have the chance to change his life, let us have a chance to talk, fix things. Maybe this time he'll change, maybe this time—

Suddenly the blue blurs, and I'm lost in the siren sound. Cars part in front of us, paving the way.

Ten minutes disappear somewhere in time's labyrinth, and the ambulance stops. We high-jump out of the car. The ambulance is tall and my feet pound onto the ground. I run to the back, because I want to see my father again before he gets rolled away, want to tell him I'm here, again, as many times as I can—that I am here, that I'm going to stay by him. Mom runs up to me and we join my father at his side.

"Dad, Dad, I'm here," I tell him in a quiet voice, and he opens his eyes again. He looks at me, and he looks at Mom. Mom delicately touches his puffy hands and says, "Bubi, it's Eliana, I'm here. Eli is here." She called him Bubi when they were married, when we were little. She hasn't said that since I was fifteen and they got divorced. Dad closes his eyes. The medics meander through a bit of rubble—the hospital is under construction. The emergency room looks makeshift; this worries me.

After my father closes his eyes, he starts snoring loudly again. It's like he's asleep and totally unconscious at the same time. I don't understand it. Maybe he took those pills—that empty bottle the medics found. I hope he did, then all they have to do is pump his stomach and that's it. Easier than fixing a heart.

"Is he always like this?" asks one of the nurses.

"What do you mean?" I ask. I'm not sure what her question is. Is she asking me if he's always sleeping? Or is she asking if he snores when he sleeps?

"Is he always like this? Does he work?" asks another nurse.

"Of course he works! He works *a lot*."

Suddenly I understand that it's the vulgarity of his body that is causing the nurses to ask me these questions. Just because he's obese they think he doesn't work, that he's stuck prostrate on a bed somewhere, always in some kind of waking sleep, like they've seen on old *Geraldo* shows.

"No, he's not always like this," I say coldly. "This is *not* his normal self. I mean, isn't it obvious? Can't you see he's sick? Something's happened! He's never like this. I mean, he snores when he sleeps, but he—he works, he goes out, he—"

"This is not an incapacitated man," says my mother. "He has a full life."

The nurses start to roll him away.

"Where are you taking him?" I ask.

"Can you all just wait out in the waiting room for a moment?" says the nurse, rolling him away from us. Nina arrives and rushes through the door. D lags behind. Mom, Nina, and I stand outside the emergency room double door, we're holding hands now, the three of us, and we don't even realize we're doing it. All my future blueprints are laughing at me, the foundation cracked on the grounds of unexpected, unheard-of chaos. Somehow we always think we have so much time, even when we're in a hurry—and now here we stand, counting the seconds and holding our breath, listening beyond the doors to the rumble of Dad's snores as they fade away, as everything plays out in beats. Numerically, and without color.

2.

My father has always snored. He uses a breathing machine now when he sleeps—a sleep apnea machine. He didn't have it when we were little, thank God, it would have freaked me out. He didn't know he had a problem, really, but I was always sort of scared of the size of his snores anyway. Like the squeaky pumping of an inflatable bed and the crashing of instruments in a discordant fall. Sometimes he would get stuck and it sounded like a choke and like all those instruments, the trumpet and drums, were now lodged in his throat.

If we'd loved him more, would he have snored so much? Maybe it was some kind of call, like an animal calls in the wild, for a mate, for love.

My mother hardly slept with him when they were married. She slept with us, me and Nina, in our pink and white room. There was nothing in the world like the pleasure of sleeping with Mom, having her arms wrap around me, trying to model my breath after hers. But the truth was, Mom slept with us because she didn't love Dad the way she should have loved her husband. I knew that even then, but Nina and I loved it that Mom slept with us, so we kept quiet about it. We'd fight over who got to be next to her on our full-sized bed. She didn't like being in the middle, so we took turns sleeping next to her. We slept like that almost every night, close enough to be cozy, our bodies small enough to avoid discomfort. Sometimes, though, Mom would make one of us go sleep with him—with our father.

I remember the feeling of anxiety and near terror at the thought that it would be my turn to sleep with him. Nina didn't mind as much, but I hated it. Mom said it shouldn't be a chore to sleep with our Dad. She used to say, "*Pobrecito*, he's sleeping all by himself." She felt sorry for him, but *she* didn't want to go, she made us go instead. That's when I'd have to venture across the cold white tile floor of the hallway and sleep beside my father, who was, then as now, clinically obese, and who snored. All my friends were afraid of my father because he was so big. I could understand.

Sometimes when his breathing would seem to choke and stop completely, I thought he would die. I don't know what I would have done, lying there, holding my own breath, if he had died on one of those nights. But he didn't die—he always managed to catch his breath again, and sometimes he would even sit up on the side of the bed and stay there sitting, sleeping in that sitting position.

I would watch him carefully until I thought he was fast asleep. Then I would try and sneak away, but just as I was near the door he'd call out and ask me, gently, where I was going. I always felt bad then, when he called out—it was always then that I realized that he had to be lonely and that he wished his kids would hug him more. It was always then that I thought his snores might be his way of calling us to him, when really all they did was repel us. It was then that my heart hurt for him and I felt sad. It was then that I wished I were the kind of person who said, "I love you."

"To the bathroom," I'd say, responding to his call. "I gotta pee."

Sometimes I would pretend to go to the bathroom and then I'd return, guilty, dejected. But sometimes I'd muster enough courage to escape to my mother, who was cuddling with Nina in our bed, in our pink room, with the circular, knot-knit area rug and the pink stereo. It was then that I felt calm. It was only then that I could sleep. Mom never made me go back after those escapes. But later, in the years he was gone from my life, while I was in high school and college, the echo of those sad eyes when he'd catch me escaping would appear, out of the blue. They still do. Sometimes I'm looking into a painting I'm making and there they are, and I miss him suddenly, want him to be by my side, wish I had bought earplugs and stayed on those nights I escaped to Mom, who was always there. I wish I had hugged him and petted his hair and said, It's okay. It's okay that you snore. I'm here and I love you. I wonder if he ever felt that, across our rift. Sometimes we were so far away from each other.

And here we are again, in the waiting room while Dad is in another room—#12, ER—in a bed, with a curtain separating him from an ancient, old Cuban bag of a woman who sees invisible cockroaches and won't stop talking.

3.

Dr. Vasquez calls one of us in. "Next of kin, please," he says. That's me. Technically, Nina and I both, but Nina is younger, so we agree—it's me.

"I just need to gather some information," says Dr. Vasquez in a thick Spanish accent. "I will call the rest of you in after. *Gracias.* Later you can come in two at a time."

Once inside, Dr. Vasquez draws the curtains of the cubicle and we stand there, in close quarters, the three of us. Dr. Vasquez ignores my father. I don't look down, I look at Dr. Vasquez. I know this is what he wants. Dr. Vasquez is cold for a Spaniard—he wants to gather facts—that's why he became a doctor and not a painter, like Picasso or Dalí, or a poet, like Lorca. There is no Gypsy Ballad here, no somnambulant serenade.

"He stopped snoring," I say.

"We anesthetized him a little. He needs a bit more, so we can intubate him."

"Why? Do you have to? He's already—"

"It makes it easier on us."

"Is it easier on *him*?"

"Him too. Now," clearing his throat, clicking his pen, "does your father smoke?"

"Yes, cigars," I say. "Good cigars. Imported."

"Does he drink?"

"Yes. Chivas mostly, he drinks Chivas. And lately margaritas at Smith & Wollensky." Right when I say this, I can tell this isn't important to Dr. Vasquez. Lately I'd gotten to know Dad better at Smith & Wollensky. We had the same Irish bartender every time, and the Irish bartender closed the gap between us, just a little more, every time he poured us another glass. The ease and grace of fermented grapes. Dad was proud I could drink like a man.

"Who was the last person to see him?"

Probably the Irish bartender.

"Nobody knows. My sister talked to him yesterday at around noon. He'd asked her if she wanted to go to an early dinner but she couldn't go because she was, um, she was practicing for *American Idol*. She's the one with the wristband. She wants to be a superstar, she signed up today, before we heard about this." Again, I've said too much and not enough. Because where was I? What if all this had happened when I was still in New York, forgetting to call Nina back, not telling Mom where I was? Disconnected. Maybe the family's right, maybe I am the cold one. I look down quickly at my father, his eyes crusty at the corners. He's secreting something, which means his body is still working, right? I don't know, maybe it's all old. He was crusty to start, on the stretcher. But now he's more, definitely more. Before my own eyes start up, I look up.

"Anything else? What kind of conditions did he have?"

"I know he had atrial fibru…fib, atrial—"

"Afib, yes. Did he take any medication for that?"

"Yes, but I don't know what it's called."

"See what you can find out."

Dr. Vasquez walks out, just like that, drawing most of the curtains, leaving only a sliver of one open, through which the old woman next door pokes her head and calls to me from her bed.

"*Señorita, señorita.*"

She's all alone. Wrinkled and alone.

"I saw the man come in and I thought, I can't believe it! A pregnant man!"

At first I think she's joking, but she keeps on.

"I'd never thought I'd live to see the day, I say to myself. So I ask the nurse, and the nurse tells me that he *is* pregnant and that he *is* going to give birth, but it's going to be hard because he's a man, that's why they brought him here."

I'm not sure what to say so I just smile awkwardly, trying not to hurt her feelings, and then begin to turn away.

"No, no, don't go. Wait. Because I have more to tell you, because then, after that, they all started to laugh, the whole staff, and I didn't think it was funny. Do you think it's funny? Playing with people like that?"

"No, it's not funny."

"Don't let them play with you. You hear, don't let them play with you. Me? I'm ready, but he's not that old. He's just very, very—"

"Fat."

"Yes, fat."

4.

Fat. Everybody in his fucking family is fat. So was I, in my teens. And then I refused. It's why I got down to ninety-five pounds the year I graduated Barnard. I looked like a boy. I refuse to be anything like them.

There's fat Dora, waddling over, the older of Dad's two younger sisters. She's joined the waiting-room fold. She's sitting next to Nina, Mom, and D, who still hasn't left Nina's side (he really doesn't have a choice; has no car).

"You can go in if you want, *tía*," I say when I see Dora, after kissing her on the cheek. "They're letting in two at a time. Someone else can go too."

Mom gets up to go. But before they make it to the ER doors, Dora turns back, pulling her shirt down over her third roll, her double chin vibrating as she speaks.

"I told Pepe to go to the apartment and see about the door, close it off or something," says Dora. "I think your father has a lot of money in the apartment."

"Tell him to bring all his medication too," I say. "They're on the kitchen counter. Tell him to bring all the bottles, every single one. The ones that aren't on the kitchen counter are lined up in the cupboard above the counter." My father's clean kitchen, neatly stocked.

Dora goes toward the ER doors, dialing as she walks.

My phone rings. It's a number I don't recognize, and what if it's the doctor we called to get Dad's heart records? I pick up quickly.

"*Hola*, hi Vero, it's Dia."

"Dia, listen—" my voice says, shaky. I want to tell her right away that I can't talk.

"Vero, Lee just called me, she wants you to call her right away, wants to start going over press material ASAP." Her voice is calm but with the directive of checking off the task at hand: have Veronica call Lee.

"Dia, listen—" I try again.

"Are you okay, Veronica? You sound… Did I wake you up? You weren't taking a nap, were you?" Dia says this with a kind tone, as if she's ruined some kind of wonderful, post-travel, deep sleep. "I can call you back."

"No, no, I never nap during the day," I say, trying to pull myself together, deciding I won't say anything about where I am, what's going on. A second of absolute clarity. Lee will freak if she knows I am this distracted. If I want to keep the show, I can't say anything. "I'll call Lee, don't worry. Thanks so much, Dia, I really appreciate you calling. Thanks."

"No problem. Oh, and hey, I saw the images, the starting images that you showed to Lee, they look great. Keep it up, really great."

I thank her and we hang up. Her pep talk depresses me. Little does she know I'm drenched in hospital white, surrounded by the clink of sterility, my father's eyes closed, not responding to our calls.

I head outside to make the phone call to New York, but realize there's no way I can talk to Lee right now. My head's in a fog, and what if someone calls with information about Dad and I'm on the phone and don't make it to the other line in time? Instead, I create a new contact for Dia, so that next time I'll know who's calling, and I turn right back around to face the waiting room, where Nina's wrist is wrapped around the worn orange armrest, banded with her *American Idol* bracelet. She stood in line all morning at the American Airlines Arena in the blistering heat to sign up for *Idol*. And then she got the call from Louisa, hysterical, that she couldn't get in touch with Dad. Actual auditions are on Wednesday. Today is Monday, just sign-up day. Maybe by then this will all be over, Dad will be fine, he'll have gotten out of this and she'll sing her heart out and do it with the sense-memory of what's just happened, and she'll win, and she'll be on TV and she'll be the superstar she's always wanted to be.

"Nina, what did Louisa say Dad said in the message he left for her?"

"She says that he had called at one in the morning and that she called him back in the morning when she woke up and got the message but he didn't answer, so she said she went by the office because she sometimes brings him breakfast there and he wasn't there and then she tried calling him again and again but he didn't answer." Nina pauses a second, catching her breath, and then continues. "She also said that on his message she couldn't understand him very well and that his voice was kind of funny and she'd thought it was just the connection, why she couldn't hear him."

"Where the hell is Louisa?"

"She says she can't leave work."

Bitch.

"What about when you talked to him?"

"He asked me if I wanted to go to Smith & Wollensky with him for lunch or something but I couldn't, I—"

"Don't worry, you're gonna be able to audition—"

"I don't care," she says, trailing off and leaning back into her seat. She'd been talking from the edge of the chair until now, with purpose, but now she was back to a curved slink. She looks tiny, even smaller than five feet two. "Do you think I even care about that?" She pauses for a minute. "Vero, he sounded sad when he called me. I told D when I hung up: my Dad sounds sad."

D nods, confirming.

"I should have gone," says Nina.

"You didn't know this was going to happen, Ni—"

"He was sad."

5.

Dad was always sad.

There's a hospital psychologist now here to ask me questions about Dad. Again, we're standing over his body. The medics found that bottle. It could have been an old bottle. From close to the divorce, when—

"Was your father depressed?" asks the shrink.

"Yes," I say.

"Was he seeking therapy?"

"I don't think he was. He was a while ago, after my parents got divorced, but not anymore."

"How long ago was that?"

"I was fifteen. I'm twenty-eight now."

"Oh," she says, nodding and jotting something down.

Thing is, my father wasn't really happy even when he had it all. A beautiful wife, two little girls who loved him, a house that sheltered him. Maybe because he didn't know how to keep it—just like he didn't know how to keep the weight off. Sometimes glass houses are broken from within. Dad never understood this. Perhaps the only time I saw him respect the delicacy of glass was at Sainte-Chapelle. Still and motionless, gasping for air.

A collection of angered yells in a home could make cracks in all the cupboards' glasses, until one day they shattered in a tempered web that could never be repaired. And the thing was that no one knew when that day would come, when the glass structures would finally fail to hold, when Mom would stop being able to keep up, dropping the glue gun from her hands. And that's when it got really hard, because color reflecting off shards is even harder to read. Maybe that's why Mom hadn't gone with us that day in Paris, maybe it wasn't because she'd really wanted to go window shopping, but because she dealt with the balance of glass all the time, and she was tired of it. She didn't want to be trapped in it, she wanted to be outside, looking in at Chanels and spectacular French couture.

Everything finally shattered. Mid-November, thirteen years ago, when my mother told my father she wanted a divorce. She'd said it before and he said he'd change, but this time was different. This time her mind was made up. Dad knew it and we knew it because of the way Dad barged into our room in the middle of the night. Nina had a track meet the next day but Dad didn't care—he came into our room at five in the morning and he woke us up, crying.

"Your mother wants to break up our family," he told us. "I have to go. She's making me leave the house."

I didn't think I really cared. I was fifteen, and I'd felt it coming. I lived outside myself then; I remember very little of how things felt on my body. What I remember is what went on in my head. I wanted to go back to sleep. But Nina was thirteen and upset.

"Where are you going?" she asked. "When are you coming back?"

Nina was the one who, when she was little, used to sprawl out on his belly like a frog while Dad watched TV. She's the one who would miss his touch and the feel of his skin. He never left her, not like he left me. The last time I remember being really close to him was years before, when we'd listen to Beatle Brunch, and drive to Perrucho's Deli near our old house.

An hour after Dad left the house for good, Mom came into the room. She was calm, like nothing had happened.

"Nina, honey, you have to get up, the meet is far, let's go, *mamita.*" Mom was already dressed in her leggings and crisp white blouse, her hair tied back, and her red lipstick set to go. Mom wasn't even crying, which didn't confuse us as much as make us feel better. Like it would be okay on this end, as long as we stuck by her side. She wouldn't fall apart. That's what she was telling us. She was stronger than Dad, and I wanted to be like her.

Nina put her track uniform on, and my mother drove her to the meet, which was in another county. She came in last.

The shrink picks up where she left off, snapping my attention to her. "I'm going to recommend a therapist on his chart," she says, "so that when he's ready to get out of here, someone can tell him his options. Someone who he can talk to." She closes the chart.

As the shrink walks away, I hone in on the hope of "when he's ready to get out of here."

Dad's chest is still heaving up and down and the snoring is back, banging and crashing through the airwaves, out of tune. I want to stay by him.

"Ms. Gonzalez, if you could wait in the lobby?" Dr. Vasquez is tapping me on the shoulder.

"Why, what are you going to do?"

"We're going to intubate him. It will help us to work with him if we regulate his breathing. That's why we sedated him, remember?"

"Yes. I remember, but he's snoring again, he's—"

"We need to do this, Ms. Gonzalez."

I don't understand it, but I give in. I don't know if I'm being a bad daughter for doing this. I'm not asking him to explain everything, I'm trusting him. He's the doctor. So I leave. Walk through the maze of the emergency room's innards and look for the swinging door that will empty out to my mother.

6.

A couple of weeks after Dad woke us up at five in the morning to tell us the news, he showed up at school, bleeding from the forehead. I was in my Honors Algebra II class and the director of students came in with a solemn severity to ask, "Can Veronica be excused, Mrs. Diaz? Her father is downstairs waiting for her. It looks as though it might be a family emergency."

Dad's forehead was cracked, blood trickling down his face. He hadn't even bothered to clean himself up. He'd gone back to our house, my grandmother's house, to beg for forgiveness, to say that he didn't want to get divorced, that he loved my mother. When Mom said that they were still getting a divorce, Dad put his head through the wall in Mom's bedroom.

A couple of days later, Mom started sleeping on the couch so that Nina and I could have our own rooms. I got the room with the hole, like a screaming, jagged mouth. We didn't have any money to repair it, and we didn't know how to fix it ourselves, so all through high school, I covered it with calendars: Monet, Van Gogh, Cassatt. Budding impressionistic lily pads, undomesticated sunflowers, mothers and children tender on sand, all of them holding their hands to the gritty teeth of the wall's cavity.

Dad didn't understand how his entire life could disappear. I still remember him crying to me on the phone every night. One day he called me from a motel room, told me he had a gun to his head. He was crying, the kind of crying that's gushing wet and oozing: "What did I do? I don't know what I did. I don't know what to do." I touched the calendar on my wall, pushing it lightly through the hole as he spoke to me, then fitting my own head softly in it. I didn't know what to tell him exactly, and my heart dropped, searching for words. Maybe this is why he'd stopped talking to me, because I hadn't known what to say. Because there had been too much silence. Or maybe we'd stopped being close later because this was too much intimacy. Nina hadn't known any of this, hadn't heard his voice so close to ending it all. It was a certain intimacy he had to try and forget. He could start over with Nina, without any of this baggage.

How to stop him from dying right there on the phone with me — the sonic clicking snap of the shot and then the clangorous drop of the phone to the floor, his heavy body thudding, burrowing through ground, making more holes. All I could find to tell him was not to die. I said, "Dad, don't do anything bad, life is good. I love you. We need you."

THE REASON my father had picked Nina and me up from school that day, blood trickling down his forehead, was to take us on a car ride, during which he explained certain things to us:

"Your mother is now a divorcée and a whore," he said, driving fast. "You two girls need to know what she's doing. She's going to be bringing other men to the house, and you'll hear her fucking other men, and you think of your father when she does that, think of what she's doing to us."

I hated him for doing this. I wished for a second he'd have died four days before, gun to his head, so we wouldn't have to hear this. And then my heart took back the thought, like a gripping sponge trying to absorb it, pick it up — that violent, frightening thought which I felt ashamed of and which had surged in me so seemingly out of my control. Was I just as angry inside as he was? I couldn't be, I couldn't let the thunder of it come over me. Right there, a decision, clear as day: the difference between my father and me would be control. I would pour it out in a rabid red, I would swish paint around like blood. Channeling everything into a grid that would line it all up. I would paint. Chaos into order, into art. Craft.

"I'm going to make your mother's life a living hell as long as I can," he said, looking straight ahead, spitting his words out, hands gripped tight to the wheel. "So help me God, I am going to make her life hell." Nina was up in front, just looking at him, tears making a path down her cheeks, quietly. She crouched so low into the leather seat that I thought the seatbelt would strangle her; her hands flat beneath her thighs. I was in the back, diagonal to her, with a perfect view of her. But when she started slinking so low, I slid sideways to the seat right behind hers and touched her head and her soft, cushy hair from behind and whispered to her by the window, where Dad couldn't see, "Don't worry." She didn't look back, but I could feel her nodding her little head in my hands, trusting me. I would be strong, like my mother.

I'd noticed a new bumper sticker on Dad's car before getting in: MY EX-WIFE DRIVES A BROOM. It was farcical. How could he have seriously slapped that on his bumper? I'd only caught it in a quick flash because we'd gotten into the van so fast. Dad was already moving the car in reverse before Nina had closed the door completely, his wheels screeching out of our elite, private Catholic school gates. How embarrassing.

"I'm so fucked up, I'm fucked up," Dad kept saying after his fit, after his clenched teeth and his spitting had softened. They were desperate and sobbing, those words: "I'm so fucked up."

"Are you okay, Dad?" asked Nina, taking her hands out from under her thighs, sniffling and touching his arm. Nina wasn't the one getting the gun-to-the-head phone calls, didn't even know about them. Neither did Mom.

I didn't say a word. I just waited for him to be done ranting and crying, and then I asked, calmly as I could, "Can you take me back to school?" I wanted to go back to the schedule, to one class after another: English following algebra, then chemistry, then break. All predictable and timed. Secure and beautiful.

Dad had started driving around in circles by then. We were going much slower now and we were all the way in South Miami somewhere, driving aimlessly. "Can you take me back to school?" I asked again, with equal calm.

"Yes," he said, looking back at me, eyes that almost made me do what Nina had done—a hand on the arm, a touch. But no: control. I wouldn't lean over.

"I want to go home, Dad. Can you take me home?" asked Nina softly. I wondered what that felt like to him. To hear her say "home" like that and know it was a place he no longer shared with us. We had different homes now.

By the time I got home from school, Nina had told Mom everything and Mom had made Nina paprika chicken, which Nina loved and which she was eating now. They had probably cooked it together. Nina loved to spread the red spice all over the chicken and then put it in the toaster oven and watch it crisp and change color.

Nina told Mom I'd wanted to stay at school so Mom let me be, but when I walked in the door, she ran to me and enfolded me, like a giant bird, an embrace very similar to Leo's but with triple the power, even though Mom is smaller. She didn't say anything at first, but then she combed her fingers through my long dark hair and said softly, "Don't worry." I nodded my head in her hands.

Those were the days when I started to wish I lived somewhere else, when I lost myself in the thick books I brought home from the library. Somehow the geometry of a cubist painting or collage, complex and pastiched as it was, was clearer than my life. I buried myself in the layers of Sigmar Polke, a painter my father didn't even know existed, whose layers were like the sky in Miami, or like the sea. Sometimes they just made you want to believe in God, bringing you joy through all of their depth.

7.

"Marta! What are you doing here?"

I go to hug Marta across the hospital waiting room, when I feel the phone ring in my pocket.

It's Lee's number. Dia told her by now that she's passed on her message to me and she's wondering why I haven't called her.

I ignore it. But my heart beats out the familiar ba-boom from a couple of days ago, echoing in the empty-hole chamber and ringing down to my stomach. Nerves shatter my insides as my internal grid smears out in a watery blue, dripping.

"Do you see what a good friend," says Mom, hugging Marta sideways, their wrists touching, matching pink watches glittering. Two of five watches, belonging to their girls' club.

"I work here," says Marta. "For God's sake, Eli, don't you remember, what's wrong with you?"

That's Marta: to the point. Always funny, always saying things that imply, *That's life, what are you going to do about it?* Marta, the social worker of the group.

Mom had just reunited with the girls' club, her high school friends we'd always heard so much about, but never met. Mom hadn't seen them since she'd moved to Texas with Dad, early in their marriage. The other four friends had kept in touch with each other, and Mom was the only lost sheep among them. About a year ago, Mom ran into one of them in the supermarket. And now they're all inseparable — Chiclets in their fifties — and they all wear their pink, fake-diamond-faced watches to prove it. They go to brunch at least one Sunday a month, but sometimes four, and they even went on a cruise together. They're all awesome.

"How are you, honey?" says Marta, hugging me. And immediately she starts to talk. She tells tales and whips you out of messes with her stories. Marta has stories about my father.

"Your mother called me. I came right away although apparently the woman forgot I was right upstairs. I've known your father since we were like this," she says, motioning the height of her hip. "Before your mother ever met him. Elementary school, can you imagine! He used to sell shoelaces to everybody."

"What?" I don't know this about Dad.

"Oh yeah, he was Mr. Shoelace. He would come into school with a box full of them and when somebody broke a lace, he'd whip out the box. *Everybody* bought shoelaces from him, I mean *everybody*, even the teacher. And when the cool ones started coming out, the ones in funky colors, your Dad had them."

That was him. That was him right there. The man could sell ice to an Eskimo. As I turn the phrase in my head, I think of Lee and the beep of her message on my phone just a few moments ago. I want to pick up the phone, call her back, talk about work, about how she's planning to sell my stuff. There is a nervous rush inside me, a new fear crystallizing. I am going to lose the show. I can't lose the show, I can't let my father sabotage this. No matter what happens, I *cannot* lose this. But then I feel a compounded guilt beating all over my body and head, to even think like this, how could I? And so I let her go.

"Ay, Ichi," sighs Mom, "he was very convincing. He should have been a lawyer."

Except all he had was a high school diploma.

"He convinced me to marry him. What a … a disconnect. I should've only ever been his friend." Mom always does that, says words like "disconnect" out of nowhere, like we're supposed to understand what that means. Mom laughs out her words a little, but her eyes sadden.

Marta sees her eyes too.

"Remember those days, Eli?" asks Marta. "Remember your desk?"

"*My* desk? I remember *your* desk!" Mom turns to me and Nina and D. "Marta had the best plastic yellow desk." Seeing our faces, she adds, "Remember, this was the '70s."

"She was so persistent: *que sí* she wanted a desk like my yellow desk and the yellow desk and the yellow desk, and 'Marta's yellow desk is so cool, I love Marta's yellow desk, the yellow plastic desk,' and on and on and on."

"But my parents never bought me the things I really needed. They had parties instead. I did my homework on my bed, which was fine, but—"

"And then what?" Marta pushes Mom slightly on the shoulder. "Tell them. You remember."

My mother takes up the story: "And then one day, I get home from school and your father's at my house, and he says he has a surprise for me. So I'm curious, and he says to close my eyes and he takes my hand, leading me to my room, and when I open my eyes there's an enormous wooden, professional lawyer-type desk in there that leaves hardly any space to walk. And your father says, 'Do you like it? I know how badly you wanted one.' And I think, yuck, oh my God, what am I going do with such a desk?"

This breaks my heart. They were just kids. What must he have done to raise that money?

Marta laughs. "Disconnects," she says. "Poor Ichi."

Ignaciano Javier Gonzalez. Ichi for short. Ichi or Icho. Bubi. Nobody called him Ignaciano. Poor Ichi.

8.

"Ms. Gonzalez, Ms. Gonzalez," the doctor calls from the ER double doors.

I run over.

"Ms. Gonzalez, we're having difficulty intubating your father. We're going to have to call in more anesthesiologists."

"Why?"

"It's very difficult, nobody has been able to. We've had two doctors down already. His neck is very short and there is a lot of skin and fat that makes it almost impossible, and his tongue is swollen. I'll keep you informed. We need to do that so we can get a CAT scan." And that's it, that's all he says, and he walks away. I feel helpless.

When I walk back, my uncle Pepe, Tía Dora's husband, has arrived with a Victoria's Secret bag, red and pink stripes, full of pills, pills, and more pills. And in his hand I see my father's cell.

"Hi, Pepe." I give him a kiss, he gives me a hug. "Can I see the phone?"

I go immediately to "calls made" and look at yesterday's list. He called Nina around noon, just like she'd said. Then there are two numbers I don't recognize. He doesn't make any calls again until 7:00 p.m., another number I don't recognize, and then Louisa at around 12:55 a.m. Then, at 12:58, he dials 944..#*7#. Pepe is looking over my shoulder.

"He was trying to dial 911," says Pepe. "The four is right there, see, right under the one."

My eyes start to water, but I try to regain my composure. If I cry, everything will fall apart. Who will be calm enough to talk to the doctor, to go inside and give the nurse the list of medications in that Victoria's Secret bag?

He didn't overdose. He was all alone. He was calling for help. He tried to call Louisa. Fuck Louisa. What was she thinking? Where the fuck is Louisa?

"Where is Louisa?" I turn to where Nina is.

"She says she'll come after work."

Dad was all alone. We didn't find him until 2:30 the next afternoon. How many hours is that? Fourteen?

"I'll be right back," I say. Marta, Pepe, Mom, Nina, Dora, and D, they all nod their heads yes.

I walk through the double doors.

9.

"My father was alone fourteen hours. Nobody heard from him since then, that's what his cell phone says. We found his cell phone. These are his medications, this is what we found, there's a lot. Some of them weren't his, some of them are old. I don't think he took those anymore. I don't know what he was taking now. There are some prescribed 2007, that's I guess what he was taking now still. Coumadin, Crestor, Xenical. That one's old, 2002, I don't know why he still had it. Another bottle of Coumadin, that's the heart one, isn't it?"

"Ma'am, ma'am," the nurse tries to interrupt.

"Bumetanide, Motrin 800, Potassium Cl 20MEQ ER tablets, Coreg—that's 2006, but he also has a Coreg from 2007. What's Coreg? Lisinopril, Clorazepate—but that has his father's name on it, his father's in a nursing home, he's got Alzheimer's. They have the same name, Junior and Senior. I don't know why he has these. Here's another one, Clorazepate, also under his father's name, it's got something scribbled on it in Spanish: *Calmante, para dormir*. Is this anti-anxiety medication?"

"Ma'am, ma'am, please. Who is your father?"

"Mr. Gonzalez, #12." Jesus.

"I'm not your nurse. Safaia is your nurse. Wait in the room, I'll tell her to go meet you over there."

10.

Dad's got tubes everywhere now. They've taken off his clothes, he's got a white sheet covering him up to his stomach. His shirt is on the chair, it has throw-up on it from before, it was there on the stretcher. I wonder if he was conscious when he threw up on himself, all by himself. He has a bruise on his belly, his wide and sprawling belly that, despite the fat, now looks swollen and yellow in parts. I can hear the sound of him hitting the tile, like a fish hitting ground, or like a person crashing against water. There's something they've put in his nose, it looks like a screw or a nail, and he's bloody all over. They put a tube through his neck, and there's blood everywhere there too. The machine is beeping in stops and starts. He's biting on his air tube and there's crusty blood all over his mouth from where he's bit his tongue. His eyes are shut, completely shut, he won't open them for me anymore. But he wiggles his feet. He's in there somewhere.

This is what living here has done to Dad. Would he have been this way in Cuba? Maybe worse, maybe better. I don't know. But this, this state he's in, it's America. A patient etherized upon a table, a huge and noisy patient no one will care for because the system is not in place to do it, because the nurses won't listen, overwhelmed instead with long trails of paper and insurance protocol. Can a doctor fix this? A messy recovery. Again, I hold onto that base — recovery — cling to it.

"Dad? Dad?"

Nothing.

"Dad, please."

He won't open them. I touch his stomach and I caress his hands, softly, his chubby, little-boy hands, his short nails. I touch his silver, more-salt-than-pepper beard and his soft flowy hair, I comb it back with my fingers. I must seem so cold to you, Dad. I'm not. I hold onto his hand. I can't remember the last time I was alone with him like this. Just me and him.

Bermuda. I was eleven. That was the first time we'd been alone together without Mom. What was the last? Dad, I'm sorry, I should be a better daughter, I promise I'll be a better daughter.

11.

Bermuda.

That was when you sold shoes in the Caribbean. You liked the Caribbean, worked like a beast there, left your sweat on the ground, let it grow. There should be plants out there named after you, you gave them breath. You taught me about work. I was the only kid in my class who knew anything about the Antilles, about the islands of the West Indies, did I ever tell you that? How proud I was that I knew where Curaçao was, Martinique, Guadalupe, St. Croix, St. Lucia, St. Kitts, the smallest island. Remember Conrad? His house by the water—a real native, you told me, not a tourist, or someone just passing through like everyone else. "This guy is for real." He was pretty cool. And the way you could handle a shoe back then, that was cool too, you used to turn it around in midair, like an expert bartender flipping a cocktail. I bet you can still do that. Bermuda was great. Was that your idea, or did I beg you to let me go? I can't remember.

Once we got there I couldn't stop going to the bathroom and giggling, I was so nervous. You were kind of nervous too, without Mom around, and you asked me if I always peed and laughed so much. But then there was Joi. When Joi came in, you said, "If you do good with her and sell her a lot of shoes, then tomorrow we go into town and buy you some real Bermuda clothes, like real Bermuda shorts." That was incentive enough. I talked and talked and sold some of your stock straight out. You were proud of me. I tried on all those shoes for her and told her what the kids might like for "back-to-school," and then I tried on the ladies' shoes and told her which colors were in season and she thought I was so cute, and I was so happy because you kept giving me high fives and doing the Gonzalez handshake with me. Slap, slap, slide-the-arm, grip the fingers, buckle the thumbs—so cool. I got off the airplane in the clothes I picked out the day after we sold out and went to that expensive boutique—that blue little suit, with the floppy, cotton shorts and the soft tank that felt so light on my skin and danced when I walked—

"Ms. Gonzalez, the nurse said you have a list of the medications he was taking?"

"Huh? Oh, yes. Here's the bag. It's all of the ones he had, it's all mixed up. Some of them are old, some of them are new, some aren't his—"

"I'll sort it out," Safaia says coolly.

"Why is he all messed up like this? Can't somebody clean up his blood? When are they taking him for the CAT scan? We've been here for hours already."

"It took four anesthesiologists to install those tubes, ma'am." Safaia lowers her eyes to me, angrily, bitter as she says this.

"So what are you telling me? When are you taking him for the CAT?"

"When we can." She cuts me off, colder now.

"What do you mean, 'when we can'? What if he's bleeding in there all over the place, in his head and in his heart and we don't even know it? We don't even know what's going on. You have to stop it. Where's the doctor?"

"Listen, ma'am, we—your father's big, it's gonna take a lot of us to move him."

"So get a lot of you moving then! What's the problem? It's not like the ER is full, it's not like we're in a Third World country. Get the fucking staff."

"I don't have to listen to you talk to me like this."

She walks away.

"Excuse me! Are you walking away from me? Where's the supervising nurse? Where's the doctor? Are you telling me because he's fat, you just don't care?"

She walks out of sight.

I run to the main desk.

"Excuse me, excuse me, I need to talk to someone."

Mom and Nina are coming in, I can see them peripherally.

"What's wrong?" asks Nina. "What's wrong!" Her hysteria escalates.

"They don't care! That's what's wrong." I turn to the nurse station. "We need to see a doctor. Excuse me. I need to see a doctor."

"Is anybody going to listen to us?" Mom begins to lose it. Nina starts to cry.

12.

It's 7:00 p.m., still no doctor. The supervising nurse tells us he's on his way. They've changed shifts. We don't have the cold Spaniard anymore, now it'll be another one. In the meantime, my other aunt has arrived, the youngest, Joe. She's sitting by my father. I'm standing by him, still stroking his belly. In my peripheral vision I catch a woman walk around the corner, toward us. She's wearing a tight black and white polka-dot miniskirt that ends so high up her thigh I can almost see her underwear. I mean it's right there. She has on a black shirt with a tight yellow belt and stiletto heels, black stilettos with yellow lightning bolts on the sides. Her hair is bleached and wired, curly and radiating around her head like some super-shuttle-express-spaced-out hairdo. She has neon-green eyes I can see from here, like a cat. She approaches. Who the hell is this? And then: I've seen her before, I'm supposed to know her. Who is she?

She walks up to Tía Joe. "You don't remember me," she says. "No," says Joe, "sorry." I can tell Joe's lying, she can be a real bitch. And then I remember everything except the woman's name. This is my father's ex-ex-girlfriend. About four years ago. *La balsera.* The one who came on a raft and the raft shook so much on the open sea that it disconnected her kidneys from her body. She told us that story over sushi one day.

"Vero," she says, "I'm so sorry." She's crying. I hug her and she says, "I have to talk to you. I was with your father last night." My attitude toward her immediately changes. She's got another piece of the puzzle.

"Excuse me," interrupts the nurse. "Two at a time."

I don't budge. I look over at Joe. Joe leaves, with an attitude, raising her eyebrows. But she leaves, that's all that matters.

"When were you with my father? What time?" Suddenly I remember her name is the name of a flower. Gardenia? Marigold? Rose? No. Lily. Lily. It's Lily. "Tell me Lilita, tell me." And she starts to cry.

She pulls me close, whispers right into my face, "I know how you are, I'm going to tell you because I know you're different than the rest of them, you're the best of them. The rest of them, your *tías*—Joe and Dorita—they gossip, they're bad, they'll think things, they'll say things, but you won't judge me. Don't tell anyone, but somebody has to know, somebody has to know."

"Don't worry, no one will know, except me. What happened?" I want to pull the words from her throat.

"Your father, he, he called yesterday afternoon, he wanted to have lunch, and I said okay. We've been broken up for a long time, but then a couple of weeks ago we ran into each other and we started seeing each other again and, well, you know."

I think of Louisa. I'm glad for a moment that she can't get out of work. My father's bedside could turn into a circus. Or a harem.

"Yesterday, when he called me—"

"When? What time did he call you?"

"It must've been around one in the afternoon, a little after maybe. I went with him, we went to that place on the beach, what is it called?"

"Smith & Wollensky."

"*Ese, ese mismo*, that's the one!"

And on and on she goes. They'd ordered shrimp.

"I told him not to eat shrimp, seafood never settles well and he said he didn't feel good, but he ate the shrimp. Your father is like that, you know how he is, he just said, 'Lilita, what are you talking about, this is the stuff of life, you only live once.'"

I imagine my father taking a jumbo shrimp into his mouth, chewing down, pleasure running through his body like the smooth intravenous ride of a heroin addict.

"He only had one drink, which was strange, and he said it to me himself, he said, 'Lily, I'm not feeling well, I can't even finish my drink. I can usually down about seven of these margaritas and I can't even swallow this one.' Can you imagine drinking seven drinks at once?"

I could imagine. I wish I had a drink right now.

"He's a big man," I tell her. "Seven drinks for him isn't like seven drinks for us."

I cut her off because I don't want to hear judgments, I want to hear facts, hear things that make sense and that make the jigsaw pieces fit, that make me understand how and why we found my father unconscious on the floor of his apartment, by himself.

"On the way home, he said that if we didn't make love, not to take it personally, that he just didn't feel well, and that he just wanted me to know that, and then he started to get a really bad headache, really bad, and when we got to his place it was even worse and he just kept saying, 'What a horrible headache.' And then it was like he was mixing things up and talking about his days in the Caribbean, and he asked me to massage his head, and I put an ice pack on his head for a very long time and I massaged his head when I could, and I gave him Tylenol and I tried to make it better, and he asked me if I would stay with him and take care of him, if I would take care of him forever, and, well, you know how it is with us, I told him I loved him but that I wanted a child. I want a child, and he doesn't want that, he always told me that couldn't be, that he already had you and your sister and he didn't need any more, but then he kept asking if I would take care of him. And then he started asking me to, you know…" At this point Lilita opens her mouth like an O, making motions with her hand and mouth, signaling a blow job.

Oh my God, I can't believe she's telling me this. My father, my poor father. He was so lonely.

"I couldn't do it, and he was asking me why and if it was because I was grossed out by him, and he kept telling me, 'Yes you are disgusted with me,' but that wasn't true, I'm never disgusted by him, it doesn't matter to me that he's, you know, it's just that, see"—she lifts her upper lip, pointing out some blue stitches on her gums—"I just had surgery last week." She wiggles around in her tight skirt, her legs dancing nervously, as she shows me.

Oh, Dad.

"But he kept insisting and I started to get a little bit scared, and I had to make a call to Cuba anyway."

It's right there that I start to tune her out. Because I understand that was the moment she abandoned him.

"You know how hard it is to call Cuba. I had to go, I *had* to go. But I told him we would talk later, and he called me again, that evening, around seven."

Which was the other number I didn't recognize on Dad's cell.

"What did he tell you? Did you see him again after that?" I ask with urgency. Calmly, but with urgency.

"I, he—he said he had thrown up, and that he had been feeling sick, but that he felt better now, and when I asked him if he wanted me to go back, he said, 'No, no, I feel better.' He didn't need me to come all the way back there, he said. And then we hung up. *Ay, Dios mío.*" She moves her long red plastic nails to her face. "I'm sorry, I'm sorry, I'm so sorry."

I hold Lily in my arms for a short while and then tell her I have to speak to the doctor, that she can wait in the waiting room if she wants, and to give me her number. I'll keep in touch, I say, which I'm not sure yet if I mean.

After her lightning heels make their last echoing sounds through the emergency room, I am left alone with my father once more, the white neon buzz of the light wheezing above me, its cold fluorescence making my eyes sting. There's a stillness all around for a slow-moving, elongated second, until I lean down to kiss Dad's cheek and go look for the doctor. Wading through the cold patch of nurses and technicians, tubes, empty roll-away beds, and hospital gowns strewn all over the ER, I walk briskly, trying to find a familiar face. There aren't many patients and there's also no doctor. But there's the supervising nurse who had helped us when we'd come in, she's filling out paperwork at the main counter. I tell her, "I just found out he'd had a headache all night long, a very bad one, excruciating. Also, he threw up."

"That's not good. Those are very bad signs together," she says, without looking up from her papers.

"Signs of what? When are we going to get the CAT scan, where is the doctor? What do you mean those are very bad signs?"

Turning around to file the papers she's just filled out, with her back turned toward me she answers, "We'll let you know when the doctor gets here. We'll let you know."

As the nurse starts to walk away from the counter, I begin to feel desperate.

I chase her. "Please, no one has told us what's going on. No one has come down to tell us what's wrong with him, or to tell us when he's going to get his scan, or what we should do, or anything. No one has told us anything, and that's all I want. Please, please, that's all I want. I just need someone to tell us where we are. Please." And I start to cry. I can't stop crying and pleading. "Please."

The nurse turns around.

"I'll call the doctor," she says, looking at me for split second, right in the eyes, and then turning away again.

I feel warm, running viscous liquid from my nose, landing on my upper lip. I wipe it clean as I walk back to my father, patting my eyes.

13.

The doctor is handsome. Young, but handsome, wearing new scrubs. He stands bedside, across from Nina, me, and Mom, as if my father's unconscious body is his desk. He sets us in our place like that, with a barrier, and he starts in right away.

"We can't put your father on the CAT scan machine or give him an MRI because those machines will only hold 350 pounds. And, eyeballing him, I can pretty much guess he's not going to fit in there."

"Eyeballing him?" I ask. "Don't you people have scales in this hospital? Bed scales? I've seen those before. You have to have those, you have to be able to weigh people to go into surgery, you don't just 'eyeball'! I mean, what kind of hospital is this? What if he weighs 349, then you can put him in the machine, right?"

My mother is silent in disbelief. Nina has already started to cry.

"We can't risk your father breaking the machine for everybody else," he says, unflinching. "That's just not the way it works."

"That's not what I'm saying. I'm saying can't you weigh him?"

"We can't. The bed scales are in our sister hospital and we don't have any here."

"Can't you transport them?" my mother yells, the vein in her forehead popping. "One, at least? You have ambulances, don't you? This is America. We're not in Haiti somewhere, are we? The man has insurance, for God's sake. Good insurance."

"What kind of hospital is this?" Nina repeats my phrase, louder than any of us. Her volume shocks the doctor; he opens his eyes at her as if scolding her. I squeeze her arm, begging her not to bring in the attitude, capital A, she tends to bring out, and always gets us nowhere fast in situations like this.

"So what are you saying, doctor?" Mom jumps in, attempting an even temper. "What are our options?"

"Well, we can take him to Jackson, where we're pretty sure there's a machine that will hold him. But it's dangerous because he's so unstable. His blood pressure waivers from very high to very low. His heartbeat is irregular and, given the x-ray we just took of his chest, we can see the heart is almost the size of his entire chest cavity. If we unhook him from the machines or airlift him, he may suffer a heart attack and die on the way."

"But what if he's lying there bleeding somewhere inside his brain?" I ask.

"He could be; we don't know that. But in order to see that we need the CAT, and in order to get him to the scan at Jackson we're putting him in danger of cardiac arrest."

"So what do we do?" Mom asks.

"I would suggest you allow him to stabilize."

We're all stunned. He can see this. He tries to put it another way.

"Some people come in here with a cut, and we put a bandage on and it heals immediately. Some people come here with a cut and they bleed longer, and it takes them much longer to heal. Everybody's different."

What kind of bullshit is that? This isn't a cut. This man is dying.

"That's your medical opinion?" Mom asks again. "To wait it out, and if he gets better take him to Jackson?"

"That's my medical opinion."

"Let me ask you something, doctor," I say. "Let me ask you something else. What would you do if this were your father?"

Dr. Young-Scrubs looks at my father, breathing through the tubes, blood crusting around his neck and mouth. And then he looks at me. "I would still wait. There's nothing else you can do, unless you want to kill him."

There is a long pause. Everybody looks at my father.

"Do you think you could get someone in here to clean his blood, then?" I say. "And do you think you could have the nurses look after him, instead of my having to go over there and beg them to watch their patient? And do you think we could have a doctor come down here once in a while, just once in a while, that's all I'm asking, to tell us what is going on?"

He nods, looks at my father again. "We'll be taking him out of the ER soon and into CCU."

"Good, when?"

"Whenever we can assemble a team to lift him onto another bed and get him there."

I want to squeeze my sister's arms in reverse, want to get her to blurt out, "What kind of hospital is this?" again, at the top of her lungs, and with the biggest Attitude she can muster. But she took the training well the first time; she's quiet as a mouse. Everyone is silent as the doctor turns and walks away. One by one, we make our way toward the waiting room.

14.

"There was a time when being fat safed his life," says Pepe, smiling, thick accent in tow.

The time with the horse.

I'd recognize the beginning of that story anywhere. Tío Pepe is telling it to Tony when I walk into the lobby. Tony, oh thank God, because I need him. His quiet self, his big eyes, his freckles, his bald little head, the cushion of his stomach padding our embrace.

"Vero never say to you that story, Antonio?" asks Pepe, in awe.

Tony looks up and gets up immediately as I walk toward him, as if he recognizes me by the sound of the squeaky steps I'm making, the fault of the "nerdy shoes," the red Crocs he'd made so much fun of me for buying. Now he's got a pair of his own—yellow ones, which he's wearing now too and are even nerdier. Tony peels away from Pepe, midsentence, no explanations. He meets me halfway, hugs me, holds me, and I thank God for him. I lift my head from his chest, catch a breath, and see that by now, almost everyone is here: Dad's two sisters, Dora and Joe, Mom, Vic, Marta, Nina, D, Pepe, and Pepe and Dora's kids, my cousins Cora and Denise.

Dora stands up. "Where is he, how is he?"

"What are the doctors saying?" That's Tía Joe.

"Are they going to move him to ICU soon? CCU?"

It's all a rush, until the cacophony of their voices becomes something blaring, like the trapped birds at Parrot Jungle. I try and get it out, tell them what I know, and then I sit down. They're outraged, they don't understand. Again, the dissonance:

"Wait, but this can't be—"

"They have to be able to do *something!*" Dora yells.

The vein in Mom's forehead is now permanent. "You have to fight the doctors in these hospitals," she says. "You have to fight, take things into your own hands. This is no time to be shy, you hear me, Veronica? We have to fight."

"I'm going to give the doctors a little bit more time, and then I'll ask again," I say, calmly. Tired.

While they yell amongst themselves, I take my cell out of my pocket, which is vibrating again. Two more texts from Lee and a voicemail from Dia at the Miami gallery.

Dia's message is polite:

"Hi Veronica, it's me, Dia, I'm just giving you another call because Lee is trying to get hold of you. She's worried, she says, because you never do this. She says you always answer right back and it's weird that you are not answering. I told her to give you until tomorrow, but she's in a panic. I think she thinks something's happened. Maybe you could just give us a call and touch base. I think that would calm her down."

From Lee, a bit more agitated:

Where are you?! I need to give you some dates! You have to do some interviews! We need to move forward, Veronica. Call me!

I can understand. The woman has just given me a solo show during Basel, and I won't answer her calls. I also realize how bizarre this is, how much like my father I must be, whether I like it or not—how Lee is having a hissy because I'm not "showing up" to work and how that's just what happened this morning when Sonny saw Dad wasn't around.

I text Lee back, decide to tell her the truth. I owe her that much, at least.

Can't talk now. My dad's in the hospital. Call you as soon as I can. Pass message to Dia, she's been calling. Everything's fine, just can't talk now.

Everything's fine. I carve out the day I've missed into the schedule in my mind. It's fine. As long as this is all over sometime soon, it'll be fine. Again: should I even be thinking this? I bury my phone in my bag, because I'm afraid to see Lee's response. Everyone that matters is right here in this hospital anyway. When I call Dad's doctor again, leaving the same message about Dad's records, about how we need them and they need to send them over to the hospital, the answering service guy finally breaks down and tells me the doctor is on vacation and he doesn't have access to those records until the office reopens, he's not sure when exactly. They'd get back to me tomorrow.

Nina, Cora, Joe, and Denise get up.

Cora, Joe, and Denise are all cowards and they won't say a word to any doctor, they'll just stand there, like fools, they're all talk. I look up at the group of them and realize that Nina is the only one of them who isn't fat. My cousin Cora is disheveled, her blonde ringlets fuzz out like a cherub halo. She's gotten really big, her double chin meeting the rim of her boyish T-shirt. She stands like a man, tapping her foot, jingling the keys in her pocket. Her blue eyes glimmer through the fat no less—they're crystal and clear and they make me sad.

What a shame it is that no one can see those gorgeous blues, hidden behind the layers of too-much-bad-eating, and hiding—hiding from Dora. Dora should let her be who she really is, accept Cora's "friend" as her girlfriend, accept her daughter. That thick outer layer would melt away. As for my other cousin, Denise, engaged to a baker, her nails loom out in acrylic, orange like a safety jacket, they make me think of Washington Heights.

"It's just two at a time," I whisper. But nobody listens.

I stay by Tony and Pepe.

"Was he telling you the horse story?" I ask.

"*Ese mismo*," says Pepe.

"What happens?"

"Tell him, Pepe." I nod, as if giving him permission.

"Well, one day Icho says to everyone, 'Let's go ride some horses,' *y todos vamos* because, you know Icho, whatever he say, whatever is we did. *Todos*—Eli, Dora, Nina *y yo, y* Vero, *y cuando llegamos*, we get to the place and there is these horses that looks very big and some very small and Eli says right away to Icho, she say, 'The girls are not riding those,' and so the girls don't get on. Eli always treat them like porcelain, so they stay behind with their *abuela*, but everyone else get on the horses. And Dora, who you know is chicken about *todo*, she get on and she start getting scared and she scream, and then Icho's horse, who already is saying, *Coño este gordo quien me lo ha puesto arriba!*"

Pepe starts laughing, squinting his eyes, and Tony joins the fold of laughter. "And then Icho say to Dora, 'Stop screaming, Dora,' but Dora keep saying, '*Mi caballo quiere comer*, it doesn't move!' because her horse was staying behind eating grass and she was afraid we would leave her. And then all the horses start to make commotion when they hear her scream and *el de* Icho *lo tira pal carajo*, throws him way off, and Icho—" Pepe can't stop laughing. "Icho, *coño*, Icho, he bounce on the floor like a ball."

"I remember that bruise," I say. An enormous hematoma. But it was true, when the ambulance came to get him, the paramedic said, "Sir, your fat saved your life."

Tony and Pepe are turning red with laughter and suddenly I feel an enormous guilt because of it, shame.

15.

"They only want to talk to next of kin, they won't talk to me, only to you," says Dora over the phone, she's the first one back at the hospital. It's 8:45 a.m. when you look at your watch. You hear what Dora says as if in a vacuum and you jump out of bed, run into the living room. You yell to your mother and sister who are pretending to nap, "Let's go, let's go, the doctors need to speak to us."

You'd all gone home at five in the morning, when they'd moved him to CCU, they'd told everyone no one would be allowed in until 9:00 a.m. Everyone thought it might be a good idea to get food and a shower, but you spent the morning, after facing Lee's response text, trying to figure out how to answer.

You OK? she wrote. *Should I give the show to someone else?*

No. Absolutely Not, was what you finally replied. *All's fine*, you repeated in a second blurp of text. *Get back to you soon. Promise*, said a third blurp.

Your mother has spent the morning with Marta on the phone. They've called all the hospitals in Miami, but nowhere is there a CAT scan or MRI machine large enough for your father. Your mother even suggests Metro Zoo.

"They must have that kind of machine there. Can't we get some kind of permit?"

Your mother remembers when they were married, when she had persuaded him to go on a diet. "Bubi," she'd said in the kitchen, "I heard about this diet that the University of Miami is doing, it's all shakes, but it also comes with nutrition classes. I'll do it with you." Your mother, who was normal and only slightly overweight, like a regular mom, she did the shake diet with him so that he couldn't say, "You don't know what it's like." Like he'd said before. He was the one who broke the diet. At the university, they had weighed him on an animal scale and your mother remembered. So do you.

"What about Metro Zoo?" she kept asking the doctors.

You find out later that Marta called Metro Zoo as soon as they opened. The zoo said, "Please, we don't do that. We get these requests all the time, we have to say the same thing each time: We can't let humans into our facilities. These are for animals. Can you let the hospital know that? Can they please—"

"But you have them? Right? You have the machines?"

"They're not for humans, ma'am, not for humans."

"Let's go," you yell. "Let's go, let's go."

Nina pulls a sweater over her head, jeans without underwear. Your mother is already dressed. All of you dart out the door, speed to the hospital. The misty remains of a night of rain in the air are sticking to you. When you get to the hospital you find the head nurse, you tell her who you are. "The doctor wants to speak to you," she says, bowing her head. You feel it immediately, by the way she moves, not a good signal anywhere.

Today the doctor is a spindle of a woman. She is so thin and her eyes so red at the rims that you think: this woman should never have become a doctor, she cares too much. The sad, red-eyed stick woman leads you into a private room. She asks, "Is there anyone else that you would like to be in here for this conversation?" You understand her tone and you call in your mother, Nina, Joe, and Dora.

Everybody sits around the doctor in a semicircle. You are the closest to her, Nina is directly across from her.

"Your father has suffered a brain death," says the doctor.

She pauses and looks around to make sure everyone understands, then continues.

"Death, by law, requires the signatures of two doctors. I have already provided mine for the brain death. The next will come, if he fails the breathing test."

"What does that mean?" The question comes in waves, once from everyone in the room.

"It means a pulmonary disease doctor will come and disconnect him from the machine, long enough to see whether he can catch his breath on his own, but not long enough for him to suffer a physical death, only to see if there is respiratory failure. When and if the second doctor signs, your father will be declared dead." She speaks directly to you and Nina, mostly. Everyone else is secondary to her. She comforts you, despite what she is telling you. Nina is expressionless until she breaks out into a sob. Somehow you understand everything, crisply. You don't cry. You say, "I understand."

"It will be up to you," she says, "at that moment, to disconnect him. He will eventually pass on his own if he has indeed suffered respiratory failure above the brain death. It will be up to you to decide when to remove the tubes. You will have all the time you need."

THE RESPONSE from the pulmonary disease expert comes later in the day: respiratory failure. You sign the papers to take him off the life support. This part is the most blurred of all.

Your father is dead.

Your father is dead, even though you don't know what killed him because they never found the right machines for him. The death certificate, they tell you, will read: brain death and respiratory failure. But you will never know the physical cause of these. Whether it was a heart attack or an aneurysm, the two suspects.

Your father is dead, but people still come to visit him. They will not remove the tubes for twenty-four hours because you have donated his organs, signed them over. It is you who has signed everything through this daze as through a thick cataract. They have to keep him breathing to remove his liver and his kidneys, which seem good, the doctors say. It surprises you they will use his liver, despite his lifestyle, his drinking, his eating. Dad will save someone's life. Your mother thinks this is wonderful. You hope this is okay with him, this decision you've made, this decision you discussed with the family, the tías, the one they approved. You think he would have liked the spectacle of it.

People see him breathing and they don't understand it's the machine. You tell them he is dead, but they don't understand. They call out to him, "Pull through, Ichi, pull through, you can do it." "Believe," they say. Mom's parents, Maman and Papan, are called in. They didn't know until now because they are old and your mother didn't want to worry them and cause them pain by telling them that Icho was in the hospital if it wasn't necessary. But now, the pain will be double. Your mother tries to ease them into the situation, until it is finally time to come out with it: Ichi is dead. They don't understand. "But he is still breathing," they say, staring at your father's giant chest as it moves up and down, up and down arrhythmically and slowly, like he's having a panic attack under water. The machine is breathing, you tell them. You're not sure you can watch his anxious chest much longer. His face is peaceful, but his chest, pumped with the visage of life, is something else.

The news reaches Tony, he runs into the hospital wing, he sees you from across the room, and his embrace encompasses you. He holds you tighter than you've ever been held, and suddenly you are secure, and the world, just for a moment, stops feeling as though it is an impalpable vapor.

Eventually, you tell Tony to go home, you will stay, continue to sign papers, meet him at home. People will continue to come and cry over your father throughout the night, you will receive phone calls from Lily and the other girls, but you will ignore them. They will continue to call you, but you don't have anything to say to them. You have already told them your father is dead. What more is there to say? People still don't understand, they pour over his body, pleading with it to wake up. You can't take it anymore, you go home.

16.

When Tony found me, three years ago, I was hiding behind a suit— ivory, sharp and smart, at least I thought so at the time. And so did he. That's when I still wore ties and long-sleeved shirts. I wasn't wearing a tie that day, but I was still going through that phase. I'd just moved to Miami and I was bartending at an art opening, a piece of a woman. New York, that siren song, had chewed on me until, beneath my suit, I was all bones. It was after I'd assisted my boss, The Poet, with a conference in Hawaii that I'd decided to come home for a while. We'd arrived in New York after the conference and immediately I knew it in the very depths of me: I can't be here. I should have left long before, but sometimes I'm just plain stubborn, and it took being away, and what had happened in Hawaii, to realize I had to leave the city, for a long time. Maybe for good. Although I always knew it couldn't be for good. As an artist, you can't leave New York for good. Lee was proof.

In the years before I met Tony, I'd stopped eating. First because I didn't have the money to feed myself properly, then because I'd lost my appetite for everything, including my life. Plus, I'd always had an issue with food. This time it had gotten bad. I hated eating beyond reason, wished it didn't exist. There were even times I thought I'd maybe chase down some pills, drop everything. Like I thought my father might have. But he hadn't, they'd tested his blood and his urine: he was clean. When Tony found me I was a knot of sadness. He would unravel me, bit by bit. I had never really been with a man before him, had refused to let men truly into my life. I thought they held women back, I hated them, was afraid of them.

"We will never do anything you don't want to do," he told me when he first had me in his arms, his naked body next to mine, his hands caressing my bony cage, toward my inward-caving stomach, down the length of my body, down to my throbbing clit, which felt as though, when he touched it, it might burst like an eardrum full of too much music. I shook the first time he placed me above him. "You're trembling," he said, and I said yes, and he helped me to sway and pump on top of him, slowly, building up speed, his hands at my waist, my flat breasts, until again the water flowed freely and he'd say, "You're so wet," and we'd lie next to each other, our bodies exhausted—mine wanting more.

He fed me. Literally. Every chance he got he served me up a plate of something. Slowly, my frame gained back its strength. One day he called me *gordita*, out of affection, and I joked that he shouldn't call me that because I might actually get fat, and he said, "Then that's what I'll call you, you need a little meat." It stuck: *gordita*. He kept saying, "*Gordita, gordita*, you're so healthy." I'd almost gotten to the bottom of my "normal" weight bracket, and that was as far as I was going. This made him happy—at least it was in the vicinity of normal. It made me miserable in my body, but it made me happy in him and it made me think more clearly and regain my life, so I let him do it. There were still problems I couldn't tell him about, still things I kept to myself—but this was the man who had saved my life.

And now, I go home to Tony. I can't wait to be in his arms. It's the middle of the night by the time I get back from the hospital, squeaking open our front door expecting the smell of home to greet me, but for a moment everything is stale and cold and the walls refuse to welcome me. The lights are out and Tony is in bed, but he hears me and calls out, "*Gordita.*" The sound of his voice is soft, I take it from the air and fold it into my shirt pocket, thinking perhaps this will force the walls of the apartment to rethink their hostile stance. I've always been able to search and find kindness in Tony, from the beginning. Why should tonight be any different?

This man who is now lying in bed, calling out, "*Gordita,* come here, come by me," and whose embrace will again make everything all right. I undress and go to him, snuggle my arm around him, my head under his armpit, taking in the distant smell of onions mixed with the sweat of his red hair. I swing my leg over his and clasp him sideways, cuddling and gripping, softly. He strokes my hair and at my knee, I can feel his penis waving itself up slowly, filling with blood, like a pulse. I extend my right hand, caressing its tip, and I feel myself full of love, and a desire to give him pleasure. This man, this man who I love so much, this man who has saved my life, who is here for me, this man. I take him in my arms, and I move my lips down to him, hard, he is still caressing my hair. My hands wrap slowly around his tight ass as my lips and mouth make their way up and down his penis, I pour myself into him, I give him all of me, until I feel him about to come and then, suddenly, I think of my father. And of Lily, and the pain my father must have felt, so all alone, and I pour more of myself into Tony and he comes in my mouth, filling it. I swallow and stay there, my face on his limpness for only a few seconds, before I crawl up to his chest and, my chest to his, I press my nose to his and take in his sweat, lying on his belly like a frog. My poor father, how could that woman leave him? How could she leave him there to die?

Dyeing

Panel 3

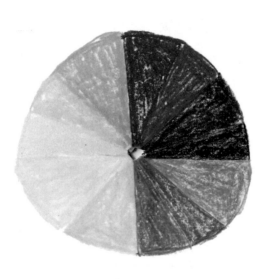

Ultraviolet.

Visible to some animals, but not humans, ultraviolet light is beyond our perception.

IT'S MONDAY again. A week since Dad was rushed to the hospital. Three days since his funeral. I try to paint for the first time since it all started. But I'm powerless in front of *Cathedral*. The entire day I stand there without a brushstroke. Somehow this drains me more than a full day of work. By nightfall, when it's time to forget it all, clean-slate-it for the next day, sleep comes quickly. I am grateful.

Until a mad gust of thunderous snoring wakes me in the middle of the night, just as it had so often during my childhood. My father, trying to speak to me, rattling me out of sleep.

But this time it isn't Dad in my head, it's Tony right next to me. Tony's body rising and falling with that clash of instruments I'd heard so many years ago. As if Dad's soul has jumped right into Tony, become the machine that breathed for him—breathed wrong.

I stare for a long time, sitting in bed at a finger's distance, as Tony's belly rises and falls, his mouth wide open. A streak of desire surges in my body to sit and flatten Tony's stomach like a *tostón*, fat spilling out of corners. A desire to climb inside his gaping mouth-hole, jam my body and shoulders through, and open up the tight airwaves that are forcing the air inside him to vibrate and make itself heard. And then a longing to gag him, squirting lubricant into his mouth, silencing the inner clatter.

A line of drool is starting to crust itself on the stubble of his red beard as a wave of nausea scampers around my stomach. My face flushes with rage, slowly, like a balloon inflating. I try to push Tony to one side or another, trying to locate him in a position where he won't snore. But every which way I pose him, he snores loud as a lion. The only thing different about Tony's snore is that he doesn't have the suffocating pauses Dad had. At least there's that.

When I can't take the screeching trumpet in my ear—not a second longer—I move to the living room. But I don't *want* to sleep in the living room. I want to sleep with Tony, like we've always slept, curled up in each other. I want his body next to mine. But more than anything else, at that moment, I'm afraid for the future, afraid for the perpetuity of all of this. A future without Tony's body beside me, without his gentle support—I don't think I could take it. What if I lose him?

Eventually, my desire to sleep next to Tony beats out my fit and I go back to the room. When I see him lying there in bed, mouth open, sheets covering half his body, I want all at once to hit him and to fuck him. It's a strange kind of excitement, wanting to fuck his brains out and say, *Now shut the fuck up or make me so tired I'll be able to sleep like a damn rock and it won't matter how loud you snore.*

I remember the ear plugs we bought when our building was under construction. I squeeze them into my ear canal, but the snores are obstinate, permeating everything—the pillow I have over my head, the foam of the plugs. And in the semi-echo that resonates off the foam plugs, droning like a bug in water, another surge rising: Tony is mine. My father has no business possessing him like that. Fuck Dad too. Fuck him if he thinks he can have so much power, even when he isn't here. For thinking he can enter corners of my life, touch them and go, taint them with fear and longing.

"Fuck you and get out," I whisper, the heat of small, silent briny tears streaming through my pillow, remembering how Nina felt, the empty sting: "We're never going to see him again." But there are other ways to make yourself felt, and Dad knew them all.

His disappearing act had started a long time ago. The first big rift: the car. It was my sixteenth birthday and he knew I wanted an old Volkswagen van. That was the dream. Like my Mom and the desk, I kept saying how much I wanted one.

He'd thrown a surprise party for me at Dora's house, which I hated. I thought I was going to see him and the family, for his half of my birthday celebration. I'd already done Mom's party the day before, where we'd stayed home and cooked and baked cake and she'd given me a book on Rothko.

When Nina and I got to Dora's that day, Nina started leading the way through the back gate to the yard, saying Dad had said to come in through the back. Then the stereo started to blare as we turned the corner into the yard. "Happy Birthday Sweet Sixteen" rang through the speakers and everybody started popping out of corners. I was horribly embarrassed. How could he not know I would hate all this attention on me? The heat rose to my face, a pink hydrangea. I couldn't help but think that this was more about him than me, but I tried to smile and get through.

He'd hired a live band and a DJ and all my friends were there, even people who weren't my friends. My sister had invited everybody in my class, and, strangely, almost everyone had come. I didn't know what to say to them. I was half ashamed of Dad's loud, unsophisticated, rough-around-the-edges family yelling and screaming and bringing out the pork and rice and beans and Cuban cake. But everybody seemed okay, so eventually I stopped worrying and even started dancing a little.

And then in the middle of the party Dad got on a microphone and said there was something in the front of the house for me. When

I got there, it was a completely souped-up, totally customized yellow Volkswagen van. "Like a yellow submarine," Dad said. I was in shock and started crying, running toward the car. The whole interior was brand new and there was even a small table in the middle of the van, inside. In the front, there was a car plate that read VAN-GO, which he'd thought up and had specially made. It had Van Gogh with a paintbrush sticking his head out of a VW van. Dad was clever like that. "What do you think, *Freakia?*" I couldn't stop crying and I just hugged him. Genuinely, not caring who was looking right at that moment. He'd gone through so much trouble. I was a brat, a true brat.

"Your dad is so cool," my friends said in intervals. "Your dad is so cool."

Nina had been the only one who knew, so when we got home with the VW Mom looked at it unbelieving, and then angrily.

"That's not reliable," she said. "This should have been a joint decision." She raised her voice, standing on the porch, staring at the van. "Nina, you knew about this? Why didn't you tell me?"

"Dad told me not to tell you," Nina replied. Mom looked like she was going to burst into tears.

"I'm your mother, Nina! You're supposed to tell me everything."

"Mom, c'mon, I love it," I said, "and he worked so hard on it, come see it." Nina took her hand and led her to the car, Mom following reluctantly.

"All that money, and it's going to leave you stranded, it's—"

"That's why I didn't tell you," said Nina. "Because you would have ruined everything."

"I'll just have to pray," Mom said, "pray nothing happens to you in that thing. Why couldn't he have just bought you a new Honda?"

ABOUT THREE months later, Dad called, yelling into the phone, "Where is your mother?" I told him I didn't know, that she had gone out with my grandparents, which was true. He raged and called me a "fucking liar." And then he started saying, "She's with that motherfucker, that Victor, that piece of shit."

I tried to calm him down and said the wrong thing, apparently: "Dad, she's not with him, but even if she was, Vic is a nice guy. He's—"

"He's what! A nice guy? That motherfucker who your mother cheated on me with, that *maricón*, he's a nice guy? What the fuck is wrong with you, Veronica, eh, what, tell me!"

We fought and yelled at each other until my throat hurt. I kept telling him to calm down, but had to scream over him just to be heard. I asked what was wrong with saying Victor was nice, did he prefer Mom's boyfriend to be an asshole, to be bad to us? Which is when he hung up the phone with a big "Fuck you!" which stung down to the marrow.

Mom got home later that night with Maman and Papan; they had gone for a drive and then gone to eat somewhere on the beach. Nina and I started telling her what happened, because my eyes were red and immediately she dropped everything and started asking if everything was okay. Then around 10 p.m., a tow truck showed up in the driveway and hooked onto the van. It was Pepe's brother, who owned a towing company.

"Icho tell me to come take this," he said to my mother when she ran out to see what was happening.

"He told you to take it?" Mom yelled at him, indignant. "You spineless pawn, you spineless man."

But Pepe's brother just kept at it, kept linking and pulling and getting it all ready to tow. Nina and I watched the whole thing from the front window, which was cracked open so we could hear everything. Mom had told us to stay inside and we obeyed.

"She loves that car," Mom said, crying now. "She really loves it. Why did he give it to her if he was going to take it away?" She turned away to come inside.

That was the last I saw of that VW, the Van-Go, the yellow submarine, or as Papan called it, the banana boat. Something very real broke that day between me and Dad.

The next day, Dad disconnected my beeper, which Mom had asked him to get for me so she could know where I was at all times, and then he cancelled the gas card he made a big spectacle of giving me along with the car the day of the party (on the microphone and all, presenting it all to me like I was a contestant winner). He never apologized. I saw less and less of him, told him I was busy studying when he called, or when he asked Nina on their outings. I never brought up the car. I knew he thought I would, that he could manipulate me with it. But I wasn't going to let him. When we did go out, when Nina begged enough to get me to go to dinner with them, or to Dora's to see our cousins, or to his half of Nochebuena, I stuck my head in a book, which Dad yelled at me for doing. I was tired of his racket, but I was still a kid really, still under the command of my parents, and it was hard to tune him out completely.

Just like Tony's snoring is impossible to silence. I try to make the most of my sleeplessness, try to paint, but nothing comes of it, not even a smudge.

I'm in the kitchen drinking cold water from a long, thick glass when I feel the urge to throw the glass across the room, watch it fly into the tempered double doors that lead to the balcony, watch the glass on the doors fracture in a web and the glass of water itself shatter, in jagged pieces, waking Tony up. But then, just as suddenly, control comes like a wave, that mantra I repeated to myself so many times over, for so many years: Just because you are your father's daughter doesn't mean you have to have your father's rage. Control yourself, go to the Internet, see how you can fix this.

Snoring, says one article, is "a cry for help"—that's what the doctors call it because it's a health warning. Linked to high blood pressure, stroke, heart disease, and diabetes. It can lead to daytime sleepiness, low energy, lack of productivity, memory loss, and loss of sex drive. Heavy-duty snoring causes sleep apnea, which my father had, and which means you actually stop breathing for a moment (those suffocating silent bits). It's most commonly found in overweight, middle-aged men, and it can be life-threatening. Tony has gained twenty pounds in the last two years. He isn't obese, but he's growing more than a very serious beer belly. And his age range is right in the danger zone: very near to forty. Also—and this is the most worrisome—80 percent of couples with a snorer end up sleeping in different rooms. I refuse to sleep in a different room forever. I will not leave him. I am not my mother.

From: Eliana Sarria
To: Veronica Gonzalez
Date: Tue, Sep 11, 2007 4:00am
Subject: Insomnia

> I can't sleep hormiga. I have to deal with the thought that continues to leap in my head and heart that somehow as i examine my conscience, at some greater level, I added to your father's death.
>
> How are you hormiga? Today was a hard day. They're going to be hard for a while, I know it. Are you okay? I love you.
>
> All my love
> Mom

IN THE HOSPITAL I had walked in on Mom lying over Dad's body in CCU. Her feet were on the ground, on tiptoes, and her upper body sprawled over his chest, her face in the nook of his neck, where the tubes breathed false life into him. Her face by his—she was crying and whispering, "I'm sorry, I'm so sorry. I'm so sorry I hurt you. I shouldn't have left you." She was talking through a runny nose and quick half breaths, petting his swollen face without looking at him directly, tucked securely under his chin, saying all along, "I'm sorry, I'm so sorry. I didn't mean to hurt you."

Ten, fifteen minutes before, Daria, another of Dad's ex-girlfriends, had come into the room. I was leaving Mom to go and get us some coffee as Daria was coming in. Mom and Daria kindly said hello to each other, but by the time I came back, two coffees in hand, Daria was gone and Mom was crying over Dad. As soon as I saw that, I tiptoed backwards out the hospital room door. When I turned around, I saw Daria down the hall talking to Nina.

I didn't know what had gone on while I was gone for coffee. Mom hadn't touched Dad like that in years. The closest they'd come was their deep hug at my college graduation. Had Daria said something? It wasn't like Daria to do something mean. Daria had loved Dad, I knew because of the way she kept saying, "No, no puedo perderlo." I believed her when she said she wouldn't be able to bear the loss of him. She had never taken money from Dad. That was the other thing: the other ones had grubbed like parasites, thinking he had more net worth than he actually did. Daria was one of the very few good ones. She'd have called an ambulance, saved his life if she'd been with him instead of the jinetera. Daria and Dad had been off and on again for a long while, but Daria wanted a commitment. Just a few months ago, just before Dad got serious with Louisa, he'd sat Daria down to talk to her, which is what I found out once I reached Daria and Nina down the hall.

"He told me he couldn't give me what I wanted. He said it could never be, that he would never get married again. You know how he is, he never got over your mother. Never, never." Daria brought a torn-up napkin to her face, her puffy eyes. She looked back and forth between me and Nina. "He always talks about her like she was different, Eli. Like she was made of fine china or something. I love him very much, but he doesn't know how to love me back. He only loves her, only her, all his life he only loved her. I told her." Daria didn't say this in a jealous way, just matter-of-fact. Nina brought Daria close to her and hugged her, soothed her. But I didn't know how Nina could touch her and be so kind. I felt a wall between me and her, in my heart, in my throat, blocking all words and only letting through small bits of air. I imagine Daria had said all of this in the same way to my mother. And it was this that brought Mom's body down to bear upon my father's.

I couldn't tell how much of Dad's love for Mom was true—really true. Maybe all of it, maybe none. Maybe Dad was just in love with the idea of my mother, his little Spaniard girl-bride with dark locks and red lipstick, skin so white you could see through it, delicate and queenly hiding behind a quiet demeanor but piercing through her dark brown eyes, the color of chestnuts. But wasn't all this a truth also—wasn't some of that very much my mother, idea or no idea, and couldn't the love of an idea be as true as anything else?

Later, Mom would hug me and Nina, when it was all over, a couple of days after we were told about the brain death, after Dad had been buried, when we were all at Mom's sitting together on the couch, Nina and Vic and Mom and me, and she would say, "If I had stayed with him, he wouldn't have died." And there was Vic sitting next to us, supporting us, petting my mother's hair and listening to all of this, not a trace of anger in him, all understanding. A saint.

ONCE, ABOUT six years after the divorce, on one of Dad's good days, he picked me and Nina up for lunch. As usual, he was blasting the oldies station, and "Cold as Ice" by Foreigner came on. Dad raised the volume and said, "Shit, I remember the day your Mom threw me out, I was driving around for a long time really upset, and this song came on the radio, and I just blasted it so loud, it was just—" But instead of finishing his sentence he raised the volume a little more, and sang out loud with the lyrics, which made my mother out to be an ice queen who would someday pay for her cruelty.

AND NOW, there she is, wandering the house in her white nightgown, writing emails at four in the morning. Her hair, the wild, frizzy mop it has become, big and untamable, let loose from the workday's gelled bun. Barefoot, she sits at her laptop, back straight, because that's what Dr. Xu tells her to do. Dr. Xu cured her of the herniated discs no one else could cure and now she trusts him more than anyone, and that's all fine and dandy although I worry about her complete abandonment of Western medicine. And, more than that, here she is, mourning, and could Dr. Xu cure her of that?

"Mom," I say right when she picks up the phone. Don't even let her say her hello.

"V, are you okay? Is something wrong?" The mother-panic rings in her voice.

"I'm fine, Ma, I just called to see how you were, just read your email."

"Sorry, *hormiga*, I shouldn't have written it, what time is it?"

"Six."

"It's so early. But I just felt so lonely for a minute and—" I can hear on the other end that she's started to cry.

"Mom, are you okay?"

"I'm okay. I'm just. I'm just so sad."

"I know, Mom. I know."

"We loved him more than we knew."

We loved him more than we knew...

I don't respond right away, there's a long pause while the thought lingers inside me.

Mom's voice has become like a little girl's, squeaky and higher-pitched than usual, but slow and deliberate too, in an attempt to caulk the cracks. We loved him more than we knew.

"Are you going to work today?" I ask her.

"I don't know. I haven't slept in days."

"You should take the day off, Mom."

"And do what? Stay home and cry?" I can see her trying to clean up when she says this, wiping her nose, straightening.

"Maybe you should."

"And you, *hormiga*? What about you? Are you crying yet?"

"I'm fine, Mom, don't worry about me. You shouldn't go to work," I repeat, wanting to make sure she stays home.

"Are *you* working?"

I haven't painted yet. Seven days now and not a stroke. Lee doesn't know. She'd kill me. Every time she calls I make sure I pick up, no matter how much I don't want to. I don't know how many times I've said, "Everything's fine." Dia sends me little text messages: *Hang in there, Veronica.* Or, *Don't worry, you'll get through.* Or, *Let time take its course. You'll be ok.* She's like a digital greeting card. Poor woman, she's nice, and she means well, but every time one of her Hallmark texts pings through, I remember how much I haven't done, how behind I am. How it's possible I might let everybody down, including myself. At one point, I even took my laptop out of the studio, so I could check my emails in the living room and not have to face the unfinished panels.

But now, with Mom on the other line, I peek into my studio, toward the last thing I'd done in *Cathedral*, a white, pale figure fixing its gaze on me, paralyzing me.

But below the ghost there are wispy flowers that look like cherry blossoms, beginning to bloom. When had I done those? I can't remember making them.

I finished that bit right before I'd even been confirmed about the show, the very morning I went to meet Dia. I *should* be painting. The show is just around the bend. And then, suddenly realizing I hadn't told Mom anything, hadn't found the right time. Everything had changed so quickly.

"Did I tell you I have a show during Basel? It's, it's a solo." My voice comes out flat and matter-of-fact.

"What? *Hormiga!*" Mom's loud and proud and excited all of a sudden.

"Yeah," I say, unable to manage even feigned excitement.

"When did you find out? With who? Isn't your dealer in New York? I thought you weren't having a show with her this year, I thought it wasn't your turn until next year?"

That's how Mom saw it. She thought Lee had a group of artists and she, fairly, had them take "turns" at whose time it was to have a show. I guess that's the way things are supposed to be, but the market changes everything. Lucky for me, this time, I guess.

"I found out right before Nina called me to tell me Dad hadn't gone to work."

Mom's voice quiets, her excitement buffering against dysphoria.

"Why didn't you tell me, *hormiga?*" And then, again, the muffled sound of her heavy heart. And then abruptly, "I'll call you back, okay, *hormiga?* I'll call you back."

"Okay, Mom, call me. Whenever. I'll have my phone on me."

From: Veronica Gonzalez
To: Eliana Sarria
Date: Tue, Sep 11, 2007 8:44am
Subject: Re: Insomnia

> "The most important thing a father can do for his children is to love their mother."
> —Theodore Hesburgh
> remember all the days you cried in the bathroom, on your knees not knowing what to do. I remember hearing you cry through the bathroom door, Mom. He didn't know how to love you. This isn't your fault, you divorced him for a reason, try and remember that now, try and think back to how it was before death put a haze on the whole thing. He was difficult. He wasn't in the same place you were, he didn't know any better; he was learning. It's not your fault.
>
> Remember how violent he got sometimes. Sometimes impossible to reason with, it's just you're forgetting the not-so-good stuff. And it's okay, but just don't make that forgetfulness make you think you did something wrong.
>
> BTW, since I know you're going to ask: Theodore Hesburgh is (was?) a priest. He was on the civil rights commission, got fired by Nixon, and was later on other immigration and anti-genocide commissions. Anyway, I know how much you love you your priests.
>
> love you, horms

WE LOVED him more than we knew. It's funny how now that he's not here to talk back—to argue, to refute and yell and throw things—it's funny what we see. Is this his essence we're looking at now, his real self, a self we loved, stripped away from his body, which we no longer have to deal with? Is there a guilty relief in his absence for me? Is it possible for me to be so awful? We loved him more than we knew. Or is it all just that he's dead? Plain and simple—gone. We loved him more than we knew.

LATER IN the day, I walk into Tony's office and I tell him about the snoring. I'd made out a fact sheet for him. There are certain things he has to do. The first thing is lose weight. He also might buy a German-engineered pillow they have online (or at Brookstone) that's supposed to help you stop snoring by opening up your airwaves.

"I snore?"

"Big time."

"How?"

"GUAAAERRRRRRRR." I try and make the loudest sound as I inhale, but it makes me cough so I try again.

"GUAEURGUARGGGGGUUUUAAAAARRHHHARHAH. Like that. It's terrible. It's really bad."

Tony looks at me, kind of smirking, leaning back in his black rolling chair. I move toward him and sit on his desk. I'm only wearing underwear and a T-shirt so the birch wood desk is cold on my thigh-skin when I sit.

"Eighty percent of couples end up sleeping in different rooms because of this," I tell him softly. "I don't want to do that."

Tony doesn't say anything. He just pulls me over from the desk to his lap and ruffles my hair a bit. He looks at me with droopy eyes full of the intent to make it up to me. His eyes make it look like his brain is frowning, but his face is still peaceful and calm and in a half-smile. God forbid we disturb the peace. Willingly, he would never. It's only at night when the unconscious mind takes over that he rattles our world with the thunder and roar of the jungle inside him.

"Okay," he says, as if that means he gets it, he'll try and do better, but most importantly it means, *Can we change the subject now? I don't want to stay in this afflicted place any longer.*

I give him two kisses, one over each eye, on his auburn eyebrows, which are slowly growing thin white hairs. Tony is salt and strawberry instead of salt and pepper.

"*Café con leche?*" I ask him.

"No, that's okay, make me something without milk. Tea."

This is always Tony's first step toward a diet. He stops drinking his morning *café con leche*, switches to warm Lipton herbal tea, and then he pastes a sign up on the wall in front of his computer that says, NO CAFFEINE. NO SOFT DRINKS. NO ALCOHOL. NO SUGAR. NO FAST FOOD. NO RESTAURANTS. NO BREAD. I've told him before that I don't think that'll work, that it's all about the portions and exercise and all that. I've told him that abstaining so intensely is only going to make him hungry and sad and then binge later. I know this from experience.

Instead of complying with the tea request and trying to go back to work, I procrastinate and tell him we should go to the supermarket, with a mission in mind: to buy low-fat and organic, trade the red, wax-wrapped round of Gouda for a red, waxless apple. He doesn't look happy but he swings his T-shirt on and we head out.

Up and down the aisles of Publix, I grab sushi boxes and yogurt, Tony reaches for the peaches and other sweet, low-calorie treats. Pointing to a bag of frozen *arepas*, he asks, "How many calories you think are in these?"

"Enough to dart a clog straight through the heart," I say, shaking my head.

We play a game. He pulls something off the shelf and I nod yes or shake my head no. It's fun for a while until my sister calls. I don't pick up. She'd called this morning and all she could say was, "We're never going to see him again, never going to see Dad again." I can't listen to that all over. Even when she was saying it this morning, I couldn't keep hearing her say it, so I told her to replace her thoughts with better ones; that would make her stronger. I don't know if I'm messing her up by telling her that. Maybe she has to mourn in her own way, maybe this horrible thing she keeps saying about us never seeing him again, maybe she has to, to be able to get through it, try and touch it.

"Did you see this!" says Tony, standing next to me in the long cashier line. I'm not even sure how we got to the cashier so fast, or how the cart got so full. Drawing me out of what I now realize was the long daze I'd been in for the remainder of our game, Tony points at the newspaper he's holding.

"See what?" I ask with effort, pushing the words out. I just want to not talk, but Tony points again to what I now see is a copy of the *New York Times*.

"*El loco este*, in Manhattan. At Ground Zero."

"What *loco*?" I ask him, until I filter what he's said and, "Oh, wow, it's 9/11. I forgot, I mean, I didn't forget. I just, when you said Ground Zero—"

"Look." He turns the front page of the paper to me.

And there's Leo! Wild-haired and dressed in his baggy clothes, waving his hands up, mouth gaping wide. The headline reading, "Young Mourner Remembers 9/11," with a subheading that says something about disturbing the peace. I can't read it completely from where Tony is holding the paper.

"Shit! I know him, *mi amor*! I know him! I lived right across the hall from him in Washington Heights. What is he doing?"

"You know him?" he asks, folding the newspaper for a second and then looking at me with that frisky little-boy look Tony gets when he wants to make me smile. "I knew you were crazy. *Estamos de acuerdo que este está loco de remate.*"

"No, no, he's a totally normal kid, he used to borrow my books and sometimes he would watch me paint. He tried to pretend, sometimes, that he was like all the other kids in the 'hood' and be all gangsta, but he wasn't because his mother had him and his brother at private school on scholarship."

"Like you and your sister," says Tony.

"Sort of, but they lived a little worse. Their Mom had like ten jobs. God, his mother hated me, thought I was gentrifying the building, even though I probably had less money than she did. Although she was probably right, I hear Washington Heights is totally gentrified now, or getting there anyway. Wasn't like that when I was there, at least not my street. What's it say? A *ver*."

"It says the police surrounded him last night and told him he'd be arrested for trespassing, disturbing the peace, and that it was against national security, because he was trying to go beyond the fences where the hole is, but he said he had his rights. Let's see, what else? It says, it says he got on a wooden platform and started reading out loud from a journal his brother wrote in, and that he said he was going to read one journal entry each day, until he read through to the last entry his brother wrote. How big is this journal? How long is he going to read for, *por dios*! And who cares about his brother?"

"His brother, Shell. He died in the towers. He'd gotten a job as a messenger and on 9/11 he was delivering a package to some executive he didn't even know."

"Shit."

"Yeah," I say as Tony starts to put the paper back in its slot, ready to put the groceries on the conveyer belt. "No, no, get the paper, I want to read the story," I tell him. Leo, goddamn, Leo! And I remember, suddenly, how he'd said right before I left how he wanted to do something big, and how that had scared me, and how I hadn't talked to him since then, and how he doesn't even know about Dad.

From: Veronica Gonzalez
To: Leo Estevez
Date: Tue, Sep 11, 2007 11:56am
Subject: Let it Flow

Leo! I read about you in the paper and I couldn't believe it. What you are doing is wonderful. I think so anyway. Keep at it. I disconnected for a bit, so sorry, and then there you were, in the paper.
     Love, V
p.s. I don't know if I should even write this right now, I've gone back and forth on telling you, sort of lingering over the keys for a while, b/c I really don't want to steal your thunder. But, I think it would be crazy to ignore it, I can't really. I just wanted to let you know my father passed away several days ago, that's

why I disappeared, everything happened so quickly. I'm really sad and for the first time I truly understand how you felt after Shell.

SMACK IN the middle of the day, Lee calls. I can hear her anxiety through the phone line—she's tapping the ground with her wiry leg and foot, the sound carrying without static across city and state borders. She must be using her Bluetooth; that thing picks up everything. I listen to the tapping through the initial "hellos" and I think, maybe it's not her foot, maybe it's her long acrylics, painted her favorite color, Eskimo Ice, lightly striking her white Mac. Her nails should have steered me away from her. Maybe I should have gone for one of those "classy" dealers who shop at Barney's and don't bother with the sales rack. Lee's a frugal little shit, buys all her clothes under fifty bucks but still manages to stand out in a crowd. Who wouldn't with those Birds of Paradise hairdos, sprayed like it was 1953 and we were all on *American Bandstand*.

But Lee sells my work like no one else has been able to. Last year after I finally handed over a body of work on consignment, she got me enough group shows to let me cut down on my day job hours and then finally quit this summer, freelance, and start to paint more. The woman got me a show during Basel, for Christ's sake. Acrylic nails or no nails at all, I owe her loyalty for that. Plus, she's not that bad. She sent me Key lime pie when I sprained my wrist last year. Then, of course, she added a note: "So your wrist's sprained, eat the pie and then paint with your mouth. Rent *My Left Foot*, that'll get you going." Or else I'd never get a solo show—that was the subliminal, clear as it always is with Lee.

Today, I feel the nicotine upping the ante on everything. I bet she's trying to quit, so she's on the gum, the patch, *and* the cigarettes.

"Veronica, you okay?" Tap, tap, tap, tap, tap.

"I'm fine."

"You painting?" Tap, tap, taptaptaptaptaptaptaptaptaptaptaptap.

I think about lying again, but I don't. Not this time. I'm pushing it, I know it.

"I'm trying. I can't."

Silence. "What do you mean you 'can't'? Your show. You said you were painting. Can you make it? Or do I have to get somebody else? I will. No mercy. Last chance, honey." Tap, tap, tap, tap tap tap taptaptptpatpatpatpatpatpatpatpat.

"Yes, Lee, for fuck's sake, I can make it. My father just died. He *just* died," I say this realizing it's the first time I'm letting her in a little. Letting her see everything is not "fine," not fine at all.

"Sorry, I'm sorry, it's just I know your father was an ass, and I don't want to see you ruin your life because—" Tap, tap, tap.

"Who said my father was an ass?"

"You did. A million times." Tap tap.

"Well forget what I said, I didn't know anything."

"Start painting, dear, you know about painting, that's what you know. Just start. And forget that message I left you about storing everything up in a little ball. Forget that too. Put it all in the paintings. Let it out."

What the fuck does she care about me letting it out? She's the Queen of the Fucking Ice Age. I don't think the woman has ever shed a tear in her life. Unless it was to sell a painting. Ice to an Eskimo. Fucking Lee.

"Fine."

"Good then, get off the phone and get to work."

Maybe it was just the kick in the ass I needed. Maybe it was Lee, maybe it was Leo. I don't know whose foot it was that kicked harder, maybe both, one for each cheek. But for the first time in seven days, I feel a jolt. A need to move.

But where to start. What color?

 Red.

Red has the longest wavelength of light in the visible spectrum. Associated with blood and everything that boils and soothes the blood—anger, passion, and love.

Tony and I made love frequently in the immediate days after my father's death. Sometimes I would take a nap in the middle of the day because I'd be so tired from not sleeping at night. When I'd wake up from the nap, sunlight hitting my eyes, Tony would be there, his toes touching mine, and before I knew it, he would snuggle up to me from behind and I would feel him, hard against me. He filled me up, he gave me peace. We lay spent. Over and over again.

"Tony, *mi amor*, want something from the kitchen? I need water."

"*Sí.*"

"What?"

"*Algo dulce.*"

I head naked for the kitchen like a somnambulist in search of something sweet.

"The cherries," he yells from bed, with the sound of epiphany.

The cherries. I open the fridge door. The suction releases and I stick my head in the cold. My hands reach for the bowl of cherries. I taste one over the sink—it's so ripe that it stains my fingers with its pulp, a bleeding red—hematite. Hematite, which comes from the Earth's crust, a heated mineral. I imagine myself digging through dirt, through the crust, then the Earth's mantle, the solid outer core, the molten iron inner core, like an ant burrowing through the rind of a blood orange. I imagine myself mixing this red, this ripe red, closing it in a jar, keeping it for later.

I eat one cherry after another. One by one, but quickly, I fill my mouth with them, spitting out their seeds into my left hand, which is cupped slightly under my chin, catching the seeds and the strings of saliva that dangle occasionally from my lip.

"What are you doing?" I hear Tony call from the room. "What's taking you so long, *gordita?*"

"Sorry," I call back, returning to the room, red-handed.

"Were you eating the cherries all by yourself?" The proof of it all over my face and hands. Tony laughs.

"Come here," he says playfully, pulling me toward him, taking the bowl from me, feeding me one cherry, then feeding himself one. I giggle. We spit the pits into the bowl, it doesn't matter that all our saliva is commingling. Tony pulls me toward him and all I want him to do is eat my ripe pussy and I think it just like that: pussy. Until I bleed, I want him to lick me until I bleed the color of cherries. I tell him, "*Cómeme a mí, dame un beso con tu boca.*"

Pulling my head back, gripping my wild hair, he takes me like a guitar into his strong arms, bending his red-dyed mouth toward my open hole and he licks it softly, sumptuously, like a *mamonsillo*, and then quickly, pulsing, it feels like a cricket sounds and I want to scream, but I don't let myself. I make myself keep the cry inside, that makes it more pleasurable. He can tell I'm coming, he can see it the way my body is moving, but he holds me back and makes the pleasure hurt until I can't stand it anymore and I rip his hands from me, and take his lips in mine and I hold his pounding hardness with my other hand, covering it quickly with a condom and stabbing myself profoundly with it, deeply. I love this motherfucker. Even when he snores. If he never lets me sleep again, I will always love him.

 Pink.

A combination of red and white. Like cherry blossoms.

MY HAND AT *Cathedral*'s ghost. The white, still formless creature is staring at me before I continue to add to the bush beneath it like a soft-petalled flame brushing its face, waking it with cherry blossoms. Finally, I'm painting. The article about Leo and Shell is pinned to the wall next to the wooden boards and every once in a while, I glance over.

I hadn't thought about Leo or his brother these past few days, like I always had before, so near to the anniversary, until I saw the article. Seeing him in New York felt like ages ago, like someone had plugged time with a big rubber stopper, except everything that was caught inside this plugged vat of time was just that, time itself, passing. Making everything feel like some Borges labyrinth, seconds and minutes collecting in pools of water so big you couldn't even feel them drop. Oceans of slow instants, one after another, with no seeming connective tissue.

What I always remembered most about the days after Shell's death was how silent Leo was. Leo was a talker, but after Shell, it was like someone knocked the breath out of him for a while. Leo couldn't put his head around it. After they took Shell's ashes home (what they thought were part of his ashes, they couldn't be sure, he'd been mingled with so many others), and the world shuffled up the remains of those two towers into buckets, shuttled them away for landfill somewhere. Ellis Island had been made of landfill too, a big part of it anyway. I wonder where that came from, what Lady Liberty stands on.

For a while, for what felt like forever then, Leo disappeared into his mother's apartment. Three weeks after the attack, he knocked on my door.

"He wasn't no old man, yo. He was—" And he cried into my arms, and I held him, and let him talk.

"I guess that's the thing, though, you just never know when you're gonna go. Wish it were the Heights that killed him, would've made more sense, you know what I mean? Not some, some shit fundamentalist crap. Niggah been shot in the Heights, I'd've got it, it'd been more expected. But the first time the motherfucker goes downtown, stupid courier bullshit he'd started up doing, with his stupid uniform, and—"

And a plane comes out of the sky and straight into a building and there goes his life from another kind of height.

"Shit, Shell," Leo whispers. "Shit! Why you gotta leave me, bro, where the hell are you? I can't feel him, V. Sometimes I think I feel him but then I know I don't and I'm just lying to myself. I don't know where he's at. I miss him, V, I miss him."

And it was like that for days. "I miss him, *pintora*, I miss him"— these words would sprout out from the center of a poem he'd been writing, unkillable weed. Or we would be drinking tea, the red papaya tea Leo had gotten used to drinking in my apartment, though he preferred soda. "At least it's sweet," he'd say. And then suddenly there it was: "I miss him, V." And there he was just a few days ago still remembering Shell and honoring him six years later. My God, will I still be feeling this empty feeling, cold-sting like I've been gutted, six years from now? Just like Dad was gutted, his organs out—did he feel that, somehow, on some level? Dad's body, so newly left to the elements, still unchewed. His hair will keep growing. His fingernails. A headless fish still flipping its tail. Shell was never chewed—he just got mangled in, ground to dirt. Dust and debris.

Did I love Dad as much as Leo loved Shell? *Loves* Shell, *love* Dad. I wonder how we're expected to do this—lose people.

From: Leo Estevez
To: Veronica Gonzalez
Date: Wed, Sep 12, 2007 5:50pm
Subject: Re: Let it Flow

> Pintora! estas en mis pensamientos, y como siempre en mi corazon. I'm thinking of you, constantly since I read your email. Listen, let me know if you need anyone or some support, I am so sorry about your dad. Please let me know, okay?
> Peace, Leo

~

From: Veronica Gonzalez
To: Leo Estevez
Date: Wed, Sep 12, 2007 7:28pm
Subject: Thank you

> Thanks Leo, that's really nice. But listen, don't worry about me, I'm going to be totally fine. Just finish what you started down there—it's a good thing.
> More later, V

 More Shades of Pink.

Pink can be as slippery as tongues, holding as many folds
and shades. Softer than red, pink speaks of nurture and our
hot nature, quieted.

"Yo, MY MOTHER wants you dead," says Leo. It's February of 2000. I
don't know who he is yet. He's just a stranger in my new apartment
building at this point.

"Excuse me?" I'm still turning the key in the locks of my door
before going down the stairs, scared basically shitless, not knowing
the voice coming from behind me.

"You heard what I said, son, my ma, she's filling the house with
brujería shit to get you the fuck outa here."

"Why?" I turn my head back to look at the voice, and it's a young
tough guy in his teens, baggy clothes to boot. I wouldn't know it was
all an act until much later.

"She thinks you're gonna raise her rent, thinks you white chicks
gonna start flooding the Heights and moving us out."

"Tell her I don't have any money." At this point I've finished
locking my door and am looking straight at him. He doesn't look so
scary. Not in his face, anyway. He's got a baggy pink polo on and jeans
with squeaky-clean white sneakers.

"How much you pay?"

"First of all, that's none of your business, second of all, I'm not white, I'm Cuban, and third, tell your mother I'm not afraid of her *brujería* because my Tía Maria is a *santera*, and Changó can do some whippin' of his own on her Dominican ass."

Right after I say it, I think he can see right through me and I want to crawl into a hole and die. I also wonder if he has a knife, and friends who can help him beat me up.

But then:

"Shit, son, and here I was thinking you're a white girl." Leo's smiling now, like he's about to wink at me.

"Yeah, well, think harder next time," I say, firmly.

I turn to walk away but Leo calls me back.

"Hey, hey, where you goin'?"

"Work. Some of us work." I continue to walk away. He follows me with small steps.

"Hey, wait, I saw you bringing all those books up here when you were moving in yesterday. Why you got all those books?"

"I like to read."

Now the kid is following me down the stairs, where I notice a trickle of blood covering ten or twelve steps that trail off into the corridor of the third floor. I try not to pay too much attention. It would ruin my act if I looked scared of a little blood.

"You a writer or something?"

"No."

"What, then?"

I decide to stop and tell him. It's the one thing that's clear in my life at that moment. Why not tell this young fool in his oversized shirt, whose mother wants me dead, what it is I have stupidly chosen to do for a living?

"I'm a painter."

"Like what? Like you paint houses and shit?"

"I wish. That would pay more." I laugh. "No, I paint paintings, you know, like canvases. 'Fine' art," I say, making fun of myself.

"No way, that's cool as shit. Can I see your paintings sometime?"

"Sure, why not, I'll be around." I laugh again and turn back to look at him. "Unless your Mom's *brujería* works and I die on the way back from work."

"Yeah, *hermanita*, don't worry, I'll try and get her to stop that shit. Plus, it's getting on my nerves, stinkin' up the house."

I'm almost all the way down the steps, when he yells out, "*Oye!*"

"Yeah?"

"What's your day job?"

"I'm just an assistant—a writer's assistant. Actually, he's a poet."

"No shit. He famous?"

"Sort of. He teaches at Columbia."

"What do you do for him?"

"Everything. And if I'm late he'll yell at me, so I gotta go, never been late before and I'm not about to let you make it a first." It wasn't true. The Poet never yelled at me, would never. But I was also never late.

Leo laughs and lets me go. I can see by the way he says "*hermanita*" and means it, that he has a good soul, that maybe he's even an old soul, heart clean as a bird's whistle. I swing the door open and off I go onto the sidewalk. It's a Monday morning and I think to myself, "Life's not so bad, even if it is freezing out here."

Seven days later, I will dodge my first bullet. But before that, Leo will knock on my door and a friendship will begin.

"*Oye, artista, artista, señorita pintora.* C'mon, open up, it's me." This time, there's a singsong that goes along with the pounding and I recognize Leo's voice. It's a voice that, in this moment, I don't even have a name for yet, but that I trust for some reason, so I go to the peephole and open up the four locks.

"Hi," I say, opening the door, but not fully.

"Hey, can I come in?"

"Depends. You gonna plant *brujería*?"

"No, I'm just here 'cuz I wanna see your crib. I wanna see where the *pintora* lives." Leo's still standing outside the door, peeking his little turtle head in. I motion him into my lair, and he follows my gesture, looking around, stopping at the kitchen, the first room in the apartment.

"You want a drink?"

"Sure, what kind of beer you got?"

"No, I mean like tea or something. It's the middle of the day."

"So? Aren't artists like *borrachos*?" Leo sits on my 1950s-style kitchen chair—silver legs, white cushion with red and pink speckles. It looks like it could've come from a diner way back in the day, or from a kitchen on *Gidget*. Leo looks decidedly awkward in it.

"How old are you, anyway?" I ask him, taking out the tea from the worn white, termite-nibbled wooden cupboards.

"Twenty-one."

"Twenty-one-year-olds don't go to high school. And why aren't you at school now, anyway?"

"Fine, whatever. I'm seventeen," he responds, ignoring the second half of the question.

"Seventeen?"

"All right, son. Give it up. I'm sixteen, okay?"

"Okay, then, we've got orange sesame tea, ceylon, Earl Grey, berry surprise, red papaya, green tea—you name it, we got it." I open my tea box (one of my father's used cigar boxes) to show him the selection.

"Only tea I know is *manzanilla*. And who's 'we'? You got a boyfriend in here?"

"It's an expression, like We, the queen. *Manzanilla*, that's chamomile, I got it right there, do you want that?"

"No way, my ma gives me that shit when I'm sick."

"So what do you want? I have tea and I have Diet Pepsi."

"Diet? Why? You already skinny as shit. I mean like too skinny."

"Thanks, I guess."

"It ain't no compliment, *flaca*. I like a girl with some booty."

"Yeah, well, I don't have one of those, and I don't really like when people talk to me like that. In fact, you should never talk like that to a girl." I snap the cigar box shut. Leo looks down and sees the tea ship has sailed.

"Shit, man, don't you have any Fanta or orange soda or something like that?"

"No."

"Can I look in your fridge?"

"Feel free."

"You ain't got nothing in here. Shit, you weren't lyin', you are poor as shit."

"I told you."

"Okay, so what do you eat, then? You eat your paints?"

"That's funnier than you know." I say this, slouching into Leo's spot in the chair, watching him try and scavenge something from a whole lot of cold nothing.

"What's that, like nerd humor?" he asks, shutting the door to the fridge, looking straight at me.

"Yeah, something like that."

"So can I see your paintings or what?" His head nudges the air, pointing toward the other rooms in the apartment, thinking the paintings are somewhere over there, not realizing there are three leaning against the wall, in the nook behind the fridge.

"You really want to see them?"

"Fuck yeah."

"I can show you what I'm working on, but it has to be tomorrow, because it's in a funny place right now, and if I show you she'll get mad at me and resist me and she won't let me work her." I get up and begin to show Leo to the door, but he's resistant.

"Who's gonna get mad at you?"

"The painting."

"You crazy? Or this how artists talk?"

I don't respond. I realize he might have caught me out, that I might be a little full of shit. A lot full of shit.

"You read all these books?" he asks, stepping into the living room without invitation.

"Yeah."

"Which one's good?"

"They all are, in one way or another, or else I wouldn't keep them, I'd have already sold them at the Strand for lunch money, like I do with the bad ones."

"What's the Strand?"

"Oh my God, how long have you lived in New York?"

"Since I was little. Long time, on and off. But just a couple of years, if you count all the time I've been here, straight, you know, without going back all the time. I mean, we still go back, sometimes, like for vacation."

"And you don't know what the Strand is?"

He doesn't say anything.

"Here, take this one, the guy who wrote it is Arenas. Reinaldo Arenas, one of my favorites. In it he kills Castro. Castrates him. It's something like that anyway—I can't really remember. I just remember I loved that book."

"Thanks." Leo turns to leave, and then, as if remembering something, "So, what's your name? You never told me your name."

"Veronica."

"Mine's Leandro, but everybody calls me Leo."

"Nice name. See you tomorrow," I say, leading him out the door. This time, he follows my lead, book in hand.

"See ya, *artista*."

And just like that, Leandro-nickname-Leo adopted me, through no choice of my own.

 Payne's Gray.

A very dark blue-gray, which can be used as a less intense mixer than black, all the better to get the right shade with.

I'VE RUN OUT of red (it's always the first to go), so I look through books. Find Matisse and Rothko and some other painters in my catalogues and art books, but they all just blur together like muddy water. Then there's *Guernica*, which makes me stop. I usually don't look too deeply into this painting. Something about it being reproduced so many times that makes me not stop at it anymore. But today I stop, and once I stop, I can't stop looking at it, running my eyes around it.

Guernica holds its dead.

Museo Nacional Centro de Arte Reina Sofia

Guernica is what the world would be like if time's arrow shot straight through the universe, pierced the sun, and caused a yellow glow to drip through space, gravitating, exhausting that colossal sphere of all its color and light. No light and too much light—that's the thing about *Guernica*. It's not black and white, it's not like people think. The white and the black merge in your eye and make the whole painting gray. It's all color and all void, all at the same time. The world collects disorder. I think of eclipses. During an eclipse the world turns platinum, they say. Like *Guernica*—like a fifteen-year-old girl's teeth under a black light, tripping on Ecstasy and entropy.

These are footprints.

The world collects footprints, like the moon collects dust. And here I am, on a hot South Florida September day, looking at *Guernica*'s footprints, wondering how Picasso put it together so that I think *all* these things? How did he show me a hundred angles at once, perspectives, points of view?

The hair of the horse is the first thing, I guess, like dry hay, making the horse look like a skinned rabbit. Its head cocked, the light spurred. Then there's the bull's head, another head—a mounted prize, proud, as if it hadn't died. Heads are everywhere in this painting, like gusts of wind or squeezed toothpaste, tails like smoke, hands like cacti, misplaced shadows. Hidden hearts, buried in the soot of a brick-lain battle. Crying, screaming, clawing forward, a knee that's bent, an arm outstretched. Charcoal lines are a chimney's breath. Big white blocks: light. There is a lot of light here. There is hope in all of this disorder. Or is it the dangling bulb of torture, waterboarding, Abu Ghraib?

Or is *Guernica* really just about ground? Foreground, background, walking ground. The ground that buries its dead. The ground must really want to talk. It's why it gets flooded and muddy when it rains and why it holds on tight to what it's got, to the roots that spread inside it, moving and growing like in the animated pages of a flip book, slowly gripping, making pictures. It's why it sprouts flowers. It's why there's a flower at the center of *Guernica*. Because Picasso knows about the ground. And about loss.

My father's grave won't have a name for six to eight weeks. That's how long it takes to process the gravestone, engrave each letter. Dad has a long name. I put the book down. I no longer have a father. Fatherless. I am nobody's daughter. How many ways are there to say this?

With the Picasso book at my feet and the dead unmarked in their grave, the return stare of the painting's surface is more daunting than ever. The only good feeling coming into my bones, through my skin, is that my studio is beginning to feel less claustrophobic than before. Before Dad died I used to come in here and bitch and moan. Say it was too small, say I was cramped, wishing I sold more, had more money. Today I like its closed-in walls. It feels like they're holding me.

Phthalo Blue.

This color can also be used as a mixer, but phthalo blue
tends to be more powerful than most colors. Hence, one
needs only to add a very small amount of phthalo in order to
significantly morph a color.

I MIX myself some ultramarine: take the phthalo, pour it into a clear
glass container, the kind you use to preserve jam—it's a really good
place to mix paints. You can see the color through the glass, and the
jars have good sealing. I add white, a gloss medium, and a little bit of
gold-leaf dust I've got left over from an old painting, the old crumpled
cover of a long-drunk champagne bottle. I've seen chefs on TV put
gold leaf on food and always wonder about eating it.

Then lime green. Next I take the ultramarine I've made, put it in
another empty jar, add more green—moss this time—get a bit of sea
green going. Take the original phthalo, pour it into another bottle, and
squeeze the last dash of crimson red left in the tube, making purple.

The quiet all around me echoes the blue. We loved him more
than we knew. Only the sound of brushes against glass bottles, tinking,
the squish and bubble-blurt of tubes squeezing. I turn the radio dial:
blue sound. I want to be surprised, I don't want my iPod, I don't want
to put on a CD and know what's coming. I want to feel the surge of

a song I haven't heard in a while, I want my lips to mouth lyrics my brain's got stored in files, classified and categorized.

Beatle Brunch is on the oldies station. The show's been on ever since I can remember. Dad and I used to listen to it on the way to Perrucho's.

"Ob-La-Di, Ob-La-Da" was my favorite, and here it is vibrating again, making my heart skip a beat. I listen to the story of Desmond in the lyrics, on his way to the jewelry store to buy a ring for his singing sweetheart, Molly Jones.

"You know why they call Ringo, Ringo?" Dad leans over the small gap between us in the truck and whispers, like it's a secret. He's smiling and his cheeks are bright pink, but his long eyebrows arch around his eyes in a way that always makes him look sad, even when he's happy, which he always was when he talked about the Beatles.

"That's not his real name?" I squeak, surprised.

We're in the black Bronco. I'm four. Dad and I, going to get Sunday-morning breakfast, radio blasting. Mom and Nina still sleeping at home. We've snuck out, making sure not to wake them.

Our lives are different than Molly Jones and Desmond's, but also the same somehow. We're on our way to the corner grocer, which is named after the owner. Perrucho always gives me a present: a slice of ham, a small rubber ball, a *pastelito*. Later, when Nina gets older, she'll start to join us, but for a long time it's just me and Dad. This was in the old house, the first house, with the big oak tree out in the front, the one I think of when I think of home.

"No, his real name is Richard Starkey. They called him Ringo because he wore so many rings." Dad tells me this with pride, like he has so much to teach me. About life, about music. And weren't they the same thing? Dad flutters his fingers like he's showing off a lot of sparkling rings. "Ring-go," he says.

I crack up. My little legs dangle from the leather interior seat, and I bop my head along to the Beatles, which both of us love.

"The Fab Four, they called the Beatles that sometimes. Your Mom liked Paul."

"Which one is Paul?"

"He's the *other* Beatle. Your Mom thought he was cute. She told her friend Marta she was going to marry him."

I giggle again.

"Does Paul look like you?" I ask.

Dad laughs big.

"Which one did you like?" I ask him.

"The legend, John. *El freakiao.*" *Freakiao* is Dad's Cuba-fied version of "the freaky one," said with more than a hint of love and a healthy dose of admiration.

Oh blah dee, oh blah daa...

"I like John too," I say.

Dad smiles and places his big, chubby hand on my little drumstick thigh with all the tenderness in the world, and for the rest of the way to Perrucho's he leaves it there, making me understand: I'm here to teach you all about music. I'm here to love you and protect you. Somehow, I know all of this by his gesture, even though I am only four. Perhaps because I am only four.

And life rolls on as the wheels turn beneath us in our black Bronco.

I turn from the painting toward my desk, and there is Dad's Montblanc pen, the one I know has an empty barrel inside, inkless. The one he always used and I can't manage to fill. I drop my brushes in the water bucket, and watch the bits of paint dilute as I try and hold back what I know is coming, but there's a force somewhere pulling it out from inside my body, like there's a magnet facing me, fighting my strength. I let myself curl into a ball on the gray-blue, paint-smeared area rug. The heaving gets louder and louder. Who cares about paint when there are invisible creatures flying around, stabbing at your heart, sucking things out of you? Who cares? And yet there are the marks, which have translated all of this into paint, onto the wood.

 Hunter Green.

The color of the hunt. In the nineteenth century hunters wore this deep green to blend with the forest. Perhaps better known as the color of US dollar bills.

DAD'S FLOOR is stone and cold. Nina and I are crouched, staring at the safe, trying out combinations. You can tell a lot about a person by the things he keeps in a safe. Dad had one on the floor of his closet. He wanted to be a gangster, wanted so badly to cash in on the American Dream. Nina and I had seen it before, knew exactly where it was. The only problem was how to figure out the code so we could get inside and see what he had left behind, organize his life.

We've looked all over his room for the digits, or a hint. But nothing. Above us, his shirts big as parachutes hang from metal bars all around. Polos, Dolce & Gabbana, Prada. Inside the cuffs, in cursive script: *Specially Tailored for Ignaciano Gonzalez.*

"What a dandy," says Nina.

"Totally." We're both laughing,

Then I spot the suit he wore to my college graduation. Dapper and proud of me. He'd surprised Mom after the ceremony as she was coming out of the bathroom. "Thank you, Eli," he told her. "Thank you for raising them so well." Then he choked up and hugged her tight. We all just stood there, watching, wondering. Where had all the anger gone? Mom's eyes didn't stop tearing for the rest of night.

"Look in his wallet again, Vero."

"We've looked three times."

"Look again!"

And sure enough. A tiny piece of paper with a number scrawled on it, 34-43-49, caught between two credit cards. I read the combination out loud to Nina and realize immediately what it means.

"It's our birthdays. Mine and yours and—"

"—Mom's."

The trinity he kept in his wallet, and safe in a box.

"So what do I do?" Nina says, breaking the short silence. Both of us are choked up, compression chambers trying not to go off. This has to get done. There might be important documents in here. Things we will need to unravel. Dad's written an *L* or an *R* under each number (left or right), and then a dash and another number: *L-3, R-4*. We try out possibilities.

34 to the left after three turns, four turns to the right, stop at 43, and so on.

After eleven tries we finally get the exact rhythm of it and open the safe.

Right on top there are two pictures. One is of me and Nina and Mom, together, in our first house in front of our stone fireplace in our Christmas outfits. Nina and I in black velvet dresses with red bows, Mom dressed in a long red dress, her long black curls falling gracefully at her shoulders, her arms around both of us. The other picture is just of Mom. She was maybe my age in the picture, in her late twenties. She was wearing a big white piqué blouse and jeans, and staring straight into the camera with a picaresque look on her face, a face that says both *This is so much fun* and *I love you.*

Under the pictures are wads of hundred-dollar bills, which we count mechanically. A poor man's fortune: $40,000.

"Didn't trust banks," Nina says out loud. Under the bills is a group of keys. So many of them. Small ones, big ones, Medecos. Keys that would take Nina and me forever to figure out which doors, boxes, and secrets they opened. And perhaps there would be keys left that we never found the locks to, secrets closed to us forever.

And then there are the guns.

"Jesus," says Nina. "I don't want to touch those. Do you know how to open them and take out the bullets?"

"No idea."

"What in the world do you need seven G-U-N-S for?"

"Protection."

All our friends used to be scared of Dad when we were small. Dad always carried his gun. Mom and Dad called it the G-U-N, until long after Nina and I could spell. Sometimes our friends wouldn't be allowed to sleep over and I knew it was because their moms were afraid of the G-U-N.

"Remember when he pulled one on Vic?" asks Nina.

How could I forget. He'd shown up at the house one day when Vic and Mom were still just friends, after Mom and Dad's divorce, and he sat Vic down on the sofa and told him that it was "inappropriate" for him to be in "his" house like this. Dad was just sitting there, with the gun in his hand, asking Vic, "Do you understand?" Vic didn't come around for a couple of months, even though he eventually mustered the courage to find his way back.

UNDERNEATH it all, at the very bottom of the safe, are the watches, which are the strangest thing of all. He'd started collecting them. Rolex, Tourneau, Cartier, high-end timepieces. Every time we saw him lately, he had a new one on. We'd always known he wanted a Rolex. Now he had two.

Ever since I can remember, Dad had wanted a Rolex. When we were little, he used to talk about it. He wanted the gold one with the blue face, that's what he'd always say. I know now that there are several variations of this kind of blue-faced watch, but I also knew the one he wanted by sight because he'd shown it to me in Bermuda, telling me, "One day I'll have one of those," tapping his finger on the jewelry store glass, "just like that one, see that one, *mamita?*"

When we got back home from Bermuda, I started a piggy bank because I thought I could raise enough money if I saved every bit of it and didn't spend money on stickers or pizza on Pizza Day at school. Dad had brought home a Rolex catalogue, so I called the number on the catalogue and I told them which one I wanted the price for. They said it was $10,000, which didn't mean much to me. It was just a number. There wasn't any reason in the world I thought my little eleven-year-old self couldn't raise any infinite number of dollars. So I had garage sales and made string bracelets to sell at school and I held car washes on the weekend, and sold lemonade with too much sugar, a Cuban lemonade, just like our coffee. Little by little, I started filling my piggy bank, which was not a pig at all but an oversized version of a glass Coca-Cola bottle. Mom had bought it and told me I would have to break it if I wanted to open it—that's why she bought me the glass one and not the rubber one with the hole at the bottom that you could take money out of every time you wanted. She was in on the secret. She knew how impossible it would be, but she wasn't going to break it to me.

When the bank got so heavy I couldn't move it, I broke it. I counted and counted. It seemed like forever, piling and wrapping all those coins. But when I was done I only had thirty dollars and sixty-three cents. This couldn't be. It was then that I realized how very many car washes and no-pizza-eating Pizza Days it would take to make up $10,000, and the impossibility dawned on me.

WHEN IT comes time to split the jewelry, Nina yells out, "I want this one, I want this one," pointing to and then grabbing at the second Rolex, a gaudy affair of a thing. "Come on," she says, "you know you'll never wear it." I don't care. And so she takes the diamond-encrusted one that we think is probably worth much more than anything else in the box. I take the original blue-faced one, open a safe deposit box in the bank, and put it there.

 Black.

Scientifically, objects are black not because they are
inherently so, but because they have absorbed all the colors
of the visible spectrum, instead of reflecting any of them.
Yet this is the "color" we so often use to outline, and make
line drawings.

From: Veronica Gonzalez
To: Leo Estevez
Date: Mon, Sep 17, 2007 3:31pm
Subject: Talk to me

> Hey there leo, so how's your day so far and yesterday; how's
> ground zero? I'm surprised no one's kicked you out yet. I've
> been following it on the news. As for my days—don't ask—I
> mean really, just don't ask—just tell me about yours. Also, Leo,
> I have to tell you, you really got me moving. Wasn't till I saw
> you in the paper that I really started painting again. Just wanted
> to say: thank you…

~

From: Leo Estevez
To: Veronica Gonzalez
Date: Mon, Sep 17, 2007 6:55pm
Subject: Does it Matter?

> Aww, pintora, don't thank me, dawg, makes me feel funny.
> Shit.

I know what you mean about them not kicking me out yet, it's like they keep giving me warnings not to get too close to the hole and after enough of the warnings I leave for the day, but they always give me enough time to do some of what I want to do down there before I go.

I get there every day at the same time, the time the first plane crashed into the first building and I'm usually able to read a full entry from the journal before the cops make me go.

Cops aren't really mean or anything, it's always the same cops on the beat, so it's like they know the story. I told them about Shell and they just say to go home b/c it's dangerous near the hole where the towers were and I shouldn't be trespassing or disturbing the peace. What peace?

Anyways, it seems like we're in the same boat, you and me. not very good days on this end either.

Sailing to Byzantium. A lot of these days I think about that poem and you reading it to me.

Every day I put on this stupid black suit, and I go down there and I'm not really sure why I'm doing it, or if it even matters.

~

From: Veronica Gonzalez
To: Leo Estevez
Date: Tue, Sep 18, 2007 11:58pm
Subject: Re: Does it Matter?

I don't know if it matters, Leo, I don't really even know what that means anymore. But if something's calling you to do this, it has to be for a reason right? I was thinking about you the other day while I was driving and passing construction sites that sort of look like ground zero. And, I just kept thinking that maybe what you're doing is a kind of prayer for your brother and that's all that matters.

Hey, by the way, I saw your suit in the pictures in the newspaper and on the internet; you look smart, in that british way they use the word... I love that word: smart.

Going back into the painting now, so have to leave you. For now.

~

From: Leo Estevez
To: Veronica Gonzalez
Date: Wed, Sep 19, 2007 7:01am
Subject: Suited Up

The suit. Yeah, it's a really classy outfit. Ma gave me the tie the day we took home Shell's ashes. I couldn't tie it that day, because it kept slipping out of my hands. Every morning now, it still tries to go away from me, slips through my dumb fingers like some icy cube, like it doesn't want to go where I'm going you know. But I have to go there for some reason, so I shut my eyes and I think of Ma that Sunday, telling me "Corazon, Corazon." and that's it, all the woman could muster. And I don't know if she was calling out to me or to her own damn heart. Ma's hands are totally transparent, blue veins coming through like they're lit like from behind, like some of your paintings, the ones you did where you put the light behind the canvas and that shit glowed like nothing else.

I know you don't know that part of my mother, how her fingers could be pearls, but take my word for it, her fingers are these long beautiful things that like to boogie, get right down and jam around things like her cucharas de madera in the kitchen; and pinches of salt. And just like that they dance around me, in my head, when I do my tie in the mornings to go down there. Listen to me, I'm babbling.

Love, Leo

~

From: Veronica Gonzalez
To: Leo Estevez
Date: Thur, Sep 20, 2007 8:14am
Subject: You're not babbling

Your emails have really been making me think. About why I'm even bothering to paint now. From the one when you ask whether what you're doing matters or not. I just kept thinking—does it? Because I've been having the same issues with painting: Does it Matter? I feel like I gave you a sort of stupid answer before, brushed over it. Because, when you asked, I feel like I didn't really know. But this morning, for some reason, I feel a little different.

This is what I've come up with: Art is important because it makes us stop. Painting is the closest art to poetry because it tries to capture the world in a few strokes, just like poetry tries to capture the world in a verse or a stanza—that's why poets and painters get along ;) Anyway, the point is, that this condensing of material makes what we do dense and full of a million little pieces and strands, and layers, like Skin. Makes people look up from their computers and cell phones, their traffic jams; 9am clock-ins, and eight-hour days. It's like, I don't know, a C-section. It's like this peeling back that matters because at the end of it there's a bundle of nerves and a whole lot of life.

Also, the other thing you made me remember was something I had totally forgotten. I do know about your mother's hands. One day, middle of summer, you know those hot, no air conditioning days. I was walking into my apartment and you guys had your door wide open. Even though it was hot, it was one of those days in the Heights that were really pretty, and you could even hear birds because everything was so quiet (a rare occurrence there, as you know).

Anyway, when I was going toward my door, I caught these flashes moving around, reflecting off a mirror in your bathroom—you weren't there; it was the middle of the day, I guess you were at school. It was your mother, her hands and elbows—her quick professional maneuvering; one memorized gesture after another, tying her hair. Her hair obeyed every command, not like the disobedient hair of maidens, or like the long unruly hair of girls in summer, or like my hair which is massive and curly and totally fucking out of control.

Josefina is not a mermaid, I thought to myself. Her hair is a tamed thing, thick and dark brown, like the nut of a shell—and it stuck in my head. That's the way I drew her when I went inside my apt. A woman with big hands, massive, but delicate. I'll look for that drawing and send it to you maybe, if I'm not too embarrassed. Sometimes you look back on old work and it's embarrassing.

Un abrazo, Vero

~

From: Leo Estevez
To: Veronica Gonzalez
Date: Thur, Sep 20, 2007 8:16am
Subject: IM?

You know we should try IM-ing.

From: Veronica Gonzalez
To: Leo Estevez
Date: Thur, Sep 20, 2007 9:15am
Subject: Re: IM?

> I vote against it. I don't know why, I just kind of like these
> letters we've started writing and I don't want to ruin it. I think
> IM would ruin it.
> xx

I'm glad we're not going to do any IMing. It would get him too close. Leo. Sometimes I'm scared he'll get the wrong idea. Or I'll get the wrong idea. I really do love our letters but I think if we IM I'll be opening some kind of door I don't want to open. Letters are strange because even though they are the most intimate of expressions, the moments in which we are most honest and perhaps true, they're also distant and not physical. Talking is physical. Letter writing is ephemeral, ethereal: art. Like Robert Lowell and Elizabeth Bishop: a distant love, a very real love, just without contact.

 Pear Green.

A speckled kind of green. Picked from a plant, prickly and imperfect.

I TURN on NPR round about ten-ish, brush in hand. They've got Leo on the radio this morning. He's getting kind of famous in a weird, cultish way, like a popular blogger who gets some attention. I catch him in the middle of one of Shell's journal entries and I listen to Leo's voice, as it reads slowly and carefully. His voice has gotten so much deeper. I didn't hear it when I saw him. His language too is different. In person it wasn't so obvious, but in the emails it is. It's so strange how someone can exist in your life for such a long time that you can watch them change, go through seasons, watch the years mark skin and language. And also how an event, a single thing that happens, can fast-forward that process, make the seasons change with more force, mark the skin deeper.

He's reading an entry Shell had written about the day he got the messenger job. It had been raining all day, Shell wrote, so he'd been looking down, trying not to get the rain in his eyes. He'd written a description of New York City shoes, scuttling around him and splashing rain. He'd written about the puddles he'd seen and jumped over, describing them as bruises that gleamed around the edges in pear green made of car oil and muck. Right away, I can see the puddles, aching. What a special mother, is my first thought, to have created these two kids. It makes me glad I didn't know Shell better when he died. That way I wouldn't have to linger and torture myself over how he thought and the things he said before they were cut off, like a radio hit by lightning.

During the broadcast, I find myself placing my paintbrush at the very top of the painting. Because I've dipped the brush in watered-down, pale green paint, colored drops hang for a second at the edge of the brush, where it meets the wood, and then they ride down the panel—rain washing over *Cathedral* like a storm. A waterfall smoldered over by heat and by the pasty sweetness of jam (pear green). The water is encapsulated and held, away from the wind. This water, this waterfall, is safe. And around it, because of it, leaves sprout and rain falls in yellow, gold-like specks of dust. No, not specks. Flecks, flecks of gold like *flechas*, arrows.

"Is that your *loco* on the radio, *gordita?*" Tony raises his voice so that it carries from across the wall between our rooms, jarring me from my thoughts, dashing a red line from my brush, straight into the water. No matter. It happens sometimes, the intrusion of red into blue.

"*Sí. Te molesta?*" I yell over, cocking my head in the direction I imagine him sitting in. Seems the only people I talk to in here are invisible.

"No, no, not at all, leave it on."

"If it does, if it's too loud, I can put my headphones on and you won't hear it."

"No, *gordita*, it's fine, *todo bien*," Tony says sweetly, and then asks, "Wanna take a break in about two hours? *Salimos a caminar?*"

"Sounds good." I'll need to get out of here by then.

 Lime Green.

Tart, cool, and fluorescent, lime is a color that lingers.

It's February 2001. Leo's sucking on a coconut popsicle in my living room. Leo introduced me to this particular brand of Dominican coconut popsicle one day on the way to the subway and I fell in love. Now he brings me one almost every time he comes. I put mine in the freezer while I'm cleaning my brushes, talking to him from the kitchen. By the time I get to mine, he'll be on his second. His second one is lime. He always eats two and leaves what, for him, is the best for last. I don't like the lime, it's too sour. This is the way it works: he brings me treats like popsicles and lollipops and I lend him my books.

"So what's on the menu today?" he asks, skimming my shelves, sliding what he's just read (*The Great Gatsby*—he says he wants to first get through the classics he never got to) back into the shelf. Something I love about Leo is that he always manages to put the book exactly where he found it. It's an admirable precision I appreciate. "*Gatsby* was awesome," he says.

"Yeah," I say, drying my hands and walking over from the kitchen. "What about Yeats? Ever read Yeats?" I ask him, dropping myself onto the living room couch.

"No."

"*The Tower*, then? That's the one with 'Sailing to Byzantium.'"

"What's Byzantium?"

"It's this place where everything is gold and nothing dies. Where everything is immortal, but fake—like art."

"What's it got to do with Yeats?"

"A poem. He wrote it."

"You gonna read it to me?"

"Don't be cute," I say, walking over to my shelf. I can feel his eyes following me. This apartment is so different from my later ones—so full of shit, everything from cuckoo clocks to old *Life* magazines. I left everything behind, thank God. Even the books. They're Leo's now. I wonder if he runs a lending library for someone else out of it, like we had going. I don't want to ask. I might get jealous.

While I reach for that Yeats book, in the same red flats I always wear, on my tiptoes, Leo does something that day that he's never done before. He tests the waters.

"You have a cute ass," he says.

I turn around really sternly, almost mean. "You ever say anything like that again and you're not welcome here anymore."

I've scared him, I can tell. Book in hand, I give him a second to gather what's just happened.

"Sorry, son. Jesus. You act like an old lady sometimes. We're not that far apart in age, you know that, *Profe*, right?"

I had to do it. That has to be clear. This will be platonic. Not that he isn't adorable, and not that sometimes I don't want to jump his young little bones, but that's just wrong, and it won't happen, not on my clock. I remember being seventeen. No way. Apart from the fact that it would be statutory rape and I could go to jail, it would also get in the way. Plus, there's something on purpose about what I'm doing, and I know it, even if unconsciously then. I know that if I create tension, he'll keep coming back. He's a teenage boy. I know I can't keep him from going home and jacking off—picturing himself touching me, jamming his fingers up inside until I began to

138

pant, then sliding his fingers out, teasing me, eventually sliding his dick in and pushing and pushing and digging and digging like some baby mole, until out came the scream I couldn't help but let go of. He would make me come loud, while he sprayed inside me, a long, strong, young spray. If I can manage this—if I can manage him taking this feeling home with him, with Yeats burning in his head—he'll never leave poetry. Or me. But if I let him touch me, he'll feel he's conquered poetry and he won't understand he never can, that it's a journey that never ends. The scariest part of the whole thing, of course—I'm not oblivious to it—is that I have to ask myself, Is this his fantasy, or mine? Even more reason to keep the distance.

"Here it is. Yeats," I say.

THEN, SUDDENLY, on the radio, there is a rush running through in waves, and the cops buckle Leo down. They've warned him, the announcer explains, but he wouldn't budge today. Incrementally, the cops had explained to newspapers, crowds, and the press, that Estevez was beginning to "disturb the peace."

"Leo, we are being told his name is Leandro Estevez, has been arrested," reports a steady journalistic voice, over the buzz of excitement around him. "It seems like quite a commotion down here. He gathered a crowd this morning, now protesting his being taken away. But after a little over a week of threatened arrest, the young man has finally been forced into silence."

 Sky Blue.

Also known as azure, it's a color full of assurance. If you're trying to match it exactly, Pantone's #2925 is a pretty close match (about 90 percent).

"Qué linda *la tarde, gorda*," says Tony, looking up at the sky. He always does this. We're holding hands and walking together, heading for the beach, down the long pedestrian Lincoln Road. I'd barged into his room, semi-hysterical, telling him *el loco*, as he called him, had been arrested. He tried to calm me down and suggested we get some air.

I follow Tony's gaze and agree it's a beautiful afternoon. But I feel uncomfortable looking up at the sky and enjoying it while Leo, poor Leo, is in a jail cell somewhere. "Leo got arrested," I tell Tony again.

"I know, you've told me a hundred times," says Tony. "Honestly, I'm surprised they didn't do it earlier."

"I'm scared for him."

"He'll be fine. They don't do much to protestors anymore. This isn't the sixties, *gorda*."

This annoys me a little, but I don't want to say anything, I don't want to fight. And is that what he's been doing, protesting? It's strange that Tony sees it like this when I see it as something totally different.

"Did you get a lot of painting done?"

"Yeah, a lot of green in there for some reason today," I respond, letting Tony change the subject.

"Johnny Cash and checks," says Tony, smiling and pulling my hand down, teasing.

"Yeah, that kind of green. But then other kinds too."

"Maybe tomorrow you can put that blue in there," says Tony, pointing to the sky.

"Yes, definitely that blue."

I lean my head closer to Tony's shoulder and he wraps his arm around me.

WHEN WE started dating, Tony used to point to billboards and shop signs and the colors of walls and say, "Do you like that one, on the pizza shop or the one next to it, the bank, more?" And I would respond one or the other, and then Tony would ask me why and we would talk about color and design for a long time. When we were in the supermarket he would ask me which magazine cover I liked best. I knew he was asking me both because I was another mind to tap into for his designs, but also because he was trying to get to know me through color. Immediately, it was a language we both spoke, and I loved him for it. Sometimes those conversations, though, would turn to Tony's other side.

"I would say 80 percent of people would choose that cover you just chose. And I would say that 60 percent of those 80 percent are women."

This is a language we don't share, but it's one that helps Tony explain the world to himself. And one that helps me, by his side, stay grounded in the checks and balances of our surroundings. Otherwise, I run the danger of lifting off like some balloon and deflating too high up into all that blue sky.

Tony doesn't read anymore. He gave up reading when he was twenty-two, "to join the world," he says. But just recently he bought himself a book and devoured it. It was Alan Greenspan's memoir, *The*

Age of Turbulence. He thinks Greenspan is *"una bestia,"* a real beast. And he means this in the best of all possible ways. "Brilliant," he says. A word he acquired from his days bartending in Cambridge, when he used to read Adam Smith and other economists while sifting through Pascal and *The Communist Manifesto* all at once.

I think it's probably a good thing Tony stopped reading for a while. I imagine he would have been almost insupportable as an arrogant intellectual traveling the world, acquiring the knowledge of pussy, along with the turn of every page and the crossing of each new border. It's funny, how some people have to do this, to learn. To grow. Usually the stubborn ones, the ones who just won't admit things unless they see it for themselves. Get mired in Russian cold to really understand what "cold" means. And yet, it's this same border-crossing that allows us to have a conversation about Gaudí and the architecture of Barcelona.

When we get to the beach, Tony points to the sky again. "Look how many colors there are there, *gorda*, right there in that patch of sky."

And he's right, it's pink and orange and yellow and blue and green. Stroking my thigh, Tony looks out to the sea and points with his head toward the waves.

"I almost died out there once," he says.

"I know, when you were eighteen." I've heard the story a thousand times, his sailor's attempt to tempt the fates. It surprises me how much he still likes to sail, after that, but then I remember I too had reason to fear the water, and still I loved it. With all my heart I loved it.

It was in Hawaii that I'd tried to tempt the sea. Hawaii was a whirlwind. And the turning point. I left New York after that.

The Poet I worked for was supposed to give a talk at a writer's conference out there and I was supposed to go along as his assistant. I think he just wanted me to see Hawaii, see how writing workshops and conferences worked. They existed for painters too, he said. It was a gift really, fully paid, a wonder, and I was infinitely grateful for it. I remember feeling young and stupid, and trying to think of new ways to thank him, every day, but thinking also that I was so lucky.

And then, on the third day, something happened that changed everything. The Poet had been drinking with me and other writers, communally, for two days, showing me the ropes, introducing me to everyone. On the third night, however, he'd picked up a cute girl who didn't belong to the conference, a waitress, and gone upstairs with her. It didn't bother me, I wasn't that kind of "assistant." But without The Poet around, I'd been left to my own devices and got drunk with another writer, an older man in his fifties, who looked sort of ageless — fine skin that was nonetheless soaked in experience, bronzed by it. Specks of white hair. Oh how I loved those specks of white hair. His writing was okay, I'd thought, nothing special. He'd read on the first night, some book about the long residues of colonial displacement in India. But when he read there was something about him that made me blush, probably the consistent thought of wanting to pull him close. He seemed, from far away, to have the softest lips. He was Indian, he'd said, as if I couldn't pick that up from the subject of his book and his accent. But really he was a mutt, a mixture of all the places he'd lived, which was my favorite thing about him, and which is what I would later love (and sometimes hate) about Tony too.

Anyway, this writer, he loved tigers and wore white linen shirts with jeans, hipster sneakers, had a small, silver hoop earring, wore circle-rimmed glasses like Gandhi or Yeats. He spoke English with a British accent, talked about soccer, said things like, "I'm not from anywhere," and in the next breath, "I may not be from anywhere, but when I die I want my ashes scattered over the Himalayas." He'd crafted himself into a cliché, I was aware of this, but he wasn't obnoxious, like some of the other writers, and his love for tigers seemed kind of honest, as if he'd possibly been one in a previous life, which appealed to me. "Beautiful creatures," he'd said with a sparkle in his eye during his reading.

On the third night, he came up to me of his own accord, saw me from across the room, he said, at the hotel restaurant, and wondered if he could join me. One thing led to another, both of us sinking deeply into a drunken intoxication, beer after beer. He ended up coming up to my room. He put on the music, radio through the TV, R&B, which I thought was a hilarious choice. But he stopped my laughter with a kiss and it was true, his lips were soft as petals. My mouth felt like it was trying to suck the spirit out of him and it felt he was trying to do the same to me.

It was my first kiss.

I was in my twenties and I'd never been kissed.

Being a fat teenager had been a misery in many ways. Men stayed away, far away—they leave fat girls alone. It's true, the good part had been that they'd left me alone long enough to think and to become myself, without interruption, undisturbed by their stupidity—without judgment, without the detrimental mark of them. But now here I was, skinny as a wrought-iron rail, but desirable because I was soft and fragile, the paradox of jutting bones and feather weight. I hated the idea of that, but it had proven pathetically true. Men liked creatures they could capture, "save," use and release. I didn't want to be used. So when the Indian writer with colonial residues slipped his hand under my shirt, I asked him to leave. Asked him to leave despite feeling a flourish of desire that almost overtook.

Just weeks before, at a Japanese temple, a monk had come up to me and told me he could see I was close to God, close to the spiritual realm, it was evident my connection was strong. I almost was not here, he'd said, on Earth. This disturbed me at first, made me think I was going to die, but the comment came rushing back as the writer cupped his long brown fingers over my soft, hard breast. And I wondered, if I slept with this beautiful writer with soft lips, would I break that bond, would I be so different I wouldn't recognize myself? Would I, all of a sudden, be cuffed to the Earth?

That night, after my earringed writer had left, I went down to the shore and jumped into the water, out of impulse, not caring that it was pitch dark, that there might be sharks. I jumped in, floral-print dress and all, a soft silk dress I'd bought in Tokyo. At first it was a rush of exhilaration, what Tony must have felt in his sailboat out at sea. But then a wave swept me from under and pushed me out, out further than I wanted to go, and my heart began to beat so hard I thought it would lodge in my throat to choke me as water tried to make its way in. One way or another, suffocation seemed imminent. Desperate and flailing, my head covered by fierce waves, I didn't have time to think of death itself, there was no flashing of my past before me, all I was thinking about was how to survive. And just as suddenly as I'd been taken out toward the ocean, I was pushed by another wave back onto the shore, thrown onto the sand. I got up and ran, shoeless, up to my room, and took off my wet silk dress, made of the spinning of a million worms, slowly and delicately. I put it in the trash and dried myself with the blow-dryer perched on the bathroom wall. I went to sleep without a shower, smelling of salt and brine and seaweed. I told no one.

As Tony continues to stroke my thigh and the wind hits my skin, my hair stands on end in goose bumps. An oozing feeling of peace comes over me. How stupid I had been, back then, to think sex would ruin everything. It had binding consequences, sure, sometimes, but sometimes that binding was more liberating than anything. I never quite understand moments like this, some life current that washes over me, crossing boundaries and all sorts of personal walls. Tony and I, whether we like it or not, are attached to life. Both of us have been through dire straits and both of us have wanted, more than anything, to live.

Leo too: attached. We, none of us, are Buddhists. Let Leo be okay, let him remain untouched in jail, let him be released quickly—a prayer. The feeling of peace, right at this moment, is overwhelming, and I want to fall asleep right on the sand here, right next to Tony, bathing in the day's last light.

IT'S BEEN four days since I heard from Leo. Yesterday was Dad's birthday. He would have turned fifty-two. Today, I can't get out of bed.

"*Gordita.*" Tony comes over every little while and pets my head as I lie in bed, asking if he can do anything, then giving me a kiss on the forehead and going back to work. I feel so bad, I don't even have the energy to tell him to just let me mourn today and everything will be okay tomorrow—I hoped so anyway.

This lasts until about eleven, when I hear Tony starting the vacuum, and I feel a surge inside me and I call out to him in a low, groggy yell, "Stop!"

I wanted to clean. Mom and I and Nina and Vic and Tony had made a mess last night. We'd eaten an Argentine *parillada*, drank champagne, and then each of us had lit a candle and put it on a cake and, one by one, made a wish for Dad.

"Don't clean, *mi amor*, I'll do it. Please, let me do it." I jump out of bed, put on my underwear and one of Tony's T's, yelling like a crazy person, "I want to do it!" Besides, why should he have to do this? It's unfair to make him. So, messy bed-head and all, I take the vacuum from his hand, give him a kiss on the cheek, and put the vacuum away, switching it for the broom. I force a smile and he says, "Okay," looking at me like he's scared of me, and then goes to his room, to work at his computer.

But then, after struggling with Tony for the birthday mess responsibility, I can hardly lift the broom. So I put on my iTunes. I can think of nothing more I want to do than listen to Billie Holiday. Slowly, the songs manage to move me across the floor, picking up the pieces of a man.

After the floor is clean, I go back to bed. Tony wakes me up at eight that evening.

"*Vamos, gorda*, let's have dinner."

 Magenta.

This color is extra-spectral as far as colors go, which means it's a mixed bag of red and blue. It is created in the brain in an attempt to fill the space between the wavelengths of violet and red light. Supposedly, it's a color symbolic of transformation.

"How ABOUT sushi?" asks Tony.

Tony hates sushi. It doesn't fill him up, he says, it's like water, "just a snack." He likes the feel of meat: real, the kind of meat that sits heavy and makes you sleepy after eating.

"It's okay, *mi amor*, we don't have to," I assure him, knowing he's just doing this to get me out of the house.

"*Sí, gorda*, you like it, *vamos*."

And so we go. I put on the first thing I find in my closet, a checkered dress I usually don't wear. I look a little like a country bumpkin in it. I only keep it because it's hot pink and white and I love the color. Nobody likes this dress but me. Tony hates it. He usually puts a "yuck" face when I wear it, but today he doesn't say anything. Everybody thinks it's too cute to be pretty, but I think it's violent. Disconnects.

At dinner I'm sitting across from Tony at a really small table outside, with a big orange umbrella hanging over us, even though it's already dark and we don't need the umbrella. I'd promised to guide my thoughts away from sadness before we left the apartment tonight, just as I told my sister to do. But lately everything is spiraling into my deep, black hole, everything is getting worse.

"You know, *mi amor*," I say, "Nina went to an *espiritista*."

"What, like a *santera*?" Tony is placing the napkin on his lap, getting comfortable in his chair, leaning back.

"Sort of."

"Shit, *gorda*."

"Yeah, I know. But you know what the *espiritista* said to her?" I say this, leaning in. I don't want to say it too loudly, but I want him to hear it.

"Who cares?"

"I do," I tell him forcefully, looking straight at him, wondering what he's really thinking about.

"Okay, okay, what did she say?" Tony asks, rolling his eyes a little, like he's indulging me.

It's just like Tony to leave everything at the surface, to keep everything on the top layer, to not want to listen to this, to not believe there's something bigger than him. I want to strangle him.

"This is just like you," I tell him, straight out.

"What is?" Tony looks confused.

Could he really not be thinking about anything?

"Nothing."

"So, *gorda*, what did the lady say to your sister?" Tony still looks confused and like he's treading water out in the middle of the ocean, land nowhere in sight.

"She said that my Dad follows her around more than me. That he's everywhere with her, guiding her, caring for her, that he's with us both, but mostly he's with her."

"*Gorda*, c'mon, please, is this why you're so upset today? I mean do you really—"

The waiter interrupts Tony to put our food on the table. I stare at Tony. I do believe it. Of course I believe it. They loved each other. What about me? Did I love him? Did Dad love me? Wasn't I the one who told everyone he was an asshole? Isn't that what Lee remembered? Of course he wouldn't be with me, why would he, what could I possibly have to offer him? And suddenly I feel completely alone. Like I'm the only one at the table, at this restaurant, on this street, in this city, and I want to scream out, scream out so loud that my voice reaches someone somewhere, even if they're far, just so I can hear their voice answer back. I stare at Tony, who, by the time the waiter leaves, has that fear face he gets. He used to get it a lot more when he was still scared of my paintings. It's the face he gets when he can't tell what I'm thinking.

"Why don't you ever kiss me?" I ask Tony.

"*Gorda*, what on earth are you talking about?"

"Why don't you fuck me like you used to fuck me?" Right when I say this I regret it. I know how crazy I sound. But I really am feeling this, like out of nowhere it's what I feel the most right at this moment. He doesn't fuck me like he used to. Sure, for a couple of days after Dad died, he loved me, really loved me. But now we're back to the dry spell we were having before my father died.

"It's because you don't *really* love me," I tell him. I'm crying now and I can tell by Tony's expression that people are looking at me.

"Of course I do. Don't you *feel* that I do?" Now it's Tony who's leaning in, across the table, trying to make this be over.

"Well why are we stuck, then?"

"What do you mean, stuck?"

Neither of us have touched our food. Tony's been holding his chopstick to his sashimi, but he's just been fiddling, hasn't taken an actual bite of anything.

"We're stuck. We're not moving to the next level."

"Are you talking about—"

"Yes, Tony. I'm—I mean, why don't you ever, why don't we ever talk about it?"

"*Gorda*, we've had this conversation before, I told you from the beginning. I don't want to get married. I just don't see it for me, it's not—"

"It's because you're afraid of blood, because you go from one surface to the next, that's how you are, happy-go-lucky-surface-man. It starts getting rough and you move from one piece of skin to the next, never going beyond the fucking surface because what happens when you get beyond the surface? There's fucking blood, Tony!" Spit is coming out of my mouth. I feel my face getting more and more hot. "There's blood, there's a lot of fucking messy blood. And what happens when Tony-surface-boy sees blood: he faints like a coward. You're a fucking coward, Tony, you're a fucking coward."

By this point, Tony has fallen silent. He won't answer back. I try and get something out of him, but it's futile. The angrier I get, the quieter he gets. The only thing he moves to do is motion for the check. I realize I'm losing it, but there's nothing I can do about it.

THE NEXT morning, Tony wakes up at six. I hear him go to the computer and start working. When I open my eyes, I feel how swollen they are. I can't open them wide, even with force. I decide to stay in bed. I stay there until noon. I know I'm depressed and that Tony won't talk to me when I wake up, he'll just retreat further and further from me and I'll have to draw him out of this. He does this every time we fight—which is rare, but when it happens, it's like this. I always manage to get him out of it, but I can't do it today. I just don't have the energy. It's like somebody's taken a straw to my blood flow and sucked it dry. All of it.

When I finally get out of bed, I make the bed by myself. Usually Tony helps me, but he just stays, staring at his computer. Usually our morning greeting is "*Buenos días, mi amor.*" And a kiss on the cheek. Sometimes he sings, "Good morning to you, I said good morning to you," silly-like, trying to get the first laugh of the day out of me. Today, though, Tony is solemnly staring at the glow of the screen in front of him.

Outside, the day is gray. I can't see it yet, but I can hear the drizzle out the window. We went to sleep in Miami, we woke up in London. I usually make his coffee in the morning. He's already made it for himself, already drank it. Before I go to the studio to work, I kiss him timidly on the cheek and say good morning, coldly. "*Buenos días,*" he responds, frigid.

"You know," I say, "I can't be the one this time, even if I said crazy things, even if I'm the one responsible, which maybe I'm not, I don't even remember exactly what happened. And it doesn't matter, I just, I can't be the one to get us out of it this time, I can't. Do you understand? Let me know when you want to talk. The ball is in your court." And then I shut myself in the studio straight through the afternoon.

"Nina hasn't been having a good week," Mom says.

"I know." Who has?

"I think she should go see Dr. Xu."

"Dr. Xu doesn't solve everything, Mom. She already went to that lady, the *espiri* —"

"Don't even *compare* that woman to Dr. Xu. Dr. Xu is a medicine man, you know what he did for my vertebrae. I—" Mom starts this "I" like she's about to confess something. She pauses and then says, "I let her go home from work early today."

"You probably shouldn't have. That's the problem with her working for you."

"You should go see Dr. Xu too."

Mom thinks Dr Xu solves everything. You're sad, go see Dr. Xu. Your leg hurts, go see Dr. Xu. You're lovesick, go see Dr. Xu. Every doctor in the world tells you you've got cancer and two months to live, don't worry, go see Dr. Xu. So when Nina couldn't stop crying for a week straight, her eyes inflated like old red rubber pool floats, Mom made her go to her Chinese miracle worker.

From: Veronica Gonzalez
To: Leo Estevez
Date: Fri, Sep 28, 2007 8:02am
Subject: Ok?

> Leo: You ok??? You home? You out? I tried your cell, couldn't
> reach you. Haven't heard from you for days and days, last thing
> I know they took you in. Please call or write.

~

From: Leo Estevez
To: Veronica Gonzalez
Date: Fri, Sep 28, 2007 8:55am
Subject: Sort of

> I'm okay. Ma bailed me out.

~

From: Veronica Gonzalez
To: Leo Estevez
Date: Fri, Sep 28, 2007 9:15am
Subject: RE: Sort of ?

> And?

~

From: Leo Estevez
To: Veronica Gonzalez
Date: Fri, Sep 28, 2007 10:15am
Subject: —

> And? I got arrested. Or did you forget?
> Now I have a record and I'm not even sure what immigration
> is going to do about it.
> I don't think I can do it anymore. I've been wondering about
> the "American Dream," and whether it killed Shell.
> I'm tired of being sad. Is this ever going to be over?

~

From: Veronica Gonzalez
To: Leo Estevez
Date: Fri, Sep 28, 2007 11:54am
Subject: Dumbass

I'm sorry Leo, but my first instinct is to tell you you're being a dumbass, I really think you should finish reading his journal out loud, that's what you said you were going to do, and that's why you had a crowd every day listening to you. So put on your black suit, wash your hands, get over the jail-bit, and ride the A train straight to the heart of the matter. And as for being sad—I don't even know what to tell you on that one. I'm not sure I feel anything but an enormous hole deep in me, getting bigger by the day, so I'm not exactly the one to be saying anything in that dept. So if you think I'm crazy, and I'm driving you to jail again, and everything I say is wrong, just ignore me.

 Orange.

The United States Department of Homeland Security uses orange to signify high risk. Second only to red. In American prisons many inmates wear orange, but so do Buddhist monks and Hindus (saffron, a sacred color that symbolizes fire, but a fire that purifies).

AN IM from Tony: *www.nycblogspot.com/wordman*. I click the link and it opens to:

9/30/2007 Blogspot, 55 comments

Leo is Back

This Morning Estevez returned to the edge of Manhattan. Some say he's over the edge but we like him that way. Today, he had a message for us and I'd, if I were you, listen up.

"I'm not budging this time, hear me Mister Bloomberg, Sir, I'm not budging because pieces of my big brother, Shell, are somewhere here, in this ash and dust and ground, and I'm not moving until I send Shell's soul up to somewhere better. I'm not moving until we all stand here and remember for a little bit all the things six years have been kind enough to let some of us forget. So this is what I have to say: I say any of you all that lost somebody here, six years ago, bring a chair. This here is Shell's. Because, hell, they aren't doing much else down here. Six years and god knows where the money's gone to rebuild. Nothing here still but a big empty hole." Then Estevez sat on the plastic lawn chair he'd been standing on to give his speech. He also said he'd be podcasting everything on his website (www.emptychair.com) live throughout the day. Comments welcome to the site, he added.

Then Estevez scattered what seemed to be a pile of orange soil in front and around him. But it wasn't, it was a pile of orange birdseeds, which soon had a flock of pigeons to it, picking them up and scattering them.

Comments Welcome:

> *Leo, you rock man, wait for me. I got a chair that looks a lot like yours. My dad died there. I'm bringing his chair he used to take me to see ball games with. Please don't go anywhere, I'm heading down there fast as I can.*

> *We love you, Leo. Stay strong my man… I'm coming with my chair.*

> *My best friend jumped out the window next to me and I ran all the way home to the upper west side; I still dream about him. My wife holds me in the middle of the night and I'm not sure what to tell her when she says it'll be okay because I just don't think it will. I'm not sure I'll ever stop dreaming about George. We rode the subway together mornings and now I'm not sure how I can stay here, in this city, with so many memories of him everywhere. I ask myself that every morning. Morning cream-cheese from his bagel all over his hands, and his face when he saw the smoke fill the office. How come I got away and he didn't? How come I didn't jump? I'll be there with you Leo, I haven't forgotten.*

By the end of the day, it's all over TV. First it was only on his website and then it was something else, it got bigger than him. Little by little, people started showing up, with chairs, all kinds of them. Red chairs, yellow chairs, wooden chairs. Lawn chairs, stools, step stools, beanbags, party chairs, high chairs. Then the "here," the place Leo was talking about, the center of loss, extended, and vets who lost friends in Iraq and Afghanistan started coming. And Muslims who'd been beat up in the days following 9/11, Muslim-Americans too, who had lost their loved ones at home because of what had happened "here."

Soon, threats were posted to the website. Comments filled with rage: "Who do you think you are, a country that can't be bombed? While the rest of the world is blown to smithereens? The Taliban was right to blow you up." And "It's not over." And "Fuck America." Comments had to be monitored, some were erased seconds after they were posted. Flagged. A red alert went up in New York City. Fox News was labeling Leo a kamikaze with a death wish, pulling down poor innocents with him. Radio stations were gathering panels and vociferating through the airwaves about where and when who should honor what and why. What that meant. American flags started to show up in windows again—a saccharine red, white, and blue, cakes and cakes of them frosting cars and people.

But Leo persisted, and little by little, as people with chairs arrived, Leo went around and gave each of them a pile of orange seeds. Right away, birds came to peck at the seeds, flying upward, dropping some of the seeds, carrying others, and soon enough, the aerial view was nothing less than striking. A view of endless chairs, people standing by their chair-side, and a patina of orange hovering over them like a delicate haze, or the remains of a benign fire. Lingering above them, birds flapping their wings, scattering light.

The cops started to come in and tried to break it apart, but Bloomberg gave an order: let it be. For twenty-four hours, he said, on this last day of September. A car bomb in the surrounding area was detected and removed, bridges into the city were put on intensive monitoring. Meanwhile, the tip of Manhattan blazed in orange, for one full day and one full night. And I couldn't help but stare at and think about the picture Old Man Matisse gave me, with its empty chair, and I pinned it next to Leo's newspaper article already on the wall, next to *Cathedral*.

"Tony, *mi amor*, did you see this, are you watching this?" I storm into Tony's room, after going through a slew of videos on CNN.com and MSNBC and all the big news sites.

"Sí, *te digo, gorda*," says Tony, watching a Leo YouTube. *"Es increíble."*

Tony's into it. You've done it, Leo, Tony's the barometer, he was the one saying this was all bullshit and a *locura*, and here he is admiring you.

"I wonder what it looks like on Google Earth," says Tony.

"Oh wow, totally! Go to Google Earth."

Looking on Google Earth, we try and see if we can zoom in and find the orange spot in the world. Zooming down into Manhattan and down to the tip, we can't see orange, only commotion, and I wonder if we'd had Google Earth during 9/11 what it would have looked like. Something like this?

Zooming back out, it's strange as it ever was looking down, over all those grids, all those lines we make, those neat blocks, so we can find our way around in the world, thick and dense as it is.

From: Veronica Gonzalez
To: Leo Estevez
Date: Mon, Oct 1, 2007 7:35am
Subject: Awesome

> Leo, what can I say? You inspired me. Keep the videos you used on the podcast—they're beautiful. Do you have more footage? I wouldn't be surprised if you get asked to show it at a gallery or someplace.

~

From: Leo Estevez
To: Veronica Gonzalez
Date: Mon, Oct 1, 2007 12:45am
Subject: Installation hoodrat

> So what are you saying, pintora? You saying I'm the artist now? Hah—that'd be something. Can you imagine? An "installation hood rat," now that's fucking funny.

I think about Shell less and less, and the years are good for that. But sometimes he just stares at me, through things. Like there's this stupid towel ma's still got; it's this orange thing that's stained and old and fucked up, but it's the towel Shell always used when he cleaned the kitchen, which he'd always try and make me help him do and I'd say something really stupid like "I ain't no woman," and he'd say, "don't be an ass, help ma out, stupid." And now the towel stares at me and talks to me. Sometimes I feel like throwing it away so it'll stop; and sometimes, I just feel like putting it all over my face and in my arms, like I was hugging Shell, you know?

Ah well, that's life, I guess: a fucking dirty orange towel talking to you.

THE WHITE-GOLD Montblanc has been eyeing me for days, asking me to fill its empty barrel.

So much has happened in the past weeks—Leo, the safe, Dad's birthday, ups and downs with Tony—the entire month of September has passed over us and all throughout, Dad's Montblanc, the one he always used, has been staring right at me.

He'd tried to give me a similar pen once, for my thirteenth birthday, and I'd just shrugged and said, "Thanks." Mostly because I didn't get it. I'd told him about a month before that I wanted to be an artist, and he'd said, "Why don't you be a graphic designer?"

"No," I said rebelliously.

"Why not?" We were in the car. "Look at that," he said, pointing at a Bacardi billboard. "You could do that. Everybody can see it."

"Dad, that's not what I want at all." I was getting upset in the seat next to him, the little vein in my forehead popping like Mom's.

"Selling is important," he said. "You have to know how to be a salesman."

"I don't want to sell out, no way. I want to *move* people. You know who Rothko is?" I said, pausing for effect. "Of course you don't," I added obnoxiously. "Rothko said that what he wanted was a person to fall apart, in tears, in front of one of his canvases."

"Why? Why would you want to bring more shit into the world and make somebody cry?" In this way Tony was like Dad.

"Dad, what I make isn't shit."

"I'm talking about Rocko."

"Rothko."

"Do what you want," he said. And then his temper set in and he started speeding and I shut up, because I got scared. I didn't want him to be mad, I wanted him to be proud of something I made and did, wanted to make the best Bacardi billboard in the world, just for him. But now we were speeding, music blasting, and I thought I might not make it to graphic design school even if I wanted to.

I'm not sure what he was doing, whether he was trying to protect me from becoming an artist, or whether he was just speeding off to the tune of his own stifled dreams, railing in frustration.

A couple of months later, on my birthday, he gave me a black Montblanc, the classic one.

I looked at him, not understanding what a Montblanc was, looking like, Why the hell are you giving me a pen?

"You know, *porque eres una freakia* and you like to study and draw, and, you know—"

"Okay."

"*Coño*, nobody can do anything right for you."

My obnoxious, thirteen-year-old self didn't get any of it. I didn't know that the little asterisk at the top meant branding, didn't know it meant my father was giving me a $700 gift even though he couldn't afford it (this was before he bought his own many years later), didn't know it also meant that it was his way of accepting what to him was his strange little daughter. I have no idea where that pen is. But now, his is staring me in the face, a white-gold, $900 affair of a pen, old and worn, with scratches. I can see it dangling from his polo shirt, on the lapel, between the buttons that made their way up his collar, in between the flaps. Click, click, the sound of the pen, when in one fell swoop he'd take it out, write down orders, jot down shoe serial numbers, sizes, boxes, amounts of containers. It's the pen he used to make money. It's the pen he used to write the letter that made me run to the bathroom and cry, hurting so much, in college. The letter that said that if I didn't agree with him that my mother was a bitch and Vic an asshole, act a certain way in favor of my father, if I didn't stop acting like a difficult child, say what he wanted me to say, do what he wanted me to do, that I could forget getting anything from him ever again. It's the pen with which he first sent me birthday cards, and the pen with which he later blackmailed me—a blackmail I refused to accept. It was the only pen he used.

A quick note in my day book comes almost impulsively: BUY REFILLS. The next day, on my way to Pearl Paint to pick up a tube of yellow ochre, I take the pen with me, and stop in by Dadeland Mall, where I'd read online there was a Montblanc store, one of the few in Miami.

When I finally get to the shop, I ask for two refills of ink and when the woman says, "Would you like me to polish your writing instrument?" I say okay. When she comes back, the age-old scratches are less visible and the pen shimmers. "Much better, no? Look how much better it looks now." I smile, but I'm not so sure and I think I might cry. I wanted the rough marks, the signs of my father's hands on it, the trace of his touch back. But then I think, he'd have done this, shined it up. Yes, for sure he'd have shined it up, and it was okay. Walking out of the store I debate where to put the pen. I had originally wanted to hang it from my shirt collar—I'd worn my own polo today, just for the occasion—but I get scared it will blow away. It's a windy day, foretelling a coming storm, even though we're almost past hurricane season now. It's just the temperament of the gods, a breathy gust, to keep us cool down here where things can get so very hot.

Click.

Inside my jacket, I click my pen in place. Click. And with that sound, the tears come. Images of my father, pulling out his pen, his watch, his arm, his face, all like in the sequence of a film, in fragments. The *Guernica* of memory trickles in and gusts of wind-blown heads are everywhere.

Once I'm in the car, the radio blares, the oldies station blending with images of Dad. Peter Frampton comes on and I hear Dad's voice saying, "Hear that? Listen to what he does with his guitar—*era un bárbaro*." I listen. "You hear that? Wow, right? That's the guitar, *mamita*, the guitar is asking us how we feel, can you believe it?" Dad always said GUI-tar, with the accent on the *gui*, like in so many rock n' roll songs, like he was black or something, which somewhere in him he was, and not just because of the courts he grew up on at Booker T. Washington, picking up handshakes he would use to create the Gonzalez handshake. He was always sort of proud of those stray black women somewhere (probably slaves, but maybe not, maybe later, post-slavery, and by choice and love) in the line of Cuban lineage that pulsed through his veins, my veins, the same women others in his family tried to hide.

Dad should've learned to play the *gui*-tar, maybe he would have been less full of rage. In him: too many soulful tunes that never made their way out.

I'M WORRIED about how to deal with the air between things, so I buy a book called *Questions of Space*. I've been thinking a lot about how the architecture of the world mirrors its place and sometimes vice versa. I read somewhere how the spiral staircases in Cuba mirror a curvy Cuban girl dancing, and wonder about the koi fish in Japan, whether they reflect the landscape (botched with bonsai) or vice versa. It's hard to figure out which is which without doing more reading: Whether the fish are like that because of breeding, a creation, or whether it's not the landscape that mirrors the fish, everything some kind of large reflecting pool.

Lately, there are these questions, standing before my *Altar Piece*. Although I still think of the show I'm preparing as a whole as *Cathedral*, I now know that the three-paneled painting I am making as part of the show is called *Altar Piece*. The impulse I had before my father died to make an "altar piece" clarifies itself after his death. I don't think, however, it's about a made-up religion anymore. It's about something else, something I'm coming to terms with in the space I don't have a name for. The space between where I am standing physically and the painting itself, between mourning and process.

According to Merriam-Webster.com, space is *a boundless three-dimensional extent in which objects and events occur and have relative position and direction.*

Sometimes I just want to say fuck it and try to free myself from space altogether. Even if it's useless. Which is always around the time I know I need a break.

"Tony, I'm going for a run."

"It's going to rain again, *gorda.*"

"No way, look at the sky. It's clear."

"They said it's off and on again, lots of rain bands."

"I'm going," I say, already tying my laces.

"Do you really think you should be running?"

"What does that mean?"

"It means you've got dark circles under your eyes, *gorda.* You should rest. You might catch something."

"See you later."

Ten minutes into the run, the sky opens its mouth and drops a bucket of massive god-spit on me, wet and thick. But I keep going. I get heavier and heavier with the weight of the rain drenching my clothes. My shoes start slipping all over, but I keep at it.

"*Mira la loca esa.*"

I hear a voice, coming from one of the clumps of people crouching under awnings, trying to keep dry, stupidly, as if the rain wasn't spraying them anyway, making its way sideways and puncturing their immaculate threads. You know flies in the rainforest can avoid the rain by buzzing through it? Tony's reaction would be like the normal ones, under the tarps: "You are not a fly." Even though when we first met, we would get caught in the rain all the time and let it soak us, holding hands and running home from breakfast and dinner, we were always getting caught in it. It was only lately that Tony started taking shelter under tarps.

As I run, I feel myself building speed, going faster and faster, feeling like I might be losing the ground below.

I hear my father's voice over me, through the loud rain:

"What the fuck is my *freakia hija* doing?"

Who are you talking to, Dad? Why are you addressing me in third person? I'm right here. "I can hear you," I say out loud.

"What are you doing, Veronica? Is that better?"

"Yes," I say, and then: "Do you really think I'm crazy?"

"Yes. But so was John Lennon, remember? And more than any of that I think you should get out of the rain. *Vas a coger una pulmonía.*"

"So?"

"What do you mean, so? You're alive. It's no fun being dead."

"Are you sad? Or are you somewhere better? Nina says the *espiritista* said you're having a hard time letting go of earthly things, that you haven't made the transition. I'm supposed to let go to help you, Dad. I don't know how, though. What am I supposed to do? Nina said the *espiritista* told us not to tempt you with things. But can I still talk to you if I let you go completely, if I say, go, go, go up into wherever you need to go, abandon everything here? Abandon space?"

"I thought you didn't believe in God."

"I don't."

"Then who are you talking to?"

"You."

"It's the same thing."

"No it's not. You're real."

"I'm invisible."

"But I can hear you."

"And what am I saying?"

"I have no idea."

"I'm saying you should stop running."

I stop running.

"You should listen to your father."

"I'm listening," I say louder than my previous mumblings, standing, looking up in the middle of a perfect rainstorm, warm and tropical, and somehow all-embracing, like little hands of rain touching me all over my body.

"You should walk into Segafredo and order a bottle of *La Viuda*."

I laugh, right there in the rain, open-mouthed, eyes disappearing like Dad's in their Chinese slant. I do as he says. I walk into Segafredo and order a bottle of their best champagne, Veuve Clicquot.

They have no customers, so the waiter, feeling bad for my soaked self, offers me a free company T-shirt and asks me if I want to change into it. I say yes. In the bathroom, I try to dry off my shorts under the hand-dryer, listening to the murmur of a man on his cell phone outside the door, now the only other customer at the bar. When I come out, dry, I sit by the window and look out as the rain pounds and slowly I sip, saying *Salud*, silently, for my father.

"Are you going to drink all that on your own, young lady?" A man's low voice—accented with a trace of Spanish—comes from my right.

"Excuse me?" The last thing I expect is someone else's voice filtering through my airspace.

"Are you even old enough to drink?" The man speaking to me is standing a couple of seats away, leaning on the bar like he owns the place. Miami-fied. His face is tired-looking, and he has on a pair of thin silver-framed glasses he's been wearing at the rim of his nose to dial his phone, and which he is taking off now as he speaks to me. On his feet, a soft leather pair of moccasins, Italian-looking. Expensive. *Un guante*, Dad would say.

"Oh, believe me, I'm old enough." And then with curiosity, "How old do you think I am?" Suddenly I'm filled with strange comfort, I don't know what it is exactly. I'm usually shy, but I feel relaxed with this stranger. I wonder, fleetingly: Has my father sent him?

"Would you like a glass?" I ask him.

"I wouldn't mind one, if you offered." He winks, still leaning on the bar. He's masculine, but polished at the same time.

"Waiter, another glass for the gentleman." The waiter immediately appears with one, as if by sudden magic, as if it was supposed to happen all along, and the waiter was just waiting for his cue.

"Thank you," says the stranger. "Cheers."

"Cheers," I say back, from a distance.

"So, what do you do?" he asks me, still standing, leaning on his right arm, his body turned toward me. I like the rusted orange, long-sleeved shirt he's wearing. It's always a chore to get Tony to wear long-sleeved shirts.

"I'm an artist. I paint."

"Oh, you're one of those." He wasn't "one of those." He had three cell phones and the conversations I'd overheard him having were about small businesses and real estate.

We talk for a bit, and he moves closer. Until about halfway through our first glass he'd been sitting about four bar stools away. It wasn't even happy hour, still daylight out. While the regular folks were chipping away at their 9-to-5s, we talked about where we were from. We talked about how we'd both lived in New York at one point. He thought I was Colombian; I thought he was Cuban. Really, I'm the Cuban and he's the Colombian. Funny how that works.

"How long have you lived here?" I ask.

"Forever."

"So that explains it."

"That explains it."

"What about you? When did you move back from New York?"

"A while ago."

"You live with your parents?"

"No. God, no. With my boyfriend."

"Oh, your boyfriend. You shouldn't live with boyfriends, you know."

I smirk.

"Is he jealous?" he asks.

"No, but he should be."

He laughs.

"How old are you?"

"Twenty-eight."

"Really? Wow, I thought you were much younger." Leaning back in his chair, he fills our glasses. "So, what about your parents? What do they do?"

"Actually, my mother's in property management. I heard you talking real estate. You should have her card." I look for her card, and realizing I've run out of them, he tells me to write out her name and contact info on his yellow legal pad, exactly like the ones Dad used.

"What about your father?"

I'm quiet for a minute. I take a drink of *La Viuda*.

"He just died," I say. "Very recently."

"Oh, I'm sorry."

The air clears a bit and I assure him, "It's okay," but suddenly everything I've been keeping cased inside me, as if my body were a mason jar, starts to bump up against the glass, making a little crack in my inner shield. My ability to talk to him doubles. I tell him everything that's going on in my life. Then I realize I'm being foolish and I say, "I'm sorry, I don't know why I'm telling you all this."

"Why? I'm listening." He leans back and listens. "What about your boyfriend?"

"What about him?"

"Do you love him?"

"Very much. Our only problem ever is that he doesn't want to get married."

I can't believe I'm telling him this.

"And you do?"

"Yes. I do."

"You want kids?"

"One day. I have to do certain things first, but I do want them."

"With a husband."

"Oh yes, they have to have a father."

"I'm divorced, I have two boys."

"How old?"

"Sixteen and eighteen." Reading the question in my face, he says, "I'm fifty-two."

"My father was fifty-one, about to turn fifty-two, when he died. His birthday was just the other day."

I tell him about how he died, and about his obesity and about my parents' divorce. And I feel warm by this man and I suddenly think, Dad would like him. And maybe it was true, maybe he had sent him. This thought has never crossed my mind before now, I've never cared what Dad thought about the men I was attracted to. In fact, Dad hated Tony, and I used to love that. Tony is quiet and calm and Dad was—well, Dad was prone to explosions and putting his head through walls. I wanted the furthest thing from Dad as possible. Tony is good and caring, and gentle. I love him.

"I love my boyfriend," I blurt out. "I'm very loyal."

"Loyal." He nods, smiling.

"I'm very loyal; I would never—"

"Have dinner with me?"

"What?"

"Have dinner with me."

"I can't." I want to have dinner with him. I'm not sure if it's the wine or my strange attraction to this stranger or what the hell it is, but I suddenly want this man to love me. To take me in his strong arms and love me. And at the same time I want to stop myself. I want to stop thinking all of this. I love Tony. I truly, really love Tony.

He finishes his glass and motions for another bottle.

"No, I can't."

"A half glass then, we'll order by the glass."

My sparkling wino self can't resist. I nod.

We keep talking, and before I know it the conversation turns to sex, and he's taking my hand in his. Here is this man, rough around the edges, tough hands and bitten fingernails, but still dressed impeccably and obviously possessing a good amount of triple-cell-phone business savvy. And I like the touch of his hand on mine. Not soft like Tony's, which is too smooth, uncallused.

"What are you doing?"

"You're amazing. You're beautiful. You're strong. You're—"

"Please." I feel myself blush.

"You really are. You're lovely." I like hearing this. Tony doesn't tell me these things anymore. He's never told me I was lovely. Lovely. What a lovely word, lovely.

He keeps holding my hand, and again that dangerous feeling runs over me, like this man could be another option. If Tony doesn't want to marry me, I have other options. And then I tell myself to shut these thoughts off and turn the "I love Tony" thoughts back on.

We talk for another two "half-glass" rounds and then I say, "I have to go."

I feel tipsy, and when I get up I lose my balance a little bit.

"You can't drive," he says, catching me.

"I don't have to, I ran here."

"You can't run. We're drunk. You'll fall over."

"It's stopped raining. I'll walk."

But before I turn to go, the stranger says, "Hey, we didn't do anything. Okay? Don't feel bad about anything, we didn't *do* anything. And I'd like to know you, even if I have to go to dinner with your boyfriend. I would like to know you."

I smile and look down, but I do feel guilty.

I wave goodbye.

As I walk home, I feel even more guilty, heavier than with the rain. Should I tell Tony? Why should I? He wouldn't be jealous anyway. He should be jealous. He's right to think I'd never cheat on him, but that's not the point. If we don't *choose* to love, we begin to allow ourselves other options, and other options are dangerous. What keeps *him* loyal? The root of all of it: he's never lost. He still has both his parents, and any kind of loss he ever went through was his choice, which is always a different kind of loss than the kind that's ripped from you. When he was eighteen and he left his girlfriend behind, the one he loved the strongest, with that kind of frenetic, youthful love, that was *his* choice. He left to travel the world, and she got left behind. He got to navigate, change gears with his stick, because he was a man with money and she was a girl in Argentina. Who cares if he still names computer files after her? Even his grandparents, both sets, died before he was born. How could he love, really love, if he's never lost? Isn't that what drives love, that fear of loss, that need for another? That's why I have to wonder about the way he loves me. He doesn't care about *losing* me, he doesn't even know what that would be like. He's trained himself to have a succession of girlfriends and start over. He'll just find another one later. What bliss to be a man. God, how I wish I were a man.

"*Gorda!*"

"Hi, *mi amor.*" I smile.

"Have you been drinking?"

I laugh in a giggle-trill, it just comes out. Although beneath the layers there is a heaviness.

"You have. Shit, *la gorda le da al drinking sin mí.*"

"It was pouring," I say, starting to lose my balance a little.

"I know," he says, catching me. "I could see from the window."

"You were watching for me?"

"I was watching the rain, *gordita*, and thinking you were getting soaked in it." Tony says this as he touches my wet hair. "They're so pretty, the small drops of rain on your hair, so still," he says.

"I'm tired, Tony."

"I know." Tony takes my hand and leads me to the bedroom.

"But I feel okay, kinda good. Kinda bad."

"*No digo yo.* How much did you drink?"

"A bottle of champagne."

"*Y esa camisa?*"

"They gave it to me."

"Segafredo?"

"Yeah."

"*Ven, gorda.*" Tony draws me toward him, takes off my shirt and my semi-wet shorts. Then he walks me to the bed, like my Mom used to walk me to the bathroom when I was little, in the middle of the night, and just like she used to dress Nina in her half-sleep. He sits me on the bed, pulls off my shoes, peels off my socks, tossing everything to the side—mess doesn't matter, mess is only temporary. Then he disappears into the other room for a minute and comes back with an orange towel. Leo. I feel myself getting sleepy. I listened to you, Dad, you see, I'm not all rotten. Tony takes my head between his soft hands, his hands that are so white they don't have pigment except the light brown freckles and reddish-brown wisps of hair. As he dries my hair, I can hear the acute sound of the shuffling terrycloth against my ears. He lays me down and covers me and puts a pillow under my head.

"*Duerme, gorda. Duerme.*"

When I wake up I think of the *espiritista* and what she said to Nina. She said to lay out a glass of water for Dad in order to help him rise up and not get stuck in transition. I don't understand the logic of it, but I go to the kitchen and fill a glass of water. I put it up high in my studio, where I know Tony won't ask me what it's doing there, where it will blend and I won't have to give any explanations. Also when I wake up, I feel the sudden urge to draw. Tony is not around and I have the apartment to myself. The quiet is inviting.

In the studio, I take the refilled Montblanc and start to draw lines out on a piece of paper, a short respite from *Cathedral*, lines that go straight and others that curve at the wrist like a chef at a batter. I want to eat my drawing, like pastry, soft-kneaded and baked dough. Going through the motions, I think about how drawing itself is like the moment at which love, which I don't always understand, is fulfilled both in its most divine and most human capacity. A masterpiece is the sum of those moments of true connection with the divine, a dialogue with God, a communion—like the wordless dialogue of wall-less stained glass spaces. I know this is why Pollock was a drunk and why Basquiat overdosed. It's because it's hard to come away from this feeling, leave through its back door into the real world. The real world doesn't have such a straight lifeline to the life force, or the spirit, or God, or whatever you want to call it. So Pollock got frustrated in the world. Basquiat took it straight to his vein and fell back into the pattern of drawing, gridding the pulse drug-lines of his interior canals, as it made its way to his head and his heart, easing the passage from art into life, filling the hole. I think it's why I stopped eating all those years ago, when Tony found me skinny as a ravished rail. I think it's why monks fast. Because when you are empty your mind goes places it doesn't go when your stomach is full, and you feel the world more, on your skin and in your nose. You see everything better. But then you're not really human, are you, if you don't go about eating and sleeping and all these necessary things, and isn't the reason we read about people like Jesus to understand that this is our plight, to find divinity in the human, the human in the divine?

By the time I'm finished with the drawing I realize I've drawn an amulet, it's what my drawings always end up being: protective charms, mystical and magical. Another image, this one more abstract, of my father holding me. Around me there's a bubble of safety. Looking at it, in the afterthought of drawing, I realize that I am all alone, that there is no one around to protect me, no male presence to fight for me and keep me from harm. Did he ever really keep me from harm, my father? He would have. He would have saved me if I was in trouble. Who will do that now? Tony? Who can't even commit enough to verbalize *I love you*? Tony wouldn't give his life for me — Tony, who is afraid of blood and who wouldn't even pay my half of the rent when I needed him to.

I feel alone.

I turn from the amulet, take out the paint, and continue through to my *Altar Piece*, entering my home-made *Cathedral* this way.

"WHAT'S THAT?" I ask Nina, pointing at a big red spot on her forehead, giving her a kiss on the cheek as she walks through my door.

"What's what?"

"That." I point closer to her forehead. "It looks like a giant mosquito bite."

"Oh, that's where all my heat goes," she says plopping on the couch, her feet dangling from the sofa. She's so short, just like Mom. Little, loveable pygmies.

"What?" I ask her, sitting right by her.

"My heat. Dr. Xu says that all this heat I have gathers right here." Nina is touching her forehead, right between the eyebrows, gently, showing me really close to my face.

"Oh, okay." I can't help but laugh. "I can't believe you're going to Dr. Xu."

"Don't be sarcastic," she says, defensive as always.

"Okay." I haven't decided at this moment whether I should or shouldn't keep making fun of her. You have to tread carefully with Nina, she's so goddamn sensitive.

"So, when he put the needle here, it bled. Everywhere else it didn't hurt or bleed, but this one, when he took it out it hurt and he said, 'You feel all tin for two.' He talks really funny and it's like you can't understand anything he says but he's *un pan*, he's so nice and I think he's helping. I took Mom so she could translate. Mom's used to how he talks."

"So what's 'tin for two'?"

"Everything for two, which apparently means that I'm really emotional and that I feel things like two times more than normal people." Nina flips her long, wavy, overly expensive haircut back over her shoulder.

"Oh." But I don't really believe her theory. We all feel the avalanche, but some of us allow it to take over, and others don't. I wish I had a boss who said go home, like Mom did for her. For a half a second, maybe less, I wish I didn't have a solo show during Basel.

"How's the painting going?"

"It's okay." I wasn't expecting us to stay so long in the apartment, and I wonder if we're bothering Tony, who is working in the bedroom, so I make a motion to move. "Why don't we take a walk on Lincoln Road or something?"

"Let's get our eyebrows done."

"Are you sure it isn't going to interfere with your high-heat spot? They're going to have to spread some very hot wax over the spot, you know."

"Shut up." Nina hits my shoulder and grabs her bag.

I leave Nina in the living room for a second while I go into Tony's office to kiss him goodbye and put on my sneaks. Tony rolls his eyes and points with them at Nina through the door. He's been listening, apparently. "She's such a diva," he says.

"I know," I tell him. "But, whatever helps." I kiss him again, quickly.

"Have fun, *gorda*. Good luck."

Is that what Nina and I need, just some luck? As I walk out with Nina, looking at her forehead I think of the red Daruma dolls I saw all over Japan when I visited. Daruma, the Japanese symbol for hope, optimism of human spirit. The round, legless monk who lost his legs by meditating so much on his way to enlightenment.

WE SQUEEZE inside the violet-walled waxing room in the back, the mandolin plucking at the air through a generic compilation of tunes called "The Calming Tide of Ancient Asia" or "Harmony" or something like that. Nina's going first, so she lays her head on the pillow and closes her eyes while I stand over her, wondering how long we'll have to wait before the wax woman comes. Watching Nina as she lies there, hands on her chest, tiny feet pointing up in her knock-off Pradas, I think she looks like a mismatched saint, stigmata on the forehead.

"Why don't you go to Dr. Xu?" Nina asks, eyes still closed. "I thought you were into all this Asian stuff."

"Just because I went to Japan and liked it?"

"C'mon, you didn't stop talking about it for forever. You almost became a girl-monk, or a nun or something because of Japan."

It's true that, in Japan, right before Hawaii, and before I left New York, I had had a moment where I thought I might be called to something—some kind of meditative life. But I didn't want to belong to any religion in particular. It was a mixed-up call, one that I couldn't clearly decipher. There was so much traveling and searching and looking for myself that year before I came back to Miami, but there weren't any answers yet, nothing to hold onto. I had shared all of this with Nina when we were drunk one day.

"So what? Dr. Xu isn't Japanese anyway. He's Chinese—totally different."

We're quiet for a minute. Nina squirms and the paper beneath her makes me think of Sundays and newspapers, Tony and *café con leche*. Suspending my hand over the heating potted wax, I let the warmth spread over my palm and think of bees and bonsai trees. Nina's led me back to Japan—six journals filled in two weeks.

"They have these paintings in Japan called *Raigo*, which means 'Welcome Arrival.' Amida Buddha is supposed to come down because of them, or through them or something, I can't remember exactly, but that's the gist anyway."

"I don't get it."

"The paintings are taken to the home of people who are dying, and the dying lie at its feet and they tug at the cords that are connected to the painting, like they're calling on the Buddha, so that their souls can be carried into paradise. They chant the whole time. I love that their souls are saved by a painting."

"You would." Nina opens her eyes and sits up on the waxing table. "Vero?"

"Yeah?"

"I'm sad."

"Me too."

"You think Dad got a chance to... I don't know."

"Tug?"

Nina nods.

"I think so," I say. "I think that's why it took him a couple of days to die, I think he was getting ready. I think he could hear us." I sit next to her on the table, both our feet dangling now like they used to off the ridge of our pool, wading through aquamarine.

"I wish he would've opened his eyes to me, like he did to you." Nina has that heartbreaking pout on her lips like she's about to cry, the pout she's had since she was a little girl.

I reach my hand out to her hand, our fingers interlace. "You talked to him the day before, you heard his voice, remember?"

"Yeah, but it's not the same."

I knew it wasn't the same. I thanked God, or Grace, the Holy Spirit, the Amida Buddha, all those things—I thank them still for that second when he looked at me.

And here, now, Nina looking at me in a way that closes all the space between us, I snuggle a little closer.

"Nina, do you remember the laundry room?"

She smiles.

"Remember the day we were talking about Cuba, and you asked me about sneaking in?"

She smiles again.

In the space between us now, I realize we know all of each other's secrets. In her smile, I know she knows me. There are those things, those vows you make only to yourself, in your own silence, to the secret ears of your own body. Your body that will never tell anyone, only hint to others with the sway of your hip in mid-strut. Those are the secrets that are full of life, like dancing in your room with the door closed. These are the things Nina and I share in that smile, the gleaming space that lives between leaves when you look up toward the sky.

 Violet.

The Chinese use violet in painting to embody universal
harmony because it is a combination of the two ends of
the spectrum, and of life forces—red (yang) and blue (yin).
Violet is also the liturgical color of Advent and Lent in many
Western churches. It is said that people with violet auras are
forward-looking visionaries.

THE LAUNDRY room was in the first house we ever lived in, the one
we lost. Almost as small as the waxing parlor, it was just big enough
to hold us in place, crouched, sharing air and breath. At first we had
only the washer, and Mom used to hang the clothes in there to dry
with the window open. But then one day she brought home a dryer.
That was the first day Nina and I slept there, because that was the day
we discovered the heat.

The laundry room was painted pale yellow, with orange Spanish
tile on the floor, which rattled beneath the dryer and sometimes
cracked underneath the washing machine. There was nothing really
interesting in this room, but we loved it, shelves with Tide and
Downy and a big bottle of bleach and violet Mistolin (which Mom
used to clean the floors, like all the other Cuban moms), a broom
and a mop, and rags, pink with red stripes. One small window. Mom

used to yell at us to get out of the room because she said we'd get sick from smelling the bleach. "*Salgan de ahí! Para qué les compramos el Nintendo* if all you do is inhale that toxic stuff?" But there was no use telling us to get out of that room because once we discovered the warmth of the dryer, there was nothing else.

The night Mom brought home the dryer, Nina and I sat by it all night while Mom was catching up on a month's worth of laundry, which she had saved for this day, which Dad had been promising her forever. We helped her put the clothes in the dryer and then we sat with our backs to the machine, our bodies shaking lightly to the rhythm of the cycles, and we started feeling really warm—beach warm—giggling. Every time Mom left the room between loads, Nina and I would start talking, the scent of Downy in the air, which smelled so much better than the soapy stuff we used in the washing machine. Nina told me about her day at school, about how Julie Prince (who had once tried to strangle her with a jump rope and later became her best friend) told her that her mom was an airline stewardess.

"Julie and her whole family get to take free trips around the world because of her mom's job."

"Where would you want to go, Nina? If you could go anywhere?"

"I don't know. Maybe Alabama. That's where the *real* Americans are, that's what Dad said. Or Tennessee, where rock 'n' roll started."

"And then we could go to Spain and visit Papan's family and visit our cousins, Celine and Virginie, in France."

"Do you think they'd remember us?"

"Totally, they're our cousins, plus we danced 'Thriller' with them, how can they forget us?"

"Where else?"

"I would visit Maryanne."

"Do you miss her?" Nina asked.

"Yeah, plus her mom told Mom on the phone that we could go and visit because Maryanne was missing Miami and that her dad's job was going really well, but Maryanne didn't like her new school."

"Where did they move to again?"

"The Bahamas."

"The Bahamas are an island, right?" Nina asked.

"Yeah. Well, islands, plural."

"Do you think we could go to any island if we could get one of Julie's mom's free trips?"

"I guess, I mean, I don't know how it works, but I don't see why one place is different from another place."

"Could we go to Cuba?"

"Cuba?"

We'd never talked about actually going there. I didn't think of it as a place any of us could actually visit, it was just a place we were from, somehow, without ever having been there. That's what Mom and Dad told us.

"Could we fly there, you think?" Nina said. "Would they let us in?"

"I think there's a fence around it and they only let some people in—the guy at the fence-door decides and then he opens the door, but only sometimes."

"What if we told them we were Cuban, that Maman and Papan and Mom and Dad and everyone used to live there?"

"I don't think they would let us go in."

"What if we sent signals from the airplane to Maman's family there, do you think they could sneak us in, do you think they could hear us?"

"I don't know. Maybe if we fly really close, really low down. Because I think that there's a sound fence too. They can't hear anything from the outside and nobody can hear them, that's why it's so hard to talk to the family over there. But maybe if you listen really, really carefully. You know, like when Maman talks to Cuba on the phone and we always have to be really, really quiet while she's doing it, so she can hear them. Maybe if we took a telephone on the airplane we could listen really carefully."

"So do you think we're ever going to get to see it?" Nina sounded desperate all of a sudden. "Will they ever let us in? Ever, ever?"

"Maybe if the guy at the fence dies or something."

"What do you think it's like there?"

"I don't know. Maman and Papan say it's really green and there's clear water and they say it's the most beautiful place in the world and that people used to dance there all the time. They say that now everyone has a bicycle. But I think it's still green and hot."

"Hot like here, or really really gross hot like outside?"

"Hot like in here, I think."

"Do you think it's still the most beautiful place in the whole wide world, like Dad says?"

"I don't know. Maybe we could find a way to sneak in and find out. Maybe we could get an airplane to drop us off in the middle of the ocean with a *salva vida*. And we could swim all the way up to Cuba and look through the fence, and come back here and tell Maman and Papan and everybody what we saw."

"Do you really think we could swim that far?"

"Yeah, sure we could. We're good swimmers. We could make a boat or something and have it waiting for us in the middle of the ocean and maybe la Virgen de la Caridad will help us."

"I like her."

"Me too. I like that her dress is big and blue sometimes, and how other times it's yellow."

And like that, we stayed until Mom came back into the laundry room and took all the clothes out of the dryer.

"What are you girls talking about?"

"Nothing," said Nina. "About the place we could go to if we could go anywhere."

"Ah, *sí*? And where would you go?"

"Lots of places," Nina said, winking at me like she didn't want to reveal our secret Cuba plans. "Where would you go, Mom?"

Mom folded the clothes for a while and said, "Here, help me fold," like she wasn't going to answer, and then she said, "I'd go to Egypt."

My sister and I giggled. Mom was so weird sometimes.

 Orange.

The color of Florida and faraway places.

THE DAY Castro ceded power to his brother Raúl, in 2006, I had just come back from seeing Dad and Nina. I had been talking to Dad more and more those days, once a week or so, and we'd made a habit of meeting on Saturday or Sunday—me, Nina, and him at the bar at Smith & Wollensky on the beach. This was the beginning of those Smith & Wollensky meetings and I wasn't sure where it was all going. He never formally apologized for what he did to me in college, the letter he sent that separated us for many years, but this was his way of saying I'm sorry, I guessed, and I wanted to forgive him, and maybe it was me, all that time, who should have tried to close the gap. I don't know—he was the father, he was the adult. But I was the educated one.

I was awkward sometimes during those meetings, wasn't sure what to talk to Dad about yet, but at least we were sitting and talking and drinking together and something was opening up. Nina could always talk to him about anything, and it was those two, really, their banter and their private jokes, that kept the conversation rolling, with me interjecting every once in a while. But it was fun somehow. I always got back heady from those visits with him, half-anxious, like I'd felt in Bermuda. But also full of hope.

"Veronica!" Tony yells from the bedroom, snapping me out of my dad daze when he hears me come through the door. Tony never yells, and Tony never calls me by my full name like that, unless something is wrong.

"What?" I run over to see what's happened. My first thought is that he's injured. But Tony is silent, mouth-opened, half-smirking as usual, and pointing at the TV.

It's the anchorman Ambrosio Hernandez, animated, breaking every rule of journalism: showing sweeps of emotion.

Fidel Castro has ceded power, says Ambrosio.

Since 1959, El Comandante has not done anything even close to this. This is huge.

He's been hospitalized, will undergo surgery, has handed the reins over to his brother Raúl. I am filled with heat, and goose bumps start to rise up on my legs and arms and I think, Could this be it? Could this be the moment my parents and grandparents have been waiting for all of their lives? Could it really be *This* year in Cuba," instead of "*Next* year in Cuba"?

Tony switches the channels to see what the others are saying.

"*Gordita! Te imaginas?*" he says.

"*Yo? Sí!* What about you, do you really get it? I mean, do you feel anything? This is crazy. Are you excited?" I'm smiling ear-to-ear like a kid, my feet taking little jumps and hops.

"I may be *un Argentino de mierda, gorda,*" Tony says, making fun of me, "but I've been in Miami ten years, and with a *Cubanita* for three. What do you think, do I get it or not?"

"We have to go to Calle Ocho," I say, standing behind him as he leans toward the TV in his chair, my hands slapping his shoulders.

"Let's go," he says immediately.

We run into Tony's car, Willy Chirino's anthem is blaring on the radio: "Ya Viene Llegando."

Chirino wrote that song, optimistically, as communism was falling all around the world in the late twentieth century. The song holds space and time for the fall of communism in Cuba—"our time is coming too," it rings. It starts with lyrics about a boy dressed as a sailor, getting onto a boat with his father, venturing to a new land, learning a new language, relocating their song, their sugarcane, their drumbeat, and it ends with a free Cuba.

I look at the car's digital clock as we're driving toward 8th Street. It's 10:53 p.m., and Tony and I are surprisingly calm, taking everything in. We're too shocked, or happy, to ruin the buzz with chatter. The radio's spouting conspiracy theories in the making. Some are saying Castro's already dead.

"*Está muerto*," one woman screams in delight on the radio. "They're just saying he's sick to give them some time to think. Real fact is the son of a bitch is dead." Some journalists try and calm the callers down, some can't help but join the frenzy.

There are calls from Cubans all over the world ringing into Radio Mambí. One guy calls in from Alaska and says, "I bet you didn't know there were Cubans in Alaska! Aha! We're everywhere! We support you Miami! We love you Miami!" The guy can't be saying this any louder—I imagine ice breaking under him at the pitch of his voice as he transfers the surge of emotions across state radio waves.

I wonder what it's like in Ohio, to receive this kind of news. Here it's special, everybody gets to celebrate with you.

When we get to Calle Ocho, we can no longer hear the radio because of the screams: "*Viva Cuba Libre!*" people are crying. Versailles is packed. Flags are waving from every corner. Cuban flags, and the Venezuelan flags of those currently fleeing Chávez and who support the Miami exile community, want to join it.

"Take pictures, *gorda*," says Tony. "*Dale*, snap some shots." I'd forgotten I had my camera. But my camera is waving all over the place because I still have the goose bumps and I can't stop smiling and my hands are shaky. When we download the pictures, they're blurry. But it doesn't matter—that's all a part of that day.

And then, in the middle of it all, I call my father. Of all people, the person I want to talk to most is him. On a loop they're playing the Chirino song again and I remember suddenly that Dad gave me the CD with "Ya Viene Llegando" a couple days before I left for college. "Don't forget where you come from," he said. Things were tense between us already, but it was a big thing for him, telling me that, giving me that CD. I played that song over and over in college, when I missed Miami.

"Wow!" says Dad, on the other line, when I finally reach him. "Wow!" That's all he can say for a while. And then: "You know what, *mamita*, you know what? I'm gonna buy a summer house in Cuba. We'll spend summers there—June and July. I'm gonna retire there and buy myself a boat and fish all day and come for a couple months to Miami for business. I'm going home. Cuba is waiting for me, *mamita*! Cuba is waiting for me to come home."

Metal spoons are clashing on pots and pans all around me.

"Are you on *la ocho*?" asks Dad.

"Totally. Cops everywhere, but they're letting people pour out into the street."

"They couldn't control it if they tried," he says proudly. "*Coño*! I didn't think I'd live to see this."

"No, they can't control this. Hear the beeping?"

"'*Tas loca*! That must be *un zoológico* down there."

"But it's great! It's great."

"I hear it," he says. "Wow. Wow."

"Love you," I say. It just comes out.

"I love you too. Be careful. People are excited. Be careful. Bye, *mamita*. Bye."

Don't forget where you come from. Which now I realize is much more than just Miami or, distantly, Cuba—it means him. Don't forget him.

I imagine what it could have been like, had he lived—Nina and me on the stoop of Dad's house in Cuba, huddled together. An empty chair behind us, but not because he's not there; this time he is, he's just taking the picture.

Silver.

A spiritual color. Color of the moon.

I PAY FOR the wax job, treating Nina, and we spill out onto Lincoln Road, Nina's red forehead dot spreading into a thick horizontal scarlet stripe.

"Yours is worse than mine, I think," says Nina, laughing. "You're getting little bumps."

"I think we're allergic to this shit," I say.

"Beauty hurts."

We walk for a while, without saying much, touching our foreheads every once in a while, looking at our reflections in storefront windows, to see whether the swelling from the wax has gone down. By the time we reach Washington Avenue, the smell of sex and last night's club scene is in the air all down the block: piss and beer, dancing sweat and 2:00 a.m. pizza crust drifting in bruised puddles made of car oil and muck. Nina leans against a building, a boarded-up strip club, and lights a cigarette.

"Do you think we knew Dad?" I ask her.

"What do you mean *knew* him?" She inhales her cigarette deeply, holding the smoke in her lungs before slowly releasing it and starting to walk again.

"You know, like really, *really* knew him."

"I think we knew the real him," she says.

"Really? I'm not so sure."

"Yeah, yes we did." Nina nods, like she's absolutely sure of this. "Remember when I used to lie on his belly like a frog, when we watched TV, when we were little?" A tear starts to roll down her face.

"I remember."

I wonder if Nina thinks that's the real him. I think of Lily and the blow job and I think of Christine.

"Remember Christine?"

"Yeah."

"Well, that's what I mean. How can we know him if he was with her?"

"What do you mean?"

"I was his daughter and he didn't even tell me he married her until later."

"They got married and a year later they were divorced, Veronica. They were friends, it was for her papers, who cares? Besides, he knew you'd be a pain in the ass about it, that's why we didn't tell you."

"Just like you didn't tell Mom about my car."

"What are you talking about?"

"It's wrong. Sometimes you have to tell. You didn't want to betray him, I understand, but by not telling us you betrayed us."

"You are overreacting. Like always." Nina takes the cigarette from her mouth and throws it on the floor, pounding it with her foot. "You're such a freak."

"No. I'm not. Can you imagine if he was married to that random woman when he died? It would be an even bigger mess. It's just so irresponsible. If you don't see it you're just being stub—"

"If you're going to start telling me I'm stupid, I'm gonna go, Veronica! You're always fucking telling me I'm stupid."

"First of all, I was going to say stubborn, not stupid, and you know what would be a good idea, Nina? If you removed that enormous fucking chip on your shoulder, that would be good."

"Fuck you."

"Fuck you."

"C'mon, Veronica! Please." Nina's eyes are watering and I feel the urge to stopper them with my fingers. I'm tired of her tears. She lights another cigarette and turns back toward Lincoln. I don't pull the cigarette from her mouth like I usually do when she chain smokes. Both of us are looking straight at the ground, walking back briskly toward nothing in particular; just back.

"There's this rock garden in Ryōan-ji in Kyoto," I tell her. I know how much she likes to hear about Japan. She slows down. "The garden is one of those zen gardens, like those miniatures that they have at the Sharper Image, except this one is real, really big and it has raked gravel and fifteen rocks, which are placed so that when you're looking at the garden from any angle only fourteen rocks are visible at any one time. The idea is that only if you're enlightened can you see all of them."

"Or if you're floating," she says nonchalantly.

And she's right. I hadn't thought of it that way. I'd had no idea what they'd meant by enlightenment, and all this time I thought I did. I'd wanted to tell her that we couldn't possibly know all of Dad when we were with him, couldn't possibly *see* all of him. But she was right, things were different from up above, you could see the whole thing. Like painting, like on an airplane, looking down at all those street grids.

"You're right, Ni. I'm the stupid one."

"You're not stupid, Veronica, you just think too much."

AFTER NINA leaves, I don't want to go back home yet so I get in my car and go for a drive through Little Havana and a sign on 8th Street catches my eye. It's a restaurant sign that's been around forever and it pulls at me every single time. UNCLE TOM'S CABIN, it reads. It's a

BBQ shop, owned by a Cuban. I remember going in once and asking the owner why he kept that name, and he didn't understand what I meant. The guy looked at me like he had no idea what I was talking about. He was just a Cuban, he said, who'd bought the place from a guy who had an uncle who had passed it on to his nephew, and the uncle was probably named Tom, he guessed.

Off the boat yesterday, couldn't possibly know about lip-smackin', cake-walkin' negroes who like them some finger lickin' good BBQ. Couldn't possibly know Harriet Beecher Stowe. Another disconnect. I didn't have the strength to explain it all, all the layers of history, and I didn't want to ruin his business, but I also couldn't quite tell what the "right" thing to do was, in this case.

This is how remnants become ruins. Somebody gets pissed, looks up at this sign, down at his skin, and wonders what the hell this little bit of the Confederacy, this remnant, is still doing here in this city, so cosmopolitan, so full of shit. Still a racist bag of—and bang, they blow it up. And there's nothing left but the ruins of a remnant and a couple of dead, clueless, off-the-boat-yesterday Cubans. And wouldn't it just end up being one big misunderstanding? Or would it be well-deserved? He should have done his research, this Cuban, owner of Uncle Tom's. Or at least he should've figured it out. Maybe it would be all my fault, maybe I should have taken him through the history lesson, ruined his business to save his life.

The Visible Spectrum.

Sometimes called the optical spectrum, it is the part of the electromagnetic spectrum that we can see.

THE TALIBAN blowing up 1,700-year-old Buddhas, Al Qaeda ramming into the twin towers, America invading Iraq, and narrower still: Dad's clothes, shoes—the things he left behind, the hole in my heart, Leo's chairs, my empty chair. So many remnants and ruins.

I look up at the amulet I've made and at the pieces of *Cathedral*, not yet complete. *Remnants and Ruins*. This will be the new name of the show. Or can be. It can change; everything can change. The underpinning of the ideas behind *Cathedral* will still be there, no matter what, even if the title changes. It's all layers, layers working toward this. This can be really good. But for now it is this—strong and loud, ringing in my mind's ear, filtering through the cracks of consciousness from somewhere I cannot touch. How to make remnants, or project the idea of remnants themselves, in and for the show?

First, more amulets for/of my father—what is left of him in me, inscribed on paper, a repetition like prayer, like the Pure Land Buddhist chant to the Amida Buddha. Then the *Altar Piece* must become a ruin. I'll have to leave it out in the sun to dry and weather and then place it like an ancient thing in the gallery. That's it. This is what it will be. Okay, so it's *Remnants*: remnants of my father—the amulets on paper—and then other remnants. An installation of his remains—like his clothes, hanging from the wall on hangers. Maybe. Or maybe some of the amulets interspersed with the photographs Old Matisse gave me, photographs of strangers, sewn on the clothes, mixing lives and history, consciousness and love, the need to record and worship. And then his shoes—I'll line up Dad's shoes. But I won't put the pants there, not with their ballooned waist, just shirts and maybe some of his jewelry, and his cigar box, filled with the amulets also. And then mix these remnants with the ruin of my *Altar Piece*.

Somehow, the viewers who come to see will have to get this, nonverbally—that this is the altar piece of a cathedral found somewhere, once scraping the sky, now in pieces. It will have to come across, in its shreds and its bits and pieces of debris. The footprints left in sand and tile floor, delicate drops after the storm, dew. Traces left after so much loss.

These are the beginnings of work. Real work. It feels good to start conceptualizing again, to start getting the show up, at least see the buds start to sprout, in my mind. Some of these ideas will go, some will stay, but at least it's starting to really come together. Still, there's something missing, I can feel it. Because what have I got? I've got the ruins of something enormous, something like religion, and then I've got the microcosm of that—the loss of my father. But what is great loss versus personal loss? Is there such a thing as small loss? And how is it different and how is it the same? I want the empty space to be part of it, the sparseness of the show with this giant painting and the installation. The space will be where the viewer puts it together. It'll be charged. But still, I'm missing a link here.

And it's not just that I'm missing a link, it's also a hesitation, a feeling that, well, that I'd be selling him. Literally capitalizing on my father—making money, commercializing his death, pieces of him, his trace and touch. And is this okay? Or is this sin? Greed in a way. Pride to meet his gluttony. Vanity, thinking I can just pretend it's mine, my own creation. I'm not him. But I'm his beneficiary, and isn't that important too, what we do with what we inherit? But again, the idea that we can possess the objects of the dead. That they're transferrable. It's twisted somehow. On the other hand, how is it different from giving it away to Goodwill and then getting a tax deduction at the end of the year? Isn't that what people do? Isn't that worse? And it wouldn't do any good anyway, the homeless and hungry aren't as big as Dad. That doesn't make sense either, to pass his things on to those who would float inside his clothes and shoes, smaller men swimming in the swollen seams of Dad's leather moccasins.

DAD'S WALLET is starting to lose his smell. I've had it in my bag because I keep needing his Social Security number. That musty smell every time I take it out, like cigars and a clean house infused into the leather. A hint of Pine Sol and a lot of tobacco. They could bottle this smell if they wanted to, call it ICHI — it would be hip among the Hemingway men. I bet Pollock would have worn it. But it's fading.

There's an oils shop near the apartment, blocks away on Lincoln Road, that looks like an old apothecary's. They have a smell there named China Lily, a suggestion of powder. The smell softens my pulse and puts me at ease. I could mix Dad with China Lily and wear him. But the remnants of his smell don't give me peace. They make my shoulders tense. It shouldn't have happened. I shouldn't be sitting here, his old polo T's spread out on my floor, taking his wallet to my nose, searching out smell like a hound. A life cut short. It shouldn't have happened. What's the point of all this? Art is useless.

How long will it take for the smell to decompose, like his body, disappear into ruins, and then to dust? I run to the bathroom because the tea from this morning is rising in my stomach. An outpouring of liquid, quick and projectile into the porcelain toilet, a fast flush.

"*Estás bien, gordita?*" yells Tony from the other room. He couldn't have heard me, must have just seen the sprint to the toilet.

"*Sí, estoy bien.*" I lie.

Back in the studio, polo T's carpeting the floor. Line them up and call them mourning and paint something on them, give them life—that human trace. Again, a quick run to—

I can't seem to keep any food or liquid in me. I too will become a remnant, dehydrate, leave only skin and bone. Will anybody feel anything when they see these huge shirts, sewn together like a kite, painted on—an old scene, idyllic, abstraction and figuration meeting somewhere in memory. Something is missing.

A need to escape into something. Another photograph—the second one, the one I didn't choose, the one Old Matisse chose for me and wrapped in tissue, the one I waited so long to look at. I allow it to surprise me:

Another scene on a stoop—all girls this time, teenagers. Four of them.

I can't stop looking at the girl in the middle of the top row, the fabric draping around her like she's desperate for its covering. And her face, so defiant. There's something of Leo in her, something of Manet and his dirty *Olympia* there too. This girl—I might as well name her. I'll name her June. June Corey, but let's say everybody calls her Fern, her middle name. The rest of the girls in the picture have names too, of course. They're not who my eyes keep going to, but they must have names if I'm to make up a story: That's Mary Nelson (top left), Unis (top right), and Sandra (bottom).

They have all been friends since the fifth grade, when Bobby Lipstein said that Fern had the face of a pig in front of the whole class. It was the day the boys were visiting. It happened once a year at their all-girls school. The boys, a couple of them, handpicked by their brother school, would be chosen to come over and switch places with a couple of the girls. The girls hated when they came, they thought boys were monsters, Bobby Lipstein among the most grotesque.

The girls' class was writing an opera because the school was "progressive" and had just hired a new music teacher with big plans and lofty ideals. She had just initiated a project called the Fifth Grade Opera, which the students would write the lyrics for, music for, design sets for, costumes, etc., all with the assistance of this new music teacher, Mrs. Maleck, and their old art teacher, Mrs. Manor. In any case, they had started writing this opera about a farm where the animals had romances and the ducks struggled through an outbreak of malaria, and Bobby Lipstein, who was nominated, for the day, to help the girl they'd selected as casting director, raised his hand in the middle of a brainstorming session and said, "I think June Corey should play the pig because she looks just like one," and everybody started laughing. But then Unis, who despite her unfortunate name (which not only sounded like but was spelled with a U, like Uranus, and was therefore too close to Your Anus) was surprisingly popular, pulled Bobby aside in gym and told him he really shouldn't have said that about Fern because it only meant that he would have to play the lice on that pig. Then Sandra punched him straight in the nose. "See who has the bloody pig nose now." Despite a bout of detentions and a near-suspension for Sandra, they had all considered it worth it. That very day, Fern joined the group (Unis, Sandra, and Mary's group), after which they were inseparable.

This picture would have been taken six years later, when they were sixteen, sophomores in high school. They always spent summers together, but this summer was different from the rest. It was the summer Fern had started making the dresses. It was the summer of the letters.

Just to give you an idea of who they were back then. Sandra was the one who stood up to everyone, the one who always had sand scratches on her legs after the summer from kissing boys on the beach. She had a lot of testosterone in her those days, in the sense that she could kiss a boy and love it and she could just leave and not get attached the way Unis got attached. Unis was the happy one, the one who bought gifts for everyone (once she bought them all Chinese parasols and they carried them around all the time because the parasols had these great blue butterflies on them that they all loved). Mary was the one who scored perfect scores on all her exams. And Fern, Fern was the one with the dead mother, who had left her husband and children the summer house they were all staying at that summer. The same summer house that had come into the family when Fern's grandfather died, fifteen years ago, when it was left to Fern's grandmother in his will. Then the grandmother left it to Fern's mother, and so on and so forth.

Every June 6, the day of her mother's death, eight days before her mother's birthday, Fern started something new. That June 6, she had started making dresses. Some people are marked. Most everybody is marked by something: a stutter, or the love of rain, the fear of lightning, a mole or a limp. But it's different when you're marked because you're motherless—the most enormous of all empty chairs. And it's not so much that it's sadder—it's desperate. It's longing for something you once had, that was close, that had made you warm, had made you angry, that scolded you, touched your skin, loved you no matter what.

It's why she felt she had to make things, why she had to start something new every year. She had to make something she could touch because what she wanted more than anything existed only in her head and sometimes even that faded a little. Fern never talked about it. Instead, she talked about moving to Hungary, and about how her father was going to buy a boat. And that summer she talked about the dresses. She said that the best thing in the world would be to be naked all the time but she didn't have enough guts for that, so the next best thing would be to wear beautiful dresses with flowers on them, like wearing spring. She talked about how different materials felt, how a certain kind of silk could feel like swimming.

Sandra didn't like very many people back then and she really loved very few, but she loved Fern. Something had called her and Unis to defend Fern that day in the fifth grade, like it was what she was put on Earth to do. Although you might say that Sandra sort of betrayed Fern later that summer, when Sandra read Fern's letters while Fern was asleep.

There was a trunk in Fern's room, which she kept under lock and key. Nobody knew what was in there, but Sandra had discovered the key one day in the bathroom, after a swim in the ocean, after a shower. She'd always been a snoop. Not in a bad way, it's not that she wanted to know anybody's business in particular. It was just an all-around, undying curiosity that never went away, no matter what. That day in Fern's bathroom her curiosity came to life, as it usually did when she was alone around another person's possessions. In Fern's bathroom there was a shell on the top shelf of the cabinet. It was pink and glossy and if you looked closely it sometimes turned to a pale cadmium orange under glare; brown toward the center. She had just taken a shower and, without thinking, she stood on the toilet seat to reach for the shell so that she could bring it to her ear and hear the ocean, but before the shell reached her ear, the key fell out. And Sandra knew immediately it was the key to the trunk.

Every day, Sandra found ways of sneaking into Fern's room while she slept or while Fern was showering or cooking or gone to the store, something pulling her magnetically to the locked-away secrets of Fern's trunk.

What she discovered was that, in the trunk, there were thousands of letters from Fern to her mother. They were an autobiography, a slow building tidal wave, like Shell's journal entries. The most recent letters were at the top. The first letter Sandra read was about wanting to fit through the center of flowers, wanting to dive in and swim all the way down the stem through the sap that was like sugar water or like coconut juice, into the leaves and then back out again. And in other letters she asked her mother questions, questions that would go unanswered. And she told her mother that she had found the fabric she had left in the attic; she would make the dresses her mother never got to make.

Mary and Unis found out because Unis woke up in the middle of the night once to get a drink of water and found Sandra by the trunk. She told Sandra that she had to stop what she was doing or she would tell Fern, because what Sandra was doing was wrong, it was invasive, and those letters were private and didn't belong to her, and how dare she steal memories and things and thoughts and images and feelings that were not hers. But Sandra was addicted and in a sense she felt she had a right, that she loved Fern, and that some of those feelings were, in turn, hers too. Unis never told Fern. Nobody told Fern.

That summer Sandra read through the life of Fern's mind. She had to restrain herself from bringing what she had read into their conversations; there were so many secrets. Sandra had to make an effort to remember what Fern had told her and what she had read. And though Fern never found out about the letters, everything had changed.

By late August, Fern had sewn together all the dresses she made, along with her mother's scarves, making them into a big parachute that looked as if it were made of human cut-outs, yellow stitching like gold. When it took to the sky it was like a bird that had come straight from mythology, floating, falling. She flew it like a kite, and pretended there was a balance between the wind and her control. Out of all of them, only Sandra understood why Fern had done this, but she could never tell Fern what she knew.

As for Sandra, she met a boy that same summer, toward the end. A boy she grew attached to. Who betrayed every inch of her body and reminded her that she was a woman, no matter how much she tried to deny it. No matter how much she pretended that a man would not hurt her. Fool her, take her, love her, leave her. No matter how much she pretended that she could resist the tides of passion and pull of love, this boy proved that pretense false, and there she was at the feet of this foreign boy, Antonio. There was no use in locking these feelings away, because she knew what happened—people found them anyway.

THIS STORY comes to me, long and full, and I know that there are bits of me in both Sandra and Fern. I wonder why Old Matisse gave me this picture, why he chose this one in particular. I imagine Leo and me walking into the photo like the kids walk into the sidewalk-chalk drawing in *Mary Poppins*. Once inside, Leo gives Mary Nelson, Unis, Sandra, and Fern his lawn chair and helps Sandra, Mary Nelson, and

Unis tie the lawn chair to Fern's parachute made of dresses while Fern looks on. Then Leo places Fern in the chair, helping her take flight, like on a hot-air balloon. Fern takes off slowly, the way things take off in silent movies, with her eyes closed. When she opens them, she's already suspended in the air, floating, looking down below at her friends, and then at the shore, further away, drenched in fading footprints. And then, at the end, she looks up at the balloon, watching the sky make its way through the brilliant yellow stitching, which flashes in front of her like shooting stars.

And there's where another part of the installation comes to me: I will sew Dad's shirts together, just as I'd thought to do, but I won't just lay them on the floor, I'll make them into a parachute, a hot-air balloon without the heat—that would be too dangerous, Lee would never allow that heat in the gallery. But I can make it look like it has the fuel pushing it up, keeping it together—that's art. Artifice. There, inside my ruined cathedral, this hot-air balloon made out of Dad's shirts. Visitors will be able to get inside the balloon—I'll need a basket—and when they look up there will be the amulet drawings, sewn to the interior, on Dad's shirts.

To make this, I will have to sit and puncture and thread the pieces of my father, and sometimes I will slip and the needle will prick me—I will not wear a thimble—and pieces of me will merge with the trace of him. It will not be sin, not feel wrong. Because it is no longer him, but me mixing with the invisible him, the emptiness left behind, filling it with something new. The way the Holy Spirit makes its way into breath and manages in Pentecostal churches to push people to the ground. Imagination. The Host holding a symbolic body at its center. It's letting go and making a sail, a flying sail for the viewer. Isn't that what Leo and I were writing back and forth about, what he made me think of—art as a breaking apart of skin to get at a thing new born?

Yellow.

The easiest color to see. People who are blind to other colors can usually see yellow.

I START with his yellow shirts, he had five. I didn't know he liked yellow so much. Indigo thread—a complementary color—to sew them together. Yellow is the color of friendship, peace. My sometimes favorite color. Yellow—saffron—the color Buddha wore after enlightenment. The color of old school pencils. I heard they were painted yellow because the graphite came from China originally, and the color yellow was associated with China. But that might be racial residue, remnants that lead to ruins. The Star of David. We say the sun is yellow because it has a yellowish color temperature. According to a quick Google search, it's the color of intellect and spirituality all at once. The color of Oshún, orisha of rivers and love, close to the heart of Cubans because of her link to la Virgen de la Caridad del Cobre. And citrine, a stone said to neutralize negative energy.

Sew, sew, sew. Slowly sew.

Sewing is not like painting, not a quick stroke or flash dabs mixed with long strokes and long hauls across canvas. There's no changing it up. Sewing is about pattern. Sew, sew, pull. Sew, sew, pull. Then come the knots.

Yellow like a canary. June. Like summer. Fern, Unis, and Sandra. The Fifth Grade Opera.

In my Fifth Grade Opera, I was a costume designer. I didn't want to do anything else. Except for production—I thought about that for a moment, being boss. But I wasn't popular enough and you had to be voted in to the position. Costume design was the next best thing, and I ended up loving it. I was in charge of costumes for everyone, along with the rush of backstage sewing when a thread tore during a scene. Fifth graders all over you, nervous, counting not only on your taste and design skills, but your brilliance under pressure. I loved the heat and rush of it, even thought about going into fashion. I thought fashion was art.

Sew, sew, pull. Sew, sew, pull.

Then it was opening night. Dad, Mom, Maman, Papan, Nina, they all came. When we were leaving, getting into the car, Dad said, "Why weren't you an actress?" He was upset. That's all he said. Not "The costumes were great." Or "What great color sense." Or "What interesting design." None of that. He wanted to show me off to the other parents. He wanted to say, "That's my daughter *on stage*." I'd disappointed him. But I didn't want to be an actress. I didn't want to shine on stage, I wanted the show to sparkle *because* of what I did behind the curtain. I wanted my brilliance to be seamless. Mom didn't say anything at first. My heart was broken.

Sew, sew, pull. Neat pull. Neat sew, sew, pull. Neat, neatly. Pristine.

"I'm going to be an actress when *I'm* in the Fifth Grade Opera," Nina said from the crowded backseat of the car. And she did just that. When her time came, Nina was an actress, she sang and she shone in the leading role. She was even in the paper, front cover of the arts section. And Dad was proud of her. She's still an actor. You don't understand, do you, Dad? I shine too, shine quietly, neatly. Sew, sew, pull.

"Nina, stop that," was all Mom said when Nina started repeating, "I'm going to be an actress" on a loop.

"*A dónde vamos?*" asked Papan, trying to change the mood in the car. "What about Versailles? To celebrate!"

"*Que lindo lo que hicistes!*" Maman shouted, almost popping my eardrum, giving me a big squeeze and giving my father the evil eye. *Bastard*, I could hear her brain-wheels churning.

I didn't defend myself. All through dinner, I held my tears back, as Dad talked about the little starlets on stage, never taking into consideration that they'd have been naked if it weren't for me. And what really pissed me off was that he didn't even notice the shoes I'd picked out for them. I wanted to tell him about what I understood that he didn't: that in order to do costume design you had to get into the psyche of characters, time, place, era. It was a *serious* job. It was smart and creative and necessary, just like putting shoes on the feet of people. I wanted to tell him all this, but I couldn't.

"You okay, *mamita?*" Mom said, leaning over to me at dinner. "You're not eating. *Come, mamita, come.*"

"You'll see, Dad, I'm gonna be an actress. I'm gonna be an actress."

"That's good, Ni, that's good," Dad said, ruffling her hair. "You're gonna be my little star."

"I'm gonna be a star," Nina sang. "I'm gonna be a star."

"Nina, come here, come *ahora,*" said my mother, teeth clenched, pulling Nina to the bathroom. I don't know what she told her in there, but Nina didn't repeat the singsong phrase for the rest of the night, hardly said a word.

Sew, sew. Pull, pull. Pull pull pull sew sew sew sew. Pull sew. Swerve, squiggle, swerve. Shit, I'm fucking up.

Pull the string out. Start again. Sew, sew, pull. Sew, sew, pull.

Ultraviolet.

Janet Cardiff's *40 Part Motet* at the Freedom Tower.

After a week of sewing, when I hear that the Janet Cardiff installation is in town, and showing at the Freedom Tower, I invite Mom to come see the show with me and Tony. Cardiff is one of the best installation artists out there and so I figure, with *Remnants and Ruins* starting to come together in my mind, but not gelled yet, I might as well grab some inspiration. Also, it's perfect to take Mom to a show there because the place means something to her. The Freedom Tower is now used for art shows and events, but it was once Miami's Ellis Island. Ever since I was little Papan and Maman, Mom and my father have been pointing to it, saying, *"Mira, por ahí llegamos nosotros en el '62."* Every time they said that, I imagine their eyes being flipped, their chests being monitored, their hair being checked for lice. Processed right along with the endless line of Cuban immigrants fleeing Castro. I hate that word, "processed." Not like art, but like sausage, or like something that's bad for you — instilled in the word — immigrants: too much sugar and salt.

The piece Cardiff and her partner, George Bures Miller, are showing is an installation piece called *40 Part Motet*. Forty tall-standing speakers in a circle around two museum-style benches. The rest of the room is empty. White.

And then the music starts, a classical piece.

Mom and I move to the center of the room. Tony stays outside the circle, stalking. He doesn't get it, and he acts like he's afraid of crossing the line into the circle. He remains on the outskirts. I try to ignore him.

The music that's playing, beginning its quiet haunt, is a sixteenth-century choral piece by Thomas Tallis. I'd read about it. Cardiff had recorded an English cathedral choir, giving each of the young men in the choir an individual mic so that she could later transfer each of their voices into one of the speakers.

Mom's standing in the center of the space and I'm sitting. She's wide-hipped but tiny, shorter than the speakers, which loom over her like black flowers. In the music, sometimes several voices join and sometimes the voices are disparate, single and solitary. Sometimes their high pitch is a screech and sometimes the choral blessing of divinity takes hold. Suddenly, Mom starts to shake. I get scared that something's wrong, so I go to her, but I see that it's not that something is physically wrong with her, it's that she's sobbing into her hands. I slowly take her in my arms, feeling infinitely larger than her. Her face reddens with tears and I want her to stop crying, but she doesn't want that, she wants to cry and cry, allowing herself to be moved by the gentle, rough, furtive voices around her.

It's over a month since Dad died. The blazing summer days have fanned themselves and cooled. Miami and its lights make their way through the large windows of the Freedom Tower and when the music stops, Mom stops crying and I wonder if Dad didn't filter himself too, somehow, his spirit, through that music.

Quietly we step outside the circle, going toward the exit, where Tony's standing, hands in his pocket, waiting.

"Something about the chorus," says Mom, "those voices in unison, like church and God, something about these walls too."

"Do you remember? Does it look different? How was it when you guys came through?" I ask her, ignoring Tony, who's just standing there and doesn't understand anything that has just happened.

"So much life, you have to have lived a life to understand that piece. A real life. I—"

"It's okay, Mom."

I'm afraid she'll start crying again, and it's not that I fear her emotion, it's that I fear her tired body might not be able to support it.

"It's just—it's so funny. It's so sad. I feel like I'm a farce, *una imbécil*, and like it's a tragedy. It's just music, I don't know why I'm like this," Mom says this to Tony. This is Mom's way of apologizing to Tony. I want to tell her to stop. Tony doesn't deserve an apology.

I wonder, at that moment, how I could be with a man who doesn't stop to look at art, doesn't allow it under his skin, let it move his insides around.

Before we got to the Freedom Tower, we'd gone to the Miami Art Museum, which was sponsoring the Cardiff show, and which had shuttles to the Freedom Tower. At the museum, Mom was roaming while Tony and I walked around together. We'd seen this piece that I tried to explain to him, a complicated thing that involved a Sol LeWitt.

"LeWitt, when he sold a piece, he sold the instructions of how to make it, so that piece there, the one you're looking at, the collector would simply buy a piece of paper that said, 'Make a diagonal blue line that meets at the corner with the red line,' etc. It's all conceptual. The buyer literally made it. So the question arises: Who is the artist? You see what I mean?"

Tony rolled his eyes and turned his back to me and walked away. Nina does this—she walks away. I can't stand it.

"Tony, that's really rude," I'd called out, louder than I'd have liked.

He turned back to me, same look of cynicism, in his Bermuda shorts and peach T-shirt. Everybody else was dressed up for the occasion and there he was: almost forty, noncommittal, in shorts and a T-shirt, a child.

But then, after it's all over, the tears and the exhibition, Tony asks Mom if she wants to go to dinner. Mom doesn't want to impose so she says, "No, it's okay, it's okay. I'm not that hungry."

"Oh, c'mon, *vamos*, we'll eat something," says Tony, putting his hand on Mom's shoulder.

"Well, okay, a little something."

"A little something, yes, a little something. Good."

And just like that I remember why I'm with the little sucker, with Tony, *mi amor*, who doesn't get art but gets this—sharing a meal, food and conversation, touch. That's his way of loving. Tony is more real than I am. Tony is not an asshole. Tony is not artifice. Tony is not art.

We go to a Cuban restaurant and Mom eats more *arroz con frijoles*, *mariquitas*, and *yuca frita* than I've ever seen her manage. Must have been the gaping hole the choir left—the tearing of skin and ground. It's always so hard to fill large, gaping holes.

"Thank you, *mi amor*," I tell Tony, as we get up from our food to go, giving him a kiss on the cheek.

"You're welcome, *gorda*."

 Red.

Despite its name, the semiprecious mineral bloodstone is actually green. It's the random spots of red on its surface that evoke drops of blood.

It's seven on a Tuesday morning, a couple of days after the Cardiff show.

"Tony, *mi amor*, I want to cook for you."

I think of my mother in the kitchen, like Leo thinks of his mother knotting his tie. Ma's breading pork and sprinkling paprika on chicken. She's boiling Brussels sprouts, making the whole house smell like farts. Mom wishes she had a bell to call us with, but I don't think she'd use it. She'd just come and get us gently, just like she wakes us up in the morning, dressing my sister for school—Nina who is still sleeping. While my father's away, away again.

On Christmas she'll make a Cuban Christmas, the sweetest *frijoles* and a *lomito* so seasoned you'd think God had blessed her hands. Maybe he did. Maybe God exists and there's no such thing as emptiness when your mother is cooking for you, when someone you love is filling that hole in your stomach that's been getting bigger throughout the day.

I call out to Tony from my studio again. He hadn't responded the first time. "Tony, *mi amor*, did you hear me? I want to cook for you." I'm in mid-brushstroke. The middle panel of *Altar Piece* and the lower end of the right panel have been going at once today. There's a covered woman in a headdress and some kind of goat appearing.

"Do you like goat?" I'm still yelling. "Do you think we could get goat somewhere? Would you like me to make you that?"

Tony appears at the door, shirtless and barefoot and wearing his swimming shorts, which he sometimes wears as regular shorts.

"What are you saying, *gordita*? I can't hear you over there."

"I want to cook for you." I'm filled with love for him, looking at him, standing in the half-light from my window.

"Tony." I put my paintbrushes down and go over to him. He makes a face about the dirty hands coming toward him, so I wipe my hands on my rag before I trace the arch of his eyebrow, and he looks at me, worried. I'm filled with love again, can't remember feeling empty just a second ago, can't remember missing things, asking myself whether when Dad was away, did I ever really miss him?

"I want to cook for you, *mi amor*."

"*Gordita*." I know the intonation of that *gordita*. It means he hates my cooking; it means he doesn't like my vegetarian inventions; it means he's a meat-and-potatoes kind of guy and he doesn't want what I'm offering. It's also mixed in with a bit of sympathy and worry, like he's lost in my weirdness lately.

"I'll cook you meat and potatoes."

"Why?"

"I want to."

"But I'm on a diet, remember? You're the one who said I had to lose weight because of the snoring."

"I want to feed you, let me. Please, let me feed you."

I give him a kiss on the mouth, and again he looks at me, sad. I wonder at his sadness, I wonder what he's doing in his head.

THAT NIGHT I dream a woman from out of nowhere, she just appears like a vapor. She comes over to me and tells me something in my ear. She says, *Tony doesn't love you anymore.*

When I wake up the next morning, I go to my studio. I work for about half an hour and when I look at my watch for the first time, it's 6:40. Tony is still asleep and I know Publix opens at 7:00, so I put on a T-shirt and sweatpants, slip into my flip-flops, and leave Tony a note telling him I'll be right back.

In the supermarket I don't know what to get. Maybe I'll make a curry. Up and down every aisle, I buy couscous and onions and turmeric and curry powder, brown sugar and cucumbers and dill. But I get stuck when I get to the meat aisle. It all looks so bloody, and I don't know how to prepare it. I can't remember what to do with it, how it cooks. I only remember its smell on the grill and Mom's kiss on my mouth, before eating, and the kiss after eating, and the kiss she made us give the food if we had any to throw away.

"There are starving children in the world. You don't throw away food. Eat it all."

"I can't, Mom, I'm stuffed," Nina would say.

Usually I'd stuff my chubby cheeks with Nina's leftovers. I was such a fat tween and teen. Infused with good eating from my mother, bad habits from my father, and a hell of a lot of anxiety.

On movie nights Dad would take us to Blockbuster Video and say, "Get whatever you want." Popcorn, gummy bears, chocolate, Pringles, Coke. I'd eat it all. For years I was fat. For years I didn't have friends because of it, always got picked last in gym class, though I could run and was a competitive little shit. But now I can't remember what it's like to be full like I was as a kid. Now I like feeling just a little hungry all the time.

The meat stares at me.

"Do you need any help, ma'am?" a hairnet-covered woman asks me from behind the meat counter. She looks like the woman next to the goat in *Altar Piece.*

"Oh, um, no. I just can't decide what to cook for lunch."

"Chicken's fresh."

Chicken is boring.

"I don't think so, not today. Do you have goat?" I ask her.

"No, ma'am." She seems shocked by my question. "I don't think we've ever had goat."

I stop and stare and wonder why goat should be any different than pig or cow.

"Lamb's always a good choice, and today we got plenty of it," she adds cheerfully.

Lamb of God, who takes away the sins of the world, have mercy on us.

"Yes. Yes, I'll take the lamb."

In the car on the way home, I call my mother. "Mom, how do you make lamb?"

"Why are you making lamb? It's 7:30 in the morning, Veronica. *Estás bien?*"

"I just want to."

"But you don't eat lamb."

"I want to make it for Tony."

Mom changes her tune. "That's good. Men like to be taken care of. The way to a man's heart is through his stomach."

Her comment makes me slightly nauseous, but at least she'll give me instructions now.

"So? What do I do?"

"Are you in the car?"

"Yes."

"Stop by, I'll write down a recipe for you."

Oil Yellow.

A color that sizzles and sometimes singes. It mimics oil in that it does not seem to mix with water when it sits on the surface of a painting. It clumps instead.

I GET back to my apartment by 9:30. Tony's still off at morning meetings, but before the digital kitchen clock clicks 10:00, the skillet's on the stove, medium heat, sizzling oil. I love the smell and look of oil, like a thick yellow paint evaporating and coloring the air with tendril smoke. Soon the lamb enters the canvas, browning at the edges, slowly. Turn, turn, and turn, trying to make the browning even, erasing the meat's rawness. A gush of water splashed in the pan brings clarity to the whole thing. I cover the lamb with boiling water. Then comes the seasoning, and then the green of it all: celery, parsley. A dash of white: onion. Cover and cook over low heat for one and a half to two hours. Or until the meat is tender.

"*Gordita!*"

I jump.

"I didn't hear you come in."

"*No digo yo.* What are you doing?"

"Lunch."

"That's meat."

"Lamb."

"Do you know how to cook that?"

"Just because I'm a vegetarian doesn't mean I'm retarded."

"Are you sure about that?" Tony laughs and gives me a tickle.

"I'm letting it cook over low heat. Lunch will be ready at one. Okay?"

"Okay." He's weirded out by this, I can tell. He thinks there's no turning back. I've crossed a line. I wish I could just say, *Listen, forget all this, this yellow oil sparkling up all over the place, forget it, it's all going to be fine. I'm going to be fine and you're going to be fine.* But the words get stuck in my throat like a big ball of clay and I say, "Good."

"*Estás bien, gordita?*" Again, there he is standing in the half-light, near me now, squeezing me. Yellow like the oil-smoke, yellow like the sun. I love you. I love you. I love you. I want to scream it out. I want him to feel it through my squeeze. I want him to know all of this. I love you.

"I'm fine." I feel a warm tear slide down my cheek. He wipes it away and gives me two kisses, two soft kisses, one above each eye, and then he goes to work in his room.

Orpiment.

Also known as king's yellow.

WHILE THE lamb is cooking on low heat, I'm back in the studio, picking up another shade of yellow: king's yellow. Sometimes it's hard to find this stuff so when I do get hold of it, I smear it everywhere, even if I get rid of it later in the painting, paint over it with brown, who cares? If only to see that volcanic flare scatter like a canary all over the canvas.

When she was giving me the recipe, Mom said she thought we should all go somewhere for Christmas. Maybe the country, maybe Disney World. Maybe we should ride horses.

I'd like to ride horses. Tony's been talking about going to the mountains. Maybe I should have suggested the mountains.

"I just think we should all take a little trip away, Vic and you and me, and Nina and Tony." Mom was very serious about the whole thing, like when I used to get strep throat and she used to tell me that no matter what, I would have to lower my pants and get the penicillin injection. "Just be thankful you're not allergic to the shot, like Papan, then it would take longer to get better."

It sounded like a good idea, the trip.

I drench the yellow in a thick layer of medium, brilliant medium with high gloss, smearing it over the entire painting, wanting the sun and the oil, wanting it viscous over everything but not so opaque that I can't see what lies beneath. While it's still wet, I begin to wipe it away with my big palette knife, and what's left behind is halo glow, pentimento.

The smell filters into the studio, reminding me.

I check the recipe: *Remove the meat with a slotted spoon.* Perplexed, I look up "slotted spoon" on Google.

A spoon with holes. Duh. I'm an ass.

Remove the meat with a slotted spoon. Strain broth. Pour two cups of the broth out and back into the skillet. Put the skillet on low heat.

The smell is rising into me like bread, expanding. I imagine it going through every vein, traveling inside my body, in through my nose and mouth, journeying through all those internal reds. The lighter brown broth and the flour mixed with curry, mixing with cold water, forming a paste.

Now I have to loosen it up, blend it in with the stock I've been saving, cook it, stirring until the whole thing is thick. Add the meat, serve the couscous, serve the meat over the couscous. Garnish with parsley.

Serves four, but only one will eat.

"Lunch is ready."

"It'll be Christmas soon."

"Before we know it."

We're sitting at the table in the living room, the small one that's really supposed to be patio furniture but which we've brought in from the balcony, where we used to eat and pour champagne all over our bodies.

"Do you like it?"

"It's good." Tony cuts up another piece, slides it into his mouth.

"I told you I could cook."

"How did you taste it?"

"I didn't. It was all visual. I can't remember what meat tastes like anyway. My Mom gave me the recipe." I pause a bit for a drink of water. "Mom was talking about Christmas."

"What about it?"

"She wants us all to go away."

"Ah, sí?"

"She thinks it would be good for us."

"It would be good for you, she's right. You should."

"She meant all of us, like me and you and Nina and Mom and Vic."

"Oh." Tony begins to wiggle in his seat.

"I was thinking maybe I could suggest the mountains. You've been wanting to go to the mountains."

"Florida is so flat. I miss the snow."

"I know."

He's cutting the meat and eating it and I'm happy that he likes it, peacock proud. I want him to hug me and lift me up to the ceiling and say, "*Gordita*, you're the best cook in the world. Nothing is more comforting than this food. I love you."

But instead he says, "I don't think I should go."

"Why?"

"Because," he says slowly, putting down his silverware, setting his napkin on the table. "Come, let's sit," he says, holding out his hand, waiting for mine to join with his, but I don't move.

"We *are* sitting."

"Here, let's go over here," Tony says, leading me to the couch.

"What's wrong? Why don't you want to go? It's okay, you know, they like you. They really like you. My Mom wouldn't have invited you if—"

"It's not that, it's just..." He strokes my hand. His face is sad. I'm worried.

"What's wrong?"

"I think we should split up."

"What?"

 Ochre.

From the Greek word *chlomós* (pale), it is sometimes
described as golden-yellow, but someone with a disease
(jaundice) might turn this color.

AFTER TONY says we should break up, I go into a state of shock. I tell
him I don't understand, I keep asking why.

"I don't want to get married. I don't think it's in the cards for me."

"Why?"

"I have to lose weight, and I have to change my lifestyle." He
seems to be fumbling for answers.

"I can help you, I can help you lose weight, we could go on long
walks."

"I need to do it alone."

"Why?" I ask again.

But he doesn't respond right away. The breaking point comes
when he explains how much stress he's accumulated from me this
past year.

"This year has been hard. I started bleeding yesterday. There was
blood in my shit, and I really think it's because of you and—"

"Jesus Christ, Tony, what do you want me to do about it? My
father died."

"I know, and I think I've been the best I could be."

"That's what love is, it's sticking around when it gets tough."

"I did."

"You're leaving."

"I felt like I wanted to break up with you before your father died, and then he died, and—"

"And you couldn't break up with me anymore."

He nods.

"I'm so sad," I say, moving my body away from his.

"I know, *gorda*, come here. I know how you are, how sensitive you are. I haven't been wanting to tell you because I didn't want to hurt you."

"I'm not sensitive."

"You are, *gordita*. I know you like to pretend you are a man, but you are not. You're—"

It enrages me, this comment, this sexist totem standing there like a wooden punching bag that would break my fist if I tried to fight it. So I don't fight, I don't have it in me this time around, I just ask why.

Why? It's all I can think to ask. Over and over again.

Tony takes me in his arms and his eyes water. But the tears don't come, he doesn't allow them to escape, they well in his ripe-red eyes and I watch them, waiting. "I was taught men don't cry. I haven't cried since I was a child" is what he always says, and I believe him. When his father dies, he will cry. He'll start to remember and he will cry like a child.

After I can't stay in his arms anymore, I walk to my studio, catatonic, and I curl up on the floor quietly. Although what I feel like doing is raging loudly like a madwoman in an asylum, and why not, the man has broken my head and heart. Like Van Gogh, full of turpentine, I want to rave. For an hour I'm like that until Tony knocks on the door, opens it slightly and says, "I have to go to a meeting, I'll be back in an hour. We'll go for a walk on the beach when I'm back. *Sí? Gordita? Sí?*"

Why should I answer?

After he leaves, I stay curled until my body starts to feel the hard ceramic of the tile on my ribs, aching. The desk Dad bought Mom, the big brown law desk, when all she wanted was a yellow plastic one. I wonder: had I tried too hard?

I get up and walk over to the table where the meal has been left and begin to pick it up, take it to the kitchen, quietly putting it into Tupperware. Everything needs to be washed clean: oil, parsley, lamb. Residue.

When everything is clean, I open the fridge, and without really realizing what I'm doing exactly, I start to stuff my face with couscous. And then I start to eat the meat. One piece after another, chewing on the animal, biting and swallowing, seeing the image of myself as a leopard in the jungle tearing apart skin. I eat until the Tupperware is clean. When I see what I've done and feel the fullness of my stomach, expanded, when I feel the grease on my face, and the food coming out of every pore, I run to the bathroom and start to throw up. I throw up for ten minutes straight—just a little under the time it took to eat it. And I'm swept over with guilt and emptiness, and loneliness, and I look down at the toilet. All that food gone to waste. How can I kiss it now? That poor lamb.

What will I do without Tony? I'll be so alone. No one to protect me. What will I do? Where will I go?

"You'll be fine," he'd said. "You're about to make it big."

Who cares about making it big when there's no one to love me, take care of me, watch over me? I can't stand this feeling, pain like a high-pitched sound making you cover your ears, fearing the blood trickle of a busted eardrum. I want to take Tony in my arms and keep him from going. I want my father back. I want to know that things aren't so transient, that the world isn't just something that passes us by. I want to be filled up again. Was I ever filled up? The hole in the heart, it's just getting bigger and wider and darker. Can you climb out of a black hole? Stephen Hawking says you can.

Lamb of God, who takes away the sins of the world.

White.

The color of new beginnings. Tabula rasa. A blank canvas.

I DON'T want to dismember my painting's three panels, its life. Not until it's done, lived out, finished, ready to move. But I probably won't finish it by the time I have to leave here. Tony says there's no rush—take my time, find an apartment, not to worry.

"I could live with you forever, you don't have to hurry," he says, kissing me softly on the mouth, brushing my hair from my forehead. But I don't understand this kiss, or this talk. If you can live with me forever, why are you breaking up with me? I don't understand anything Tony says anymore.

Tony says, "We can do this the wrong way and make it hard for each other, or we can do it right and not hurt each other." I nod when he says this, I will be strong. I am a civil woman, a smart woman. I am not a hysterical woman, I will not throw a fit. We will not hurt each other. We will slowly undo ourselves from the knot of union, we will unwind, we will separate our lives. Slowly, intentionally, with love.

"Yes," I tell him, "let's agree to not hurt each other."

But he has already hurt me.

As the days go by, my body begins to detach itself from him. A shell of myself has sex with him — debris, rubble, just a big wide open hole, searching for landfill. And I begin to feel a certain and very particular kind of desperation to leave my situation and find a home. I need, at least, four walls to take me in, protect me from storms, shelter me.

I decide to move to my father's apartment.

But I'm scared. I'm scared of all of his things surrounding me there. His wallpaper. The smell that is disappearing from the wallet but that will be concentrated in his apartment, a scent of heaviness but also of relief, that he has not totally vaporized into nothing. I would have to gut it. Rip out the wallpaper, paint it white. I would have to start over. Erase the traces. Live simply.

I walk into Tony's office and tell him, "I think I'm going to move in to my father's." He looks up from his computer, sad eyes like a damn dog.

"I think that's a good idea. I can help you. I thought you should, but I thought it was something you had to come to on your own."

"Please, Tony, don't pretend to know what's best for me," I say as kindly as I possibly can.

"I'm sorry."

"I'll let you know how long it will take to move his stuff out of there and prepare the apartment for my stuff. Then we can move everything of mine in there together."

"Take your time, *gordita*."

NINA IS the only one who knows about me and Tony. I had to tell her.

I had to make a deal with her to stay in the apartment. I would maintain the place, pay insurance, make all special assessment payments. We would figure out the rest later.

"There's a housing crisis on the rise," I tell Nina. "No use selling now anyway."

"Yeah, I guess. Besides, you need to stay there, it's okay." Nina gives in to the deal easily. Nina is a better person than I am. Sometimes I really think this is true.

"Hey, don't tell anyone, okay? I still have to live with him until I fix Dad's place and get rid of all his stuff and move in there, so, you know."

"I won't tell anyone, you know how I am. To the grave, darling, to the grave." Nina says this with Garbo drama, and then asks, "Vero, are you okay?"

"Not really. I'm really sad." I fight the cry-ball that begins to rise in my throat, attempting to block the words from emerging. "This is worse than losing the first house."

"Isn't that funny, how when you *choose* to make a home with someone it's a bigger deal to lose it. That's why I don't live with men anymore. You wanna marry me, put a ring on my finger, then we'll live together."

Maybe she's right. My sister is wiser in love than I am.

"You're going to be fine, you know," she says. "It's just your first time."

"Yeah, well, I don't want to do it much more, I can't."

"Everybody says that."

"I'm not everybody. Really, I can't just keep doing this. I only ever wanted to do this love thing once."

"That's just because it's your first time."

"Stop saying that. Who makes up the rules and says this has to be done over and over again? I say we go back to arranged marriages. You can love anyone if you really want to, right? Everybody has a good side."

"Yeah right, Veronica. You of all people. You would have murdered Dad if he'd even tried anything close to that."

"Well, can you imagine who Dad might have chosen!"

"Well, cheer up, buttercup, at least you're not handicapped."

I laugh.

For the first time since Dad died, Nina sounds like herself.

You HAVE to lift the door and jiggle it to get it opened. It's a little off-center from when they kicked it in. The apartment is dark, and the air conditioning doesn't work. The remains of the paramedics are all around: a bag full of some kind of fluid I'm scared to touch, heart monitor stickers I don't have a name for, iodine spills on the stone floor. Had we all lost our minds—why had we left all of this when we'd come to see the safe, and all the other times we'd been in here? I guess we couldn't deal with it, the cleaning up, the erasing of the puzzle pieces, like the erasure of the lamb's rawness. I'm not sure I can deal with it now.

The blinds are all closed and when I finally get them open I can't believe the view. Water and skyscrapers, I feel like I'm at the tip of Manhattan, except the sky is more blue, and the clouds look like the cotton candy you buy at the Dade County Fair, so soft and sugary it melts in your mouth. Why in the world would Dad block this view?

"He was a very private man," the security guard told me when she saw me, parking my car at the valet. She knew who I was, said I looked "exactly like him, except for you being paper-thin," a slight Caribbean accent tracing her words like smoke. Her name tag read, Ms. BABS.

When I look at how much stuff Dad had, I want to cry. I have to get rid of all of it, nothing can remain. Everything he owns has a tinge of yellow because of the cigars he smoked. Once, his great silver hair had started to turn yellow, but he nipped it in the bud, went to the doctor and the doctor said it was his cigar smoke, getting into his hair like a cat's tail. They gave him something to put in it and it stopped turning yellow.

He has a little bar he made in the back room, surrounded by shaded windows that cast a cool blue tint over everything. One of the chairs at the bar has a loosened top. I imagine that's the one he sat on. Unable to support his weight, the screws started to unsettle. I can see him sitting there, cutting the end of his cigar with his cigar clip, lighting it with his mega-torch lighter, letting the cigar rest in the corner of his mouth, setting his hands in front of him, one on top of the other. Until I open all the windows and the vision of him goes up in smoke.

It struck me, that thing Ms. Babs said about Dad being private. My father wasn't private, he was just paranoid and depressed. And embarrassed. Like what Daria said about when he'd bought the exercise bike and wouldn't try them out in the store. She kept telling him to get on one and he started turning red and sweating and he told her to go wait outside, please. He ended up buying the most expensive one, figuring that one would support him.

EVER SINCE I can remember, he locked himself in. When we were little he locked us in too. In the first house, we had gates on every window, and a gate indoors too, between the bedrooms and the rest of the house. Nina would sleepwalk, I'd forgotten that. Dad was scared she would just walk straight out into the street, so he gated us in. Every night, they would lock it before we went to sleep, or before Nina and I took to the Nintendo set or movies on our pink TV and Betamax. *Chip and Dale*, *Mary Poppins*, and *Dirty Dancing* were all we watched for a while, on a loop. Nina would sometimes put on jeans, Keds, and a white T-shirt showing her midriff, and she would singsong, "Come here, lover boy," just like in *Dirty Dancing*, and then she would dance to the scene when Baby walks over to the Patrick Swayze character, all sexy. Nina was seven.

One day, in the middle of the night, we all heard a twangy metallic boom, and Mom and Dad came out of their room, and I came out from mine, and there was Nina face-up on the floor in front of the gate, with a big red mark on her forehead. She'd sleepwalked, hit her head, and now she was seemingly unconscious (either that or still asleep on the floor).

"Be careful," I said. "You're not supposed to wake up sleep-walkers." I'd read that somewhere.

"She's not asleep." Dad looked at her, worried.

"How do you know?" I asked.

"Nina?" My Mom was trying to make her come to, all of us hovering over her. "Nina, honey, Nina."

"Mom, what if she's still asleep and you wake her up and she dies or goes nuts?"

"Veronica, stop it! Stop it, *ni digas eso!* She couldn't have slept through that bang, it woke everybody up."

"Move, *muévanse!*" Dad finally yelled, picking Nina up and taking her to their room, putting her on the bed. "Eli, bring the ammonia your mother gave you."

In the room, the yellow light of day started merging with the night's gray, filtering slightly over us, dawn.

Mom ran into the bathroom to get the gate key that dangled from a nail on the wall next to the mirror. When she came back from the kitchen, she had a little white sack-stick in her hand that looked like a cotton suppository. She cracked it and put it under Nina's nose and Nina opened her eyes and looked at each of us. Then we all rushed off to the hospital for x-rays and CAT scans. She was fine, except for the enormous *chichón* she had on her forehead for weeks to come.

LIKE A somnambulist waking up and not understanding where she is, I'm standing on a chair starting to rip Dad's green and white wallpaper off. It comes off in crooked chunks, still stuck to the wall. It's harder than I thought. Sweat begins to bead on my arms, my forehead, hands. There's a gluey white old mucus behind the paper like old cum. Bathroom scum. It gets under my fingernails and makes me angry. I don't want to stick to this wall. My hands suction like the empty hollow of plastic; I have to force them off the wall to go to the kitchen, get a knife, and start trying to scrape it all off. Get it clean. Scratch, scratch. Do it, remove it. Nothing. A drowning desire to take the room apart, wishing for claws, wanting it all to go away, dissolve. Longing to be home, with Tony, but then Tony isn't home anymore. This is home, dear God, *this* is home. I can't believe I have to do this, with the show so soon. Will I even have time to manage, I don't know, but I can't stay at Tony's anymore, it's erasing me.

Dad's entire apartment is now drenched in a bright, glaring sunlight from all the windows I opened, but the furniture and the shards of wallpaper still look dark and dull and gray. The only thing shining is the knife in my hand, which is rusted near the grip with a reddish-brown, oxidized stain. Red ochre. Dried blood. Mud. It's like everything in here's been living in the gray for too long to change. The thought petrifies me still, like some Greek god-turned-tree trunk. The first release I get from my thoughts, I drop the knife. It clashes on the stone floor.

Picking up my bag, leaving the apartment, darting for my car, and driving back toward the beach, the road is blurred the whole way there. Not remembering if I'd locked the door. It doesn't matter. Not anything really real that anyone could steal, not a piece of sky, not the twanging sound of Nina's head hitting metal, not hard light. Maybe I just have to let the space marinate in the sun for a little. Maybe I just have to let the light seep into the apartment and warm the place up. The same as with *Altar Piece* — orpiment spread all over, giving it glow. Then putting it out in the sun, making ruins, too much sun. A ravishing.

Either that, or I'll have to hire someone to do the job for me.

"How DID it go?"

"How do you think it went?"

Locking myself under the covers, I pray for immediate sleep, grateful for the darkness of Tony's room.

In the morning, for the first time ever in Tony's room, I feel as if the light is trying to press through the black hole of blue-black paper Tony has lined the windows with to prevent computer glare. The light battles, but doesn't win. Tony's staring at me, but I feel like he's not solidly there, like it's not him, just a shell of him, and like my head is an astro-cartooned bubble in space. This is not the man I used to hug in the shower, letting the water fall on us, cleaning us, binding us with steam and grace. Who are these two people staring at each other?

From: Veronica Gonzalez
To: Leo Estevez
Date: Fri, Nov 2, 2007 9:14am
Subject: Dumped

Tony dumped me. I'm moving in to my father's.

~

From: Leo Estevez
To: Veronica Gonzalez
Date: Fri, Nov 2, 2007 9:52am
Subject: Re: Dumped

Argentino de mierda! Are you okay? Most importantly, do you
need anything?

~

From: Veronica Gonzalez
To: Leo Estevez
Date: Fri, Nov 2, 2007 12:00pm
Subject: Re: Dumped

Just a new heart. And a little hope that the guy I hired to pull
the wallpaper out and paint my dad's apartment shows up and
finishes on time. We'll talk soon, I'm a little overwhelmed right
now. I guess I don't need anything. Just a little time.

~

From: Leo Estevez
To: Veronica Gonzalez
Date: Fri, Nov 2, 2007 6:00pm
Subject: Good luck

Okay. I'm here if you need me, anytime (I mean that). For
real, pintora.

I know he means it. I don't know why I believe Leo, he's never
had to prove himself to me, as a friend, not really. But there it is,
this feeling, somewhere in my gut, telling me it's true. And there's
Tony, who is supposed to love me, telling me the opposite—I am not
here for you, not for the long run. And yet here I am, still at Tony's,

painting while the newly arrived *balsero* I hired fresh off the boat removes Dad's wallpaper and paints the whole apartment white. I don't have time with the show coming up to do it myself and he says he'll do it all for $400, including patching up the walls and fixing any light fixtures. I can't believe it's so cheap until I realize the *balsero* hasn't figured out you need money in America, this isn't Cuba. But I don't say anything, I accept the price. He'll have to figure that out on his own. Just like Tony says, "It's part of the game."

The game. What the hell does that mean?

Maybe it's what Tony's playing at now. Because days go by and sometimes it feels like we aren't breaking up. Although really it's just like sitting in a waiting room knowing you're going into surgery. I make him his coffee, he kisses me and wishes me well every morning as I head into the studio. We talk about politics like we always do. The possibility of Obama in the White House excites us and takes our minds off ourselves. We shower together and I scrub his hairy chest peppered slightly with white and red Pollock splashes of hair, his balding head. At night, he fingers me like an angel, playing with my clit like he always does, with what I now realize are perhaps too many years of experience to ever settle down with one pussy to dig his fingers into forever. Except for sometimes when he looks at me and I think, could that expression be what I think it is: "I'm not sure I want to let you go." It's a Morse code of confusion that runs through me when he does that—little wild red ant pricks all over my body . ... I don't know.

The *balsero* says he'll be done soon. Which means soon I'll start to transfer my possessions. I've almost finished sewing the shirts to install as a hot-air balloon in the gallery later. Now it just needs the basket, but I won't be quite done with the painting yet when I move, it will have to finish its life (or begin another) somewhere else, sadly, and without my choosing. It angers me how little choice I have in it all.

AND BEFORE I know it, in a purple haze, it's all done—the whole of it, the *balsero*'s done painting and I've moved my things. All done— the breaking with Tony and the new physical distance between us, growing as I drive away from his apartment. I know the only place I can really go, that will keep me from bursting inside, breaking at the seams, is toward my half-built *Altar Piece*, to finish it and then destroy it.

 Tokyo Purple.

This is the color of the "floating world" produced by the
Edo period in Japan.

IT'S HARD to find grounding at first, painting out of Dad's apartment —
my apartment.

Altar Piece rants at me in black spots that are really purple,
Coltrane-blue sometimes: sultry and seemingly safe but dangerous
like a 1980s New York night. The purple has gotten cavernous, pinned
by visceral pinks that intestinalize around the squiggles of the purple
swivels in brain-like waves of motion. Have to add more light later.
It's too dark now, but can't quite find where the yellow is, where the
beam lives, or comes from, or shines on or through. The light source,
basically—it's lost. Will have to petal flowers in here later, curving
their soft-touch pollen pistils into the fold, to lessen the blow. But for
now it is all dark like the moon would look if it didn't glow, like the
royal root of rhubarb. Plasma not yet iridescent. Purple temples lined
with gold, Shinjuku traffic, octopus—succulent. Plastic wrapping
like the suction of my hands on wallpaper remains: Sticky. Creamy.
Scummy. Stuck. I wonder if my legs will both swing off from all this
chanting, pleading, begging. Tug, tug. Brush, brush. Sew. Sew. Tug.

Brush. Sew. Tug. Brush. Love. Brush. Brush. Brush. Brush. Brush. Brushh. Shh. Shh. Shhhhhh.

"I THINK we should move him."

"Who? What?"

"Your father."

"What are you talking about, Mom?"

The morning is still in my eyes when the phone rings. I haven't even made it to *Altar Piece* yet. Water's in the microwave, and I'm reaching for the teabag in a blur. No more coffee for Tony, it's just me now and tea. Mom's voice is agitated.

"Nina and I talked about it. I'm going to look into it."

"You mean his body?"

"Yes. It's too far away."

"I know, it's in butt-fuck, but that's where he chose."

"But it's so far from us."

"I mean, look into it if you want, Mom, but it's going to be expensive. I mean, it has to be."

"Maybe. Maybe not. Remember he's in the penthouse. Which means they don't have to dig him up. They just literally have to move him. That's not such a big deal."

"Maybe, but you know how those people are. Business of death and all that."

"I know, Nina said the same thing. She said they capitalize on death."

"Capitalize on death, yeah." Nina steals my words.

"Okay, so that's it. I'll look into it."

"Okay."

There's a short pause. I dip the green tea bag in the almost-boiling water, in and out, like a buoy.

"How are you, *mamita*?" Mom asks finally after a long, breathy pause. "Are you okay in your dad's place?"

"I'm fine."

"You know, you can come and sleep over if you want, if you get sad."

"I know, but I just don't think I should, you know. I'm too old."

"You're never too old to sleep with your mother. Never."

Mom is getting adamant. I know I'll have to hang up soon or the tender feeling I have will turn to aggravation. But I also know I'll probably end up staying the night over there, if not tonight, sooner or later. And probably more than one night.

 Indigo Blue.

The color you see glinting off a non-recorded DVD,
dispersed by it.

THE WORD "cloying" is in my head, like a headache trying to scratch
its way out, an old papyrus-scroll tragedy calling for somebody's eyes.
Raw and red: my eyes hurt and burn. I long to be held, or for my head
to crack open finally, give birth to a happy thought. I wonder if this is
what an aneurysm is like, lonely and painful and like every filed-away
memory is emerging from somewhere inside the brain, exploding in
live-wire action, synapses clashing, all at once, and trapped inside
your skull.

Every day I find a trace. Today, it's a DVD. The cover has red
letters spelling out CASA JUANCHO. I don't recognize the handwriting,
but the name is an immediate torrent. Casa Juancho was Dad's
favorite place to go on his birthday, a Spanish restaurant with orange
terracotta tile and the smell of cured, salty ham hitting your nose at
the door. *Jamón serrano*, just like at Perrucho's. Sometimes Dad took
Papan to Casa Juancho, even after the divorce, because Dad used
to say, *"El viejo sabe disfrutar."* Papan and Dad, eating *camarones al
ajillo* and drinking sangría and Rioja until they were red in the face

like they were Don Quijote and Sancho Panza. Dad lifting his glass to Papan over and over again, oil saturating everything. Oven-warm, we would linger, closing the place down. "*Vengan otra vez*," the owner would call out.

"*Esta es la vida, Gallego, la vida, no?*" Dad would wrap his chubby hands around Papan. And wasn't that the thing, the stuff of life, the thing we could not live without—food. Bread, water. The things that, garnished with enough oil, could slide down into us with all the pleasure in the world, simmering and sifting through space and time, carrying the brunt of memory with it. The very thing that would kill him.

THE FIRST audible sound in the DVD's soundtrack is a voice, unrecognizable, and then a face I recognize. It's not the face the voice is coming from, the face is Louisa's, with her son, next to Dad. And then a pan to Dad and a close-up, his eyes squinty and happy, pupils almost disappearing into those Asian eyes he got when he smiled. I pause it for a moment, folding the laptop screen, asking myself, Can I do this?

Unfolding the screen, the voice again saying, "So here we are, to celebrate this special day." The camera is still on Dad and the voice is still the stranger's. Then the voice says, "Look how well Louisa has done for herself. We wanted to show all of you what life is like here in the United States." On my father's paycheck. In our restaurant. "What a good man," the strange voice says—Louisa's mother, I deduce by now. And then out comes a paella, like a painting, red and sizzling orange. Pieces of fish and steam surfacing. "A special paella to welcome Doña María to Miami," says Dad, his voice floating in the background, fighting, along with the trace of his face, to engrave itself in my head. The camera leaves the paella and eventually skips and follows them from dinner to Dad's apartment, for after-dinner drinks. And there is his home, before I stripped it to pieces, before I gave his furniture to the condo maid, before I tore out his wallpaper and erased his memory, made everything white. A horrible daughter. And then, to either rescue me or tear my heart asunder, my father says, "Look, Doña María, look at that over there, underneath the Cuban frames. You see the dollar over there? That was my first dollar."

There is a zoom to the dollar and my father's voice in the background: *"Cuando yo era un chamaquito,* I'd gone out into the street to shine shoes, with an old plastic bag full of tools, and when I came home, I'd made about ten bucks, which I gave to *mi mamá.* I didn't know it, but she kept the very first one she counted that day. And when I turned eighteen, she gave it to me and said, 'Keep this, this is the first dollar you ever made.' She kept it that whole time, can you believe it?"

I can feel the emotion in Dad's voice and suddenly the vision of him sitting on the side of his bed, crying into his hands when his mother died. My mother standing over my father, taking his head to her chest. Nina and I standing by the bedroom door, frozen. Our father was crying and the world was falling apart.

Sitting in his bar, now my office, I look toward my right at the framed dollar. One of the only things I kept of his, and out of all the things in his apartment, it was the only thing he chose, on this DVD, on this day, to record. I didn't know that story. I knew it was his first dollar, but I didn't know it was his mother who had saved it for him, for eight years, until the day he became a man and went out into the world without her.

 Indigo Blue.

Most likely, this color started out its life in India. The human visual range is not as sensitive to this color as it is others. In fact, some claim it should not be called a color at all, but a shade.

IT'S MID-NOVEMBER and we're nearing the final stretch: the last two and half weeks of work.

I know I have to stop thinking of the apartment as Dad's place and start thinking of it as mine, but it doesn't feel like I'm actually here, it just feels like I'm floating above everything.

The studio at Dad's is set up differently. I'm trying to keep it out of the sleep space. It's in a corner of the living room, divided by a Chinese folding screen, which is white and indigo blue, heavy and made of porcelain. But it has blue little flowers, tiny buds, and delicate birds on it that have always made me happy. Matisse-happy. The people who make this color, this blue, their hands turn purple with the indigo plant the dye comes from. I wonder what they're doing now, across the world—mixing paints, like I am, getting more and more blue. The screen was Maman's. I once watched her as she looked at herself, naked, in its mirror. Going into her room, I stopped at the door, watching her stare at her own reflection: her wrinkled, droplet breasts, her white pubic hair. She said I could have the folding screen, that I should have it because I was the only one who loved it almost as much as she did. When I was little, I used to hide behind it. I guess I'm still doing the same thing. I wonder what Maman was hiding from?

Anyway, it separates the mess of the paints from my neat living space, that's all I need. That and this thick brush, an extension of my hand.

When I can't sleep I come here. Especially when I feel the full force of the empty space beside me. I know that my natural state is to be curled up in someone, loving someone. Tug, tug. Tug, brush. Tug. All the way until morning.

"HORMIGA."

The sound of Mom's voice is soothing on the phone.

"What are you doing?"

"Painting."

"Vic had an excellent idea," she says, getting excited. "He says why don't you come over for dinner every night!"

"Not every night, Mom."

"What about tonight, then? I bought you pineapple, and Brazil nuts, and veggie dogs, and cauliflower."

"I'm painting."

"You have all day to paint. Are you going to paint *toda la noche también*? We can have a slumber party. Nina will be here. *Yo duermo con ustedes.*"

Something in me wants to jolt over there right now, curl up in her bed. Forget about painting, forget about Tony, forget about Dad, just be with my mother, have a fight with my sister about which one of us will sleep next to her. Vic can sleep on the couch, he's done it before.

"When will you be home from work?" I ask her, giving in.

"Around seven. When do you want to come?"

"I'll go like at eight."

"I thought you liked to eat early?"

"Not really." Not anymore. Not since Tony got me used to eating late. Sometimes as late as ten. Latin time. I used to eat my last bite of food at five, and anything after felt like a travesty, dirty. I couldn't stick a morsel in, not even coffee, only water. But Tony changed all that with late-night trips to El Rey del Chivito.

SITTING HERE in front of *Altar Piece* now, without Tony's invisible presence in the other room, or the sound of his shuffling, is unnerving.

The first panel is done. Completely done. I feel it. It's over. I miss Tony.

I keep having this recurring dream of blindness. It used to happen before I met Tony, and it's not that I'm totally blind in the dream, it's that colors start to bleed into each other and I can't clarify anything in space, everything blurry and floating in some stinging netherworld. In last night's version, I was trying to drive but I kept swerving all over the place, unable to see if I was even on a road. It's always painful, like a sharp pebble piercing beneath the lid, dust and shampoo and acid in your eyes, which you can't get out. I hate these dreams. They say Monet created impressionism because he was losing his sight. A slight reduction of the movement, I know, but...

I should be happy about finishing the first panel, but I have to finish the second and third panel in just a couple of weeks, which is so short, considering how long the first panel took. Plus, I have to give this first one to the elements for a while, which makes it problematic to finish the second panel and the third without this one. Unless I photograph the first one and place a large photo as a reference. Yes. Tomorrow.

Because today I have to get out of this painting, it's suffocating me—a nervous mess of melted plastic, shaking its head, dipping me in resin, polymer and pigment fusing, clinging. I wish my profession was clean and spotless. Like Leo's, he only has to sit down and write, not get his hands dirty. Like Tony. That's the first thing he told me when he found out I was a painter. "Good thing about my profession is I don't have to get my hands dirty." And I thought, What a sissy thing to say. But now I wish I could say that. I wish I could get a manicure that wouldn't get ruined in five seconds flat. I wish I could be more feminine. I wish I wasn't always sweaty and filled with clusters of paint and unwashable color spots stuck to my hair. I wish I wasn't a painter.

I don't mean that.

Tony said to me, after I left, in an email, "Sometimes I wish you would have chosen me over your art."

What the hell does that mean? It enrages me. How dare he make me choose? The people we love are supposed to support what we love.

And yet Art feels like nothing now, right this second. One panel done—so what? Without someone to share it with, I'm not sure what any of this means.

But my painting is full.

Maybe too full. So full I have to get out of here.

Leave the ropes, stop tugging. Go home.

 Gold.

All that glitters…

EVERY HOUSE Mom has ever had, every apartment, it always looks the same. Like a combination of all those pages she marks in interior design books: a combination of country French and chic contemporary. Antiques matched up against clean white plates. The floor in her current house is black wood (a floor they couldn't afford and probably shouldn't have bought, but that's Mom for you). This place is small compared to our first house and my grandparents' house, and all the places Mom and Vic rented in between, but it's cozy, and most importantly, it's theirs. They own it, bought it together. A real home.

There's a round table, nooked in the kitchen, that feels like Papan's library used to feel. And the prints Mom chose to upholster the sofas with are floral—bold reds and whites. Maybe my mother too, somewhere inside her, is also an artist. Mom and Dad, hidden hearts, opening doors for us. My heart breaks as I sit at the table, the smell of paprika chicken, a couple of veggie burgers, and vegetables sopped in oil and garlic wafting in the air. We're waiting for Nina to come out of the shower. She still lives with Mom, and I wonder how long she'll live and work with Mom. Vic isn't home yet. It's just Mom and me, stirring the veggies in garlic, roasting, pouring wine. We don't talk much, but I can see Mom is happy I'm home. Her shoulders are at ease and she's let her hair down from the workday's bun.

The three of us finally sit down to dinner (Vic said he'd be late, to start without him).

"The Rolex is fake," says Nina right away, almost as soon as we sit down.

"What? What are you talking about?"

Mom starts to laugh. She spits a piece of broccoli out.

"Mom already knows."

"I'm sorry, it's just so funny." Mom's eyes begin to well with tears; her cheeks are red with the blood rush of laughter.

"Swallow, Mom," Nina says, and then stares at Mom while Mom tries to control herself. "C'mon, you're freaking me out."

"You're such a freak, Nina," says Mom, calmer now.

"I wonder where I get that from?"

"So, what's with the Rolex?" I ask.

"Dad's, it's fake."

"What?"

"The one with the diamonds. It's a fake," says Nina. "I went to the store and I asked them to fix the buckle for me because I wanted to wear it, and the guy was trying to be all nice, saying he didn't think he could fix it, and then when I asked him why not, he said, 'Well, ma'am, it's not an actual Rolex. It's a very good imitation, but it's not the real deal.'"

"I wonder if Ichi got screwed." Mom stops laughing.

"Or maybe he knew," says Nina, "and thought what the hell, it does the trick."

I start to laugh a little bit too, and then my sister joins in, and soon we're all laughing around the table spitting out cauliflower, broccoli, pieces of veggie burger.

"It's a fake, oh my God, it's a fake," Mom says still laughing, green all over her teeth.

"Swallow, c'mon guys, swallow your food," Nina says between her own bursts of laughter.

We don't even hear the door, but soon Vic is standing over us saying, "What's wrong with you three?"

Double, double toil and trouble.

"Nothing."

"The Rolex—"

"It was a fake!"

And then more laughter.

Vic looks at us like we're crazy, gives my Mom a kiss on the forehead, and then walks toward the bedroom, saying, "I'm gonna take a shower, girls. Save me a veggie burger."

"He's so good," Mom says, and then she leans over and whispers to us, "Sleepover, girls, why don't we have a sleepover?"

And we do.

Vic spends the night on the sofa, and Mom sleeps between me and Nina, the three of us cuddling like we used to do in our pink room.

Lying in bed, thinking of Dad and his gold Rolex, the first one, the one that is now sitting in my new safe deposit box, I feel an overwhelming sadness for everything we laughed at just a couple of hours ago. I know in my heart that first one is real.

A WEEK to go. The second panel is almost finished. There are feathers rising from a phoenix at the bottom, some endless bird. The feathers rise up to the top, to the ghost, who I still don't recognize. I can't tell who it is, the white bulbous face, Dad or Tony or Shell—or nobody. Or somehow all three. Or if it's just some part of me, somewhere, something watching over me, some kind of grace or god Mom has sent me, like a witch.

The floating feeling is everywhere still. A feeling of being above everything, which makes me think of Leo and the way he had those birds scatter the birdseed, and how that linked itself, in my head, to the photograph of Fern and the hot-air balloon, which is almost complete. I don't have the basket for the hot-air balloon yet, which makes me think: Leo, what if I use Leo's chair, the one he used down at Ground Zero, Shell's chair? What if he made a really good, edited video of what he did and we run it as part of *Remnants and Ruins*, as a part of the whole installation? What if it was *Altar Piece*, and the video projections of Leo's project, and then in the middle a combination of both (the unifier), my hot-air balloon made out of Dad's enormous shirts and Shell's chair as the basket. That would be the thing that was missing, the thing that brought together large-scale loss and intimate loss, and it would tie everything to the title of the show, *Remnants and Ruins*—the remnants left of Dad's death, and of Shell's, linking up with what killed both of them—obesity and 9/11. A picture of America, and at the same time a very personal voyage into mourning and prayer. Faith of some kind lingering over everything—the faith of the kamikaze Muslims, my faith, Leo's faith—constructive and destructive.

Maybe Nina was right—you could only see things fully when you floated above. Maybe this floating wasn't bad, it was just a way to get out of the gridlock and get through this. Someday, I would land back on the ground, and when I came back, I'd know where the fifteenth stone at Ryōan-ji was hiding.

> *Veronica*: Leo, I was thinking…
> *Leo*: Wait, are you IMing me?? Could this be?!!!
> *Veronica*: Yeah, but listen, I was thinking and thinking and
> *Leo*: Yeah, you're always thinking. 'bout what?
> *Veronica*: I'm almost done with my painting and I was thinking
> *Leo*: Oh my god, this must be big, with you IMing me.
> *Veronica*: What I was thinking is that you should come over
> *Veronica*: And we should collaborate, and that maybe we could use some of that footage you have
> *Leo*: What?!
> *Veronica*: of what you did down at the trade center and we could mix it in with my painting, and the big thing I made out of my father's shirts.

Leo: come down where?

Veronica: To Miami, you fool.

Veronica: What do you think? Can you come over? Did you film it? Am I babbling?

Leo: V, you're babbling for sure but I'm really excited about this!

Veronica: So, do you want to and do you have the whole thing on DVD?

Leo: YES and Yes

Veronica: So come then, get your ass on an aeroplane

Leo: I'm there faster than you can say square

Veronica: You're more square than you know, you know

Leo: Ultra dork. I learned it from you

Veronica: No, no, you're a natural. Do you have the tapes?

Leo: You already asked me, V, I got it all on "tape." They're DVD's by the way, "fool." Anyway, how many times you want me to tell you, I got them girl, got 'em. We can do this. I can't believe it!!

Veronica: You're excited. This is good.

Leo: I love you artista.

Veronica: Me too Poeta. Now get your ass over here.

A SMILE on my face, a Bubble Yum pink feeling at the thought that in a couple of days I'm going to see Leo and we're going to work together and soon the work will be done, and it will be opening day, and everything I've worked for will have come to something. A solo show during Basel. A solo show that I've decided to share with—

And then an IM from Tony stops me, just before shutting off the computer.

Gordita, come over.

The message shocks me, but I feel a thrill in my body, like nothing could be better in the world, like, my God, could this be happening, could he have realized the mistake he made?

WHEN I get to his apartment, my heart is beating fast. He opens the door and the sight of his green eyes and his round face and his red eyebrows glinting—they all make me want to burst out. But I hold it in, and make myself quiet. More quiet than when we met because if I open my mouth, I'll choke.

"*Hola, gordita,*" he says, standing there in his shorts.

Why is he still calling me that? I'm no longer his *gordita*. It broke my heart, not being his *gordita*, and now here he is, calling me this. Kissing me on the cheek, he says, "Come in." Behind him the small outdoor table, the round one with the brown mosaics that we bought off Craigslist from a guy who was moving from the beach, moving to London, where he wouldn't need patio furniture—it was a flat without a balcony, he said. It would be gray anyway, Tony said. When Tony lived in Cambridge he'd fallen in love with an older woman, a bartender who didn't want him—just like now, he didn't want *me*. Except he'd invited me over, and here I was.

He sits down on the blue, plush couch and tells me, bowing his head a little, that this is where he's been sleeping, he hasn't been able to buy a bed yet. On the table in front of us, he's set out my favorites, cherries and blue cheese, carrots and hummus. He's laid out two bottles of wine and a medley of veggies, marinated with an extra virgin olive oil lemon vinaigrette, the only thing that could get me to open my mouth. But I still fear the tears. Words fail to follow the bites and swallows.

"Remember when we first met," he says, "and we were walking down Lincoln Road for like ten minutes *y me preguntastes* if it was okay that you didn't talk. Sometimes you wouldn't talk to me for more than twenty minutes, thirty minutes at a time." Tony laughs a little, looks down. We are sitting on opposite ends of the couch. Not even our auras are touching.

"And you'd joke—"

"That I'd found the perfect woman."

Quietly, I spit out a cherry pit.

"Do you want to go outside?" he says.

"Okay. Bring the wine."

"*Claro.*"

And there we are, facing the lounge chairs on the balcony, the green ones where I'd gotten naked for him, who cared if the world saw? The lawn chairs we had drunk champagne on, where I'd told him my secrets, and read him pieces of my journals. Where he'd told me travel stories and explained about how he was the black sheep in his family and how he would never return to Argentina because it was as gray as London and depressing and there was no opportunity and his father had cheated him there. Cheated him out of what belonged to him, the family business. Tony had ideas for it, said he could have morphed it, moved it into the globalized world. He might have failed, an experience that would have been good for him, I'd thought. But I'd also thought he was smart, and in such a different way than me: knowing what shares to buy, what stocks to invest in and when. I'd never heard someone talk so clearly, from point A to point B. The world wasn't muddled for Tony. It isn't muddled for him. Which is why I don't understand why I'm here. I'm confused but I want to kiss him. Since I got here I want to kiss him, like we used to before he stopped. I want to let him do what he wants to me, remember how to trust him.

Tony lies down on the green lounge chair, head up. I'm still standing.

"*Ven acá, gordita,*" he says, reaching out his hand. I go to him, letting myself fit right back into the mold of him.

When I finally touch him, his lips are as soft as I remembered. I wanted to be part of him again, and here we are, beginning this merger. I don't know why I would have agreed to come if this wasn't what I'd hoped for all along. Did I really think I could be near him and not love him with every part of myself?

In the morning, when I wake up, after having him in me all night, I smell my own morning breath and I taste like him. His armpit sweat has parts of me in it, pieces of my violet scented cologne, parts of my own sweat. I want him to want me like this forever, hold me and never let me go. Tell me he wants to keep me in his arms, that he wants this love.

"I haven't been with anyone since you've gone," he says.

"I can't be just one of many," I tell him.

"I haven't been with anyone since you've gone," he repeats.

I don't know what to do.

All I want to do is stay in his arms.

But how long will it last?

If I tell him that he'll have to decide, because I can only stay with him if there is the possibility of making a life together, I know what he'll say: We can't. But he'll invite me again, he'll say, "*Gordita,* come over." And I'll be confused at all the mixed messages. And I'll wonder, again, what I'm doing here. Again, me: a proud, strong woman, with a career on the horizon, and a life, and a brain. An old woman now. What am I doing in the arms of a man who doesn't want me, not really? Or who doesn't understand what it means to love because he thinks he prefers his "freedom" to love? But really, isn't love the greatest freedom? And maybe he does love me, I know he does, he just doesn't know how to keep it. He's never lost. I have to keep remembering that.

I allow myself a fantasy: We stay together, until the day, one day, down the line, when we are fairly long married, and we decide, after enough solo shows, that I am ready for kids. After Europe and Asia, and Africa, after all those shows, I'll feel his dick, without a condom, and he'll come inside me, freely, his liquids in mine and we will, then, really be one, together, making a little something else, a mix of us. A baby. A beautiful, healthy baby. I'll have a decent belly, cute and round, popping out right in front of me like a tulip bulb. I'll touch it and sing to it, and he'll touch it and whisper sweet things. Jesus! He would freak if he knew what I was thinking, about how much I want his sperm inside me, how much I want to feel the hotness of his penis in me, him in me, in me, in me. Don't take him away.

"Good morning, *gordita*," he says quietly, his warm words on my face, breathy on my earlobe.

His hands already inside me, this is how he wakes me up from the half-waking dreams I've been brewing in bed, and soon enough there

I am, wet in his hands, his fingers buried, burrowing into my hole. Please, God, I don't want to go. I don't want to get left. I don't want to lose. I don't want to lose anymore.

After we're, once again, spent, we lie in bed for a while, in morning sleep, and I dream, again I dream. This time, with my father. There he is, sitting outside his shoe store. I walk up to him, in shock, stand in front of him, without words. Truly numb for a moment, struck dumb. He doesn't say anything either.

"But...," I finally mumble.

You're dead, I want to say. But I don't. Half because I can't and half because I'm hoping that he's not dead, that he's still alive, and words are a powerful thing. To verbalize it—You Are Dead—it might make it real. Soon, my father opens his mouth like a wooden marionette, like God is pulling his strings, and he tells me, "It was a trick, the whole thing was a trick."

He just wanted to see how much we loved him, he explains.

"Did we pass?" I ask him, angry. "In death, do we love you enough? Do we?"

I wake up in a sweat and I turn to Tony.

"Please, please don't touch me again, unless you really want me to be part of your life. Forever. Please, just don't trick me. Don't trick me. Stop tricking me. Stop it."

"I'm not tricking you, *gorda*. What are you talking about? *Yo te quiero mucho*."

"But can you stay with me? Are you going to leave again?"

"Nothing has changed," he says slowly. "We still want different things. You want marriage, and I don't think that's for me—"

"Then why did you ask me to come? Why are you doing this to me?"

He doesn't say anything, he just looks at me with his eyes glossy, like he's about to cry. But he doesn't cry, he holds it back, just like he holds everything back. He doesn't let any of it go beneath the surface or dig up from underneath. The tears won't break, his surface is too tough. But mine, mine is torn to pieces.

THE HOLE in my heart widens. I didn't think it was possible. If it gets any bigger, will the edges of my heart spread so thin that the heart will disappear completely, or will it just make Siamese holes, bound by a thread—one for Dad, one for Tony?

Two days without Tony since I told him not to touch me, and I feel like I'm on fire and like I'm hurting so much I can't stand it. I'm so thirsty, but no matter how much water I drink it doesn't go away, it's like I'm embalmed, full of salt. There is so much I can't seem to touch in my life right now, so much ground shifting from under me. In my mind: an image of the stigmata, the wounds of people who feel Christ's wounds, and I wonder why I'm thinking this except to think that it's religion's way of explaining the wounds of very deep love. I miss my father. I've missed him almost my whole life, but when he was alive he was always out there, somewhere, physically, so that there was always the hope that someday we could get back together, as father and daughter, the real thing. And maybe we did that at the end, a little, but now he's gone and the opportunity is gone to do it fully, when it was there all along. Tony is still there. Am I supposed to try harder?

LEO SHOWS up at the door dressed in a bright red T-shirt. He's got a black Yankees cap on when I open the door, but he pulls it off as soon as his eyes meet mine, revealing a clean and newly shaven head, shiny. He's neater than he was the last time I saw him, a sharpening of rough edges. But he's still got the bags under his eyes, dark circles that say he's tired, but don't reveal what he's tired of—not to strangers, not even to me.

"Hey!" he says, taking me in his arms, strong, and then loosening his grip a little. "*Artista*, you're too skinny again, it feels like sugar when I hug you, like you dissolve."

"It's the breakup diet."

"Asshole."

"Well, what can you do? You can't force people to love you." And then, feeling self-absorbed, I usher him in. "C'mon, don't just stand there, come inside, take your shoes off. Come in."

"Wow," he says, dropping his old black, dusty duffle by the door and moving around the place with a timid strut. "V, shit. You done good for yourself. This is a long way from WaHi." His eyes are such a light brown, like a delicate insect's wing. You can almost see straight through them when the light hits him, as he looks out the windows.

"Yeah, a long way," I say. But I think: it's not really mine. I didn't really make it here myself. This is my Dad's sweat, on this floor, on these walls—painted over maybe, but his pentimento shining through nonetheless.

"View's amazing, reminds me of New York a little."

"It does, doesn't it? I thought the same thing when I first saw it."

"Didn't think Miami had anything to do with our old New York."

"It doesn't."

Walking toward the windows, he looks down at the water.

"Look at that water!"

"I realized that's what I missed the most when I came back, you know. Those waves, that water, it's—"

"It's beautiful," he jumps in as I join him at the windows.

"Kind of makes you wanna drift away."

"Drift away, huh?" He makes fun, catching onto the edges of my melancholy, which is clear, apparently, despite my trying not to show it.

"Yeah. So, do you want the tour? It's short—about five seconds long."

"Okay." He laughs a little, sticking his hands in his pockets, more shy than before. A part of me knows it hasn't been long since I saw him, but another part feels like there are swamp-gulfs of time between us that can never be filled.

"You wanna drink?"

"You got a beer?"

"Presidente. Light."

"Light? Shit. Ah well, it'll do." Leo winks, which is unnervingly charming.

"I guess you're old enough now, huh?"

"Guess we've known each other a while now, V." Again, he digs his hands into his pockets. "I was thinking that when you came up, after you left. I had that long bus ride back to the apartment, and I kept thinking how long we've known each other and how much's happened. I know it's sort of old mannish to think those things, but…"

"No country for old men, remember," I say

"Right. Guess we're both getting old," he says, pausing a little. "Or getting to be old friends."

I nod, a genuine smile coming to my face, and then there's a spot of quiet, nothing except the un-suctioning pop and fizz of the bottle cap bust.

"Here you go."

"Thanks." He sips. "So? The tour?"

"Right. The tour."

AT NIGHT, I want to give Leo my bed and take the couch, but he refuses and tells me, "*Estás loca?* Uh-uh, no. My mamma raised me right, yo."

I nod.

"You know Shell would've been twenty-seven this year?"

"Wow," I say, sitting by him on the couch.

"It's funny, you know, the things you think about. I remember on his birthday this year I couldn't get this fight we had about sneakers out of my head. I was young and stupid and I used to shine my white sneaks and not want to get them dirty, just like all the other kids in the hood. I was really obsessed with them."

"I remember your white sneakers."

"Yeah. Well, Shell used to look at me shining my shoes and avoiding puddles and he used to tell me not to be a dumbass, to look at Bill Gates, who wore natty sneaks with suits, and he was a gagillionaire."

I look at Leo's shoes by the door, a pair of old Adidas, raggedy and worn.

"You know the guy who runs Basel, Sam Keller," I say, "he does the same thing—sneaks and suits. He's Swiss. They've got style." I stand up and start to make the sofa bed, swiveling a pillow into a pillow slip and fluffing.

"Do they?" he asks, immediately getting up to help me with the bed, the sheets, the pillows.

"Oh yeah. Look at my Swatch! Did I show it to you? It's new. I love it." I put my hand in his face, he smiles.

"It's white. Never seen one like that before." And then he pauses, looks at me and says, "Just be sure you don't get too whitewashed."

"Hey! I'm not whitewashed, whaddya mean, whitewa—"

"Okay, okay. But you're a nerd, that you are. Totally a nerd."

"Maybe," I say, feeling the night outside the window, filtering through, blanketing the apartment. "I want to live there, you know."

"Where?"

"In Switzerland. It's wonderful there. They tax the hell out of you, but everything is clean and straight and right."

"Opposite of America," says Leo, sitting on the newly made sofa bed, squeaking.

"Exactly." I sit across from him.

"But, hey, you know what? America isn't so bad. I mean, look at Barack, right?"

"Yeah, look at Barack."

"You think he'll make it?"

"Be our president?"

"Yeah."

"That would be something, wouldn't it?"

We look at each other for a while. Leo's still sipping the beer he's been nursing for an hour. Kid doesn't drink much, I can see that. I, on the other hand, am on my third glass of wine. I realize just then that we're smiling, both of us, at the thought that a black man could be president in America. Damn, that *is* something. It shouldn't be, but it is. And suddenly I have the goose bumps and I get excited and realize that tomorrow, when I start the third panel, I have to get some hope, of some kind, in there.

Eventually, I give up trying to convince Leo to take the bed and give in to the fact that he'll be sleeping on an uncomfortable sofa bed that pricks his back for over a week, until we're good and done with our collaboration, until after the show opens and, two days later, he hits the road again, on his way back to the Big Apple.

I hand him another pillow, a towel, an extra blanket, and the freedom to take whatever he wants from any corner of the house.

"So tomorrow, we wake up and get to work around six. Is that good for you?"

"I say that's what I'm here for."

"And then, in the middle of the day, when we're dripping in paint and theory and art, we take a little break and I'll take you to one of those hole-in-the-wall places on Calle Ocho where the food's like it's been stewing in your grandmother's kitchen for days."

"Sounds like *un sueño*, V. I can't believe I'm here."

"I think you'll like it here."

"I already do."

LYING IN bed, I look out into the darkness, unable to see the water. The only thing visible in the window is a reflection of my room, and distant lights like cricket glows. I wonder what Monet's cathedral would have looked like, had he painted it in this light.

"V, SHIT, what time is it?"

"Sorry," I whisper. "Am I being too noisy?"

My hands are on Maman's screen as I shift it around.

"That depends. What time is it?"

Leo is groggy and hoarse and he looks like a little boy sitting there, sheets over his body, squinting. I think of his mother again and how her hands wanted to fix things for him, knot his ties for all his days without Shell, and without her, when the time came. And suddenly the flowers I was planning for the third panel, the wild bloom, begin to wilt and I wonder how it will turn out, with all these things rushing through me.

"It's 5:30," I say.

"I thought you said six! I set my phone for six."

"Yeah, sorry, I just wanted to carve out a spot for you to work, you know, because our process is going to be different. I mean, you're gonna have to be on my laptop editing the videos and the pictures and I'm gonna be full of paint, over here, right next to you, so I just wanted to—Sorry, forget it, just go back to sleep."

"It's cool, *artista*, I'm up, I'm up. Art's about discipline, right? All about discipline."

"Yeah, I guess that's right."

"See, I remember almost everything you used to babble about when I'd go borrow your books."

I can't think of anything to say except, "Want coffee?"

"Yeah."

In the kitchen, making the coffee, I can't help thinking about Tony. Heat the milk: a minute and twenty-three seconds in the microwave, skim off the top of the milk (Tony doesn't like that part), eat the creamy top layer from the spoon, then one spoon of Nescafé, one spoon of sugar, and when it's a light *café con leche* brown, a sprinkle of coffee right on top that'll stay at the surface and look like cinnamon.

I told Tony not to call. Unless he decided he wanted to spend the rest of his life with me. Told him Leo was coming and I'd be working straight until the opening. He hasn't called. Shit, how I miss him, just now, his smell and his "Good morning" and his eyes and his auburn beard, glinting in the sun. If we moved to Switzerland together he could let his beard grow until he looked like a Viking, and I could nuzzle my face in it because it would lose its prickly feel, so long and bushy and orange-red. The half-wild, half-wilting flowers of *Altar Piece* gather the pollen of Tony's beard.

I have to force myself to stop thinking about him, and get back to Leo, who's come so far to bring his video to my—our—installation. New York to Basel.

"Okay, here you go." I hand Leo a white mug.

"What about you?"

"I don't drink coffee."

"I feel like a *chulo*."

"Don't. It's my pleasure. If you like it, I'll make it like that every morning. If you want more milk, less sugar, or more sugar and less milk, just tell me, I'll shift the recipe around a bit tomorrow."

Leo laughs. "The recipe, huh."

WE AGREE that the collaboration will be like this: I will work on *Altar Piece* and *Altar Piece* will, in the end, lean on one of the walls. My father's sewn shirts will air-balloon in the middle of the room with my amulets sewn on the inside of the balloon. Then there will be Shell's chair, linked to the balloon (the chair is being shipped over—Leo mailed it so he wouldn't have to carry it on the plane). The chair segues straight into Leo's work and gives Leo two walls to project the images of the video he took at the tip of Manhattan. He'll have to edit them, decide their size and colors, give it a title. On a small, podium-like table, lit with a single spotlight from above, there will be *Shell's Journal*, which people will be able to read through. We agree they will be able to do this with their hands, without gloves. None of that archival bullshit. This will be something you can touch, leave your prints on.

We work with our backs to each other. He's working on editing his project, I'm working on panel 3. The show is in less than a week.

"I'm calling my video *The Manhattan Project*," he says.

"That's a great title."

"I was thinking about applying to Columbia and I was reading about things that went on there and how they made the A-bomb there in a basement or something, and it was called the Manhattan Project, so I thought why not call it that."

"It's a great title. Really good. Wait, wait, did you say you're applying to Columbia?"

"Yeah. I'm gonna be kind of old for a freshman, but who cares, I guess. I'll be that cool transfer student that took some time off or something, right? I been working on my application, and I'm thinking I should write my essay about this project." As soon as he finishes saying this, I remember Shell was going to apply to Columbia after a couple of years at City College.

"I'm so happy, Leo." Without realizing it, I'm jumping up and down and hugging him. Inside, I'm saying a little prayer that we can sell his piece at the show so he can take the cash with him for Columbia.

"They haven't accepted me yet or anything, relax. And anyway I was thinking, you know, since you're an alum and I'm gonna need two recommendations, if you would—"

"Yes! Yes. Absolutely, yes!"

I hug him tight again, until he stops me and says, "Okay, okay, back to work, back to work! You gotta finish that third panel so you can let it rot."

The other two panels are rotting well, but I'll have to rush this one, pour something on it to quicken the process.

The third panel blooms, dies, and blooms again, all in a matter of hours. Petals appear everywhere. Wilting, tilting flowers, some are bright and alive and others growing back: all of them blazing.

THE CURTAIN rises on another day. I make Leo's coffee. He's cheerful and clicking away at his computer. Groggy eyes and happy heart, pacing to the rhythm of possibility. Crack and peel my morning banana—potassium. And then it's back to the painting board, flipping through the exhibit catalogue for *Painting at the Edge of the World*. I am drawn in by Julie Mehretu's painting *Dispersion*. Hers is the language that makes sense now, the opposite of one-point perspective. The microchip, dust and debris. Douglas Fogle, the curator of *Painting at the Edge of the World*, writes, "Painting has never gone away, but, like a virus exposed to an antibiotic, has mutated, importing its genetic code on an entire new generation of descendants....Why do painters still paint? For me the reason is clear. Because the world is flat."

Brilliant.

Flat as a flat-screen plasma and a computer monitor.

Flat as Google's homepage, deceptively simple—the problem with globalization. Primary colors, with an empty, blank slate, a virtual window that leads you into a world, the result of complex programming hiding beneath the surface. Maybe if I'd never gotten those one hundred color crayons from Papan, this would all be different and I wouldn't be able to understand that behind the blue, red, yellow, and green, there's magenta and a rusted ochre, and a lavender the color of a wind-blown day in Switzerland.

(Basel!)

The twenty-first century—our fractured, blurred, pixilated window onto the world. So many options, which one is true? Does painting have power? How can it represent the world?

To write poetry after Auschwitz, says Adorno, *is barbaric.*

Is it?

The trace of my hand across the canvas.

Marlene Dumas writes that "Painting is about the trace of the human touch," that's what makes it better than any other flat plane. The fact that a hand has been there, loved it, and is now loving you as you take in the painting.

"You know what's really cute, V?"

"What?"

"You drool when you paint. You get really into it and you drool."

"Great."

"No, seriously, it's really cute. I always wonder what you're thinking, it's like I can almost hear your little wheels turning. Right when you start and you're staring at your painting or a book, your tongue sticks out of the side of your mouth. I love it."

FOR DAYS we work like this. Work, work, break, work, work, work, booze, snooze. I reach for books on the shelves. Sol LeWitt, Paula Rego, Picasso, then all the abstract expressionists, and all the collage monkeys, and Van Gogh. It's partly Van Gogh's fault, the wilting flowers in the third panel, I know it. Sometimes I open a book and get that feeling that makes my brainwaves ram into each other, bursting. It's this feeling of joy, pure and simple. Something like: how in the world did a human make that, that mark, tight, right there, unjamming a portal door somewhere, stretching its sketch into a keyhole and: magic. How in the world were those colors mixed—layered, layered, and more layered? That line, what the fuck—did it come, suspended on a golden chain, straight from heaven, like perfect vertical grace landing on canvas? When that happens, I grunt and pass the book back, over my shoulder. Leo knows to take it and look at the pages, the ones marked with my drool.

"Motherfucker," he'll say, slamming the book down after staring at the marked pages.

"Exactly."

We don't look at each other—eye contact is almost only at lunch and during the time before sleep, during our nightly booze before the snooze.

ONE DAY, for lunch, we eat in Little Haiti, but it's not Haitian food, it's Dominican. It's all a jumble, Miami. Crossword puzzle without clues. Sometimes it's hard to match the letters vertically and horizontally to make words and sense of the whole thing.

"How do you know so many of these places?" Leo asks me when we get to the dive.

"My father, he used to love *fondas*," I say, stopping to point at a table by an open window. "What about that one?"

"What are *fondas*?"

"Just all these places, home-cooked, look like kitchens and they only have one dish."

"So your dad used to take you slummin'?"

"I guess." I laugh. "We used to go to Cuban *fondas* all the time, which I hated. He wanted us to love them like he loved them."

"But you wanted McDonald's."

"Exactly. Or, I don't know, even French food would've been better."

"Brat."

"A little. But then it was weird because when the Cuban *fondas* started disappearing, my father would get really pissed off and say, 'This is Little Honduras now, not Little Havana,' and he'd get cranky and he'd do something weird like take us on the highway and say, 'Fuck this, let's find a Cracker Barrel.'"

"The hick place?"

"Right. It was so weird. But then he'd get all excited about the 'American' food and the 'country steaks.'"

"He had him some crossed brain cables."

"And then later, he'd turn around and fall for a Colombian girl and pick up her accent. Or we'd be driving in Little Havana and he'd take me and Nina to a Mexican joint without any doors and bare concrete for floor and tell us, 'Eat up, girls, this is the real deal. It's not Taco Bell, right, *güey*?' And he'd look at the Mexican waiter, who seemed to know and love him and who gave us free *cervezas*. And then my father would overtip the waiter like there was no tomorrow. 'Poor guy,' he'd say, when we were leaving, getting into the car. 'I remember that shit. *Un americano de mierda* spit on my mother once, can you believe that?' He'd say things like that, out of the blue, and everything would make sense."

The dish at the Dominican place is *gallina*, which is basically chicken, but from looking around at the other patrons' plates, it's like they caught it in the back, cut its head off, plucked it, cooked it, and served it up right there. Leo places an order of *gallina*, but I stick to some fresh-squeezed juice, papaya and orange, lots of pulp. There's no ice and no dessert in this place, and there are flies buzzing around the kitchen. Looks like a shantytown off a roadside in Africa, or in the Caribbean, and it looks like whoever the owner is, he put the thing together himself, nail-and-hammering pieces of wood, coloring them in a turquoise and pink afterwards. But it's great, and I know Leo likes it. He's got a smile wide as a country meadow on his face.

"You're so weird, V, you bring me to these joints and then you don't eat."

"I like being here more than I like the food. Like cooking shows. Watching somebody cook is like watching somebody make a painting."

"Funny how this shithole is home for so many people, you know," says Leo.

"Yeah."

"I mean, look at that guy, it's like he doesn't even belong in Miami, but here he is. In this place he merges with the furniture and the plants. Could be my damn *abuelo*, sittin' on his back porch in La Dominicana." The old man Leo's looking at—old blue T-shirt, faded red cap, *gallina* in hand—is swallowing memory, right here, an oasis in the middle of a foreign city.

THAT NIGHT, staring at *Altar Piece*, wine in my hand, beer in Leo's, Leo asks, "You miss him?"

"Which one?"

"Both."

"More than I thought I could, but each of them differently."

"Yeah. One's never coming back."

"And the other one's out there somewhere, with a part of me."

THE MORNING of the opening, the sound of a Frank Sinatra belt is coming from next door. I wake up to it but stay snuggled in bed for a while, letting Frank take me to the moon on an imagined snaky trail of 1960s cigarette smoke. It reminds me of the man who moved in next to Maman after *la vieja* Leonor died. The tenor who would hardly ever practice in his house, he would leave early in the morning to what I imagined was a rehearsal room. Or, now that I think of it, maybe he was just going to his day job. Usually, inside his house, he just played scratchy records of foreign voices and unfamiliar Italian stories told in song. Sometimes, though, he would wake me and Papan up, singing really early in the morning, and I would rush to the window and open the old wooden blinds and we would watch him, listening through the gardenias Maman had planted in memory of *la vieja* Leonor.

For some reason, John next door, an ex-actor-turned-lawyer, has decided that instead of his usual techno, he's going to play some Sinatra today. It seems appropriate somehow. Just three days ago Leo and I delivered the work—paintings, balloon installation parts, journal, and projections. And just last night we'd finally finished installing the balloon, tired and chewed-up as tobacco. Listening to the clarity of Sinatra's voice, I dance out of bed. For a second Frank makes me doubt myself, makes me wonder why I'm a painter and how it is I wasn't made a trumpeter or a composer who could read the ant-like patterns of scores. And then I realize that it's because I was meant to see the world in color, translate Sinatra into a great big promising splat of yellow paint. And also perhaps because my father never taught me to read the music he loved, because he didn't know how.

Leo was so excited last night, like he was about to fly to the moon and back.

As soon as I walk into the living room, there's the sofa bed, perfectly made up already, and Leo's picked up the leftovers from last night's celebratory mess. Yesterday we'd picnicked on the floor, raising glasses and chiming, "To tomorrow!"

"So, today's the big day," I say as soon as I see him, near the bathroom door.

"Good morning, *artista*," he says, blue boxers and a white v-neck on, beaming like a headlight, bright and neon, reaching for the razor.

"Good morning, *artista*," I giggle in my PJs. I feel like a ten-year-old on her way to Disney. And not because I haven't been before, but because I get to show Nina the good stuff—the rides that are worth the wait and the ones that aren't.

"Ha!" Leo says, razor fisted in his hand. "I guess today I *am* an *artista*."

I laugh. "That you are. That you are."

I'm filled with the desire to take Leo in my arms and say thank you. But he beats me to it. He turns from the bathroom, dropping his razor, and runs into the kitchen and comes out with a white African daisy and a bowl of strawberries.

"Thank you, V," he says, gifting me.

"Oh, Leo, you're, you're just the best ever."

"I was watching the Discovery channel about how in Denmark they have this thing called *hygge* and its supposed to mean cozy and warm or something, it's not really translatable, but they were saying how they have strawberries in the street for sale on the honor system, things like that, like you can take a strawberry and then just leave some money." He's panting and ranting and it looks like his heart is going to pop out of his chest and fall straight into my hand, painting the daisy red. "And the strawberries they showed on TV, I mean they weren't like this, they were so ripe-looking, I wish I could've gotten some of those for you." Leo stops for a moment. "It's funny, looking at the strawberries I kept thinking, shit, I haven't seen the world."

"I love strawberries," I say, biting into a really soft and juicy one, no bitterness at all, no pit, just the most tender thing. I'm dripping.

"I know you love them. How could I forget."

"Forget what?"

"Remember the year you showed me the cherry blossoms in Brooklyn, how we went to eat after, and I thought you were so weird because we went to Yaffa Café and all you ordered was a bowl of strawberries and a Bloody Mary?"

"I don't remember that."

"I do. I wrote a poem about it."

"You never showed me that! Do you have it? Can I read it?"

"Not until you show me the drawing of my mother's hands."

"I'll show you now." I say this running to the box I know it's in.

LEO STARES at the simple line drawing, his eyes red, like if they were cloth, they'd be bursting at the seams, verging on a break, but not quite. There's that thing I told Dad about Rothko, and for a minute I wonder whether I don't have everything I wanted. How can I feel so lucky and so empty at the same time? Last night I went to bed thinking that I didn't want to go through with the actual opening. All the work was done already, what was the point? But I have to go, because of Leo. For Leo. Then, snapping out of thought, without thinking too much about it, I knock on the wall: "Hey, John!"

No response.

"Hey! John!"

"Yeah," replies a distant echo.

"Turn it up, we wanna dance."

John turns up the volume and I put the strawberries aside, take Leo in my arms and we start to waltz to "They Can't Take That Away from Me."

I start to sing along, miming the lyrics of the song with silly abandon. Crooking my pinky out, mocking a tea drinker, taking off an invisible hat. We're totally committed to the dance. Leo can dance to anything, pouring all of himself into the movements with a smile as big as Mars on his face.

"You can't sing for shit!" yells Leo, over my voice and Sinatra's.

"I know!" I laugh up a genuine guffaw of a laugh, straight from the gut. It hurts. "But who cares?"

Leo dips me and I dip him. And then he joins me in the singing. And like that, with all the childish soulfulness that comes with the dips and dives of dancing, we tell one another the way we've changed each other's lives.

At the end of the dance, we stand looking at each other and bow, like two kids at cotillion. And then "My Way," Dad's favorite Sinatra tune comes on, and now it's me who's bursting at the seams.

"Hey, come here." Lee whispers me over, pulling at my hot pink silk shirt, bought just for the occasion. Magenta, but brighter. She's balancing two glasses of champagne in her right hand. "Take one."

"Hay is for horses, Lee."

"Yeah, well then neigh, neigh, neigh, and clink, clink," says Lee, holding up her glass. "You did it, kiddo, you did it. There were times you scared me a little, didn't think it was going to happen, but..." She's nodding now, a strange old-fashioned sage-nod that makes me feel tenderness for her somehow. She didn't drop me. She stuck with.

"I know," I say, already a little tipsy. "There were times there I didn't think I'd make it either. But, well... To Basel!" I watch Leo just a few feet away, surrounded as he is, in front of his *Manhattan Project*, next to Dia, who Lee has assigned to the piece. "Sell it," she'd told Dia in front of me. "I'm going to be really busy with Veronica's work, I need you to be in charge of the kid's." Dia, looking a little scared, took up the baton, straightened her shirt, and said, "Okay."

A swarm of skinny, mothy girls in soft skirts and flowing hair flutter around Leo, drawn to his gleam, buzzing at the gem of him, fluorescent in his yellow polo.

"Not just to Basel, much more than that, hon," says Lee, drawing me out of my small spell.

"Yeah, what can be more than Basel?"

"Jesus, kid, ice to an Eskimo, remember?"

"What? You sold something? It's been fifteen minutes."

"Fifteen minutes. *Altar Piece*. Bam. Sold. Done. New record. Buzz is creation, my dear, and I've just put out the hive. Plus I'm on the brink of lining up two solo shows for you for next year. International. Geneva and London. Those aren't definite yet, but probable. Meetings tomorrow. Tell me you love me. No, wait, wait, don't tell me yet, wait till I tell you who bought *Altar Piece* and then tell me you love me."

"Who?" My heart is beating like a set of maracas in the middle of a cha-cha-cha.

"Who bought it, Lee? Don't leave me hanging, it's cruel."

Lee's playing hard to get, watching me suffer. Smiling like it's the end of the world and she's been given some special pardon that will wipe away her sins. Then she points her long, hibiscus-pink-nail-polished finger toward *Altar Piece*. In front of the painting are—

"The Romells? You sold it to the Romells?" A wave of shock runs over me, and then a tingle, like when your leg has been numb and the feeling starts to come back, tiny sparkles all over me.

"You can make out with me now, thank you."

I take her cheeks in between my hands on impulse and I kiss her on the lips, fast, and full of suction. Lee's cracking up inside, I can see it, but she feigns calm; she's better at hiding it than me. "Now I have to go re-do my lipstick," she says.

"What a pro, Lee, my God, I can't believe they liked it. I thought because the title made reference to religion that it would be that much harder to sell. I don't know what to say." It's hard to pinpoint another rush like this. My first big-time sell. The thing that will lead to museums. I try to calm down, but my breath loses pattern, a train off its rails.

"You're welcome."

"Thank you, Lee." I touch Lee's arm and she winks at me, looking down at the oversized Rolex on my wrist. But she doesn't say anything about the watch—she knows better. Instead, she points to the flower in my hair and says, "Nice touch, by the way."

"Thanks. It was a present."

"From? You're not back with what's-his-face, are you?"

"No."

"Good. He's an asshole."

"Who said he was an asshole?"

"You did."

"It's from Leo."

"Oooh." Lee looks at me askew.

"It's not like that. And speaking of Leo, any nibbles on his piece?"

"Not yet. His is a harder sell. I'll have to help Dia in a little, she's new at all this. She's hanging in, but she's green. Nobody knows who the hell he is. And you know people forget what they read in the paper in three seconds flat. But don't worry, he'll get a nibble, even if it's from me." Lee's eyes look over at Leo, up and down, as she sips her champagne.

"Down, poodle, down."

"Oh stop it, he's adorable. But don't worry, I know my boundaries."

"We're not fucking, Lee."

"Really?" She looks at me like I'm lying.

"Really, I'm not lying. We're not fucking."

"But he's been staying at your place."

"On my couch."

"Hmm. Interesting."

"Just sell him."

"Oh, don't you worry, the night is young." Lee starts straightening up, her line of vision shooting over me. "See the Scholtzs over there looking at *Balloon*, next to David Horvitz and Francie Bishop Good? I better go talk to them. I might call you in for backup. In the meantime, go talk to your new collectors." She winks and points to the Romells.

The Romells have moved away from the painting toward the center of the room, amid circles of strangers drinking champagne. I can't believe all these people are here for me, for us.

"I gave them the summary of what it's about," says Lee, "but they'll want to hear something from you. So go."

"Okay, I'm going, I'm going," I say, lifting my glass. "To the youthful night."

"Cheers." We touch glasses again. Lee sips slowly, her glass basically full (I know she'll nurse that thing for the rest of the night). And off to work she goes, the wonderful wizard of Oz.

Dave and Martina Romell are standing right in front of me — prim and proper and rich. I'm petrified.

"What was the inspiration for the piece?" asks Martina, all in black, sharp in her hip, plastic-rimmed glasses, big, red wooden bracelet circling her wrists. Obviously the woman knows a thing or two about aesthetics. Plus, she looks like a nice person. I shouldn't be scared of her.

For the price they've paid they can ask me my Social Security number for all I care. But I hate this part, this talking about the art. They're going to hate me and then they're going to hate the painting. They'll think I'm retarded and weird and socially awkward and then they'll go ask Lee what the warranty is for *Altar Piece*, and there will be none, and they'll despise the painting even more and never show it in their collection.

Combing all of my registered vocabulary, I finally fumble across:

"It's hard to put into words, because it's such a different language — painting. All art is translation, but with literature it's always easier to talk about because there aren't so many layers of translation. What I mean is, literature is still made of words, not marks. Well, sort of, but getting into that would be getting into semantics. And yet, somehow, mark-making was our first form of communication, so I should be able to talk about it, it's just... Well, it's a different animal." Am I boring them to death?

"Interesting," says a woman's voice that, just seconds before, wasn't even in the conversation. "Hi, sorry, I couldn't help but overhear. I'm an arts writer. I write for the *Miami Herald*."

"Oh, hi. Nice to meet you," I say.

"I'm doing a story on your show. I've been talking to Lee and Dia, but I'd like to get a bit of your voice in the piece, if you don't mind."

"Oh, okay, great," I say, more excited than I'm letting myself show. *Stay cool, cat* repeats in my head as if I were a beatnik or something. I have no idea why. It's *Stay cool, cat* and *Stay cool, cat*, on a loop in my brain.

"You mind if I listen in?"

"No, no," I tell her, trying to draw my confidence back up.

"These are the Romells," I say stupidly, immediately regretting it, as if I'm the only one who knows them, when we just met three seconds ago.

"Yes, we've met, nice to see you again," says the reporter, graciously. "So you bought *Altar Piece?*"

"Yes. It's beautiful," says Dave, "plus Chris told us to do it. We do everything he tells us to."

Chris Kotze. Curates their collection. South African. Art snob. Thank God for Chris.

"So you were saying?" asks the reporter. "About language and how painting is another language and—"

"Oh, I was just—" and then my heart stops. Right there.

Stop.

It drops the cha-cha-cha, the arrhythmic blues, the patternless jargon, it just plain stops as I see him, green-eyed and smartly dressed in a baby-blue long-sleeved shirt: Tony. He's let his beard grow. Is that for me? Why is he here? He sees me, waves. I wave back, softly, almost imperceptibly.

"It's like the things that connect us, they're so thin and so delicate," I say, flipping my attention back to the Romells and the reporter. "But they're made of something gold that shines somehow, that's why I sewed those polos together with thread that looks like it could break easily—but it won't break, it's stronger than it looks, just like a diamond. That's in the other piece over there, in *Balloon*. But there are similar ideas in the pieces, in dialogue with each other, hashing things out."

"And why those shirts?" Martina asks.

"They were my father's. He passed away several months ago." Dad, who slipped away and covered himself in tents of ballooning flesh, so he didn't have to feel his losses, the things that slipped through his fingers, the yellow glow he couldn't touch, or keep or— "And I wanted to project what loss feels like in these pieces, in the whole show, really. Which is hard to do. And which is why I felt like I had to forcefully age *Altar Piece*, rush it into ruin."

"I'm not sure if I should bring this up," says the reporter, "but it all reminds me a little bit of Albert Speer. You know his theory about ruin? Did you have that in mind at all, or am I just completely off?"

Albert Speer: Hitler's architect, who took into account what his buildings would look like ruined as he was conceptualizing them. In other words, he thought about what would happen to them once time had passed and ravaged them, what kind of "monument" he would leave behind, thereby infusing them with the self-importance of their future—ruin value. I didn't want to go there, not directly. Because of fear the Romells would take it the wrong way. It was bad enough there was religion involved, and politics, but now this mention of the Holocaust. Never mention Hitler while selling art (unless you're a Hollywood producer). But it was true, I'd come across it. *Ruinenwerttheorie*. Speer and Adorno. And the way it all blends and builds—theories one on top of the other, the way our minds work.

"Yes. I did think about that. And that's the thing, that dangerous line of human creation, right? How the things we build, our monuments, can leave prints and crumble, how they can sing out in glory or they can obliterate so thoroughly, so horribly. That's why I asked my friend Leo to bring what he did down at Ground Zero." Leo's performance amid ruins, most of which have been completely picked up and erased, not left to awe passersby like Rome's ancient shards of empire sitting, anything but dormant, next to soccer-fan graffiti and tourist gelato shops. Melted metal isn't marble. Although soon there might be a memorial—and what exactly did that do? Or mean?

"So," I continue, "the whole thing is connected then by this idea of loss, on both a small and large scale."

"Is there such a thing as small loss, really, especially in death?" asks Martina, and suddenly I'm glad she's the one who will own *Altar Piece*. It's a good feeling, that click.

"That's right, I don't think there is," I say, looking behind them at *Altar Piece*, on the other side of the room, which is no longer mine, but theirs, which will live out its days of life and ruin somewhere else entirely, and perhaps most of its years in an art storage bin that tries to prevent, paradoxically, ruin.

"I also get a strange hopeful feeling, somehow, when I look at *Altar Piece*," says Martina, longing for a positive edge to all these hard angles.

"Yes. *Altar Piece* is the piece of *Remnants and Ruins* that is both most glowing and most sad for me." As I keep talking to the Romells I can see Tony still standing in the background, hands in his pockets. He's been watching, his eyes burning into me. "It's the piece I love the most in the show," I say, "because it's the piece I got my hands most dirty in." Gloves of red paint surfacing after sinking into skin and love and loss and failure, palpable somehow in paint. Altar pieces in old cathedrals, always painting our heavens, hells, and purgatories. "There are so many layers," I say, "I can go on forever." Excavating, discovering, plowing, planting. "But that's the germ of it, anyway."

"Thank you," says the reporter.

"No," I say, "thank you."

I search the room for Leo, who's standing by Lee now, Dia having switched places with her and taken her own spot by *Balloon*. Lee's getting closer and closer to Leo, slowly erasing personal space. Not that Leo's little Dominican self has much of that anyway. He's okay. A sweep across the gallery, and Tony's still standing alone.

"If you'll excuse me, I've just seen someone I know, and—"

"Don't worry, dear," says Martina. "Enjoy your opening, congratulations. We're very happy with the piece."

"Do you mind if Chris gives you a ring," Dave says, "so you can tell him everything you've been telling us, maybe a little more? For our catalogue. I'm sure he'll want to include you."

"Of course, absolutely, anytime," I say, handing the Romells my card.

Soon enough, I'm walking toward Tony, without thinking, just one foot in front of another until we meet, right in front of my painting. All roads, it seems, lead to *Altar Piece*.

"Wow," he says, "it turned out wonderful. *Está lindo el cuadro. Estás linda tú.*"

"I sold it. To the Romells," I say, ignoring the compliment about how pretty I look. His eyes are red. He looks tired.

"Congratulations, *gordita*." He's been around me enough to know who the Romells are, what they mean.

God I want to hit him. *Gordita. Gordita.* How dare he?

"This is it, you made it," he says, proud and smiling, and sad.

God I want to jump him. *Mi amor.*

His beard is glowing red. The gesture of growing it, brittle bits of sawgrass touched by spotlights. I want to paint him.

We stand, quiet for a bit.

"You want champagne?" I ask him, knowing he'll say yes, about to turn around to get him some, when suddenly Leo is beside me, touching my upper arm.

"Is everything okay?" asks Leo.

"Oh, it's fine. Leo, this is Tony. Tony, Leo."

"I've heard a lot about you," says Tony, extending his hand. Leo takes it grudgingly.

"Uh-huh. Yeah, I've heard some things about you too."

"Not all bad, I hope." Tony is bad at banter. He just says this because he thinks it's what he has to say, but it doesn't seem right coming out of his mouth.

Again, a moment of silence. This one nervous.

"I'm gonna go get us all some champagne," I say, smirking.

"Let me," says Tony. "Would you like some too, Leo?"

"No, that's all right." Leo's standing like a tough guy now.

"Nothing?"

Leo gives a subtle shake, no, and Tony walks toward the bar.

"Leo, it's fine," I say.

"Really?"

"Go and be with your fans. Look at them! They're waiting. Go sell that thing. Plus, look at Lee, she's over there by Mike Mantellis—he buys lots of new photo and video and digital stuff. Go talk to them."

"Okay. Who the hell is Mike Mantellis?"

"Don't worry, just be yourself. Guy's loaded up the ass, but talks like he's from Brooklyn. He's a developer, I think. Just go. He'll like you."

"Okay, V, but you just say the word and I'm here by your side." Leo looks me straight in the eye, then gives me a kiss on the cheek. Walking away, he points to his surroundings with both hands, grins, and says, "I can get used to this."

"*Gordita*," Tony says, handing me a flute of champagne, "the Captain asked me if we wanted to go sailing tomorrow. We never got to go. Remember we had planned to, when you got back from New York?"

"You want to go sailing?"

"Tomorrow."

"I don't know."

"I told him yes already."

"I'm not sure that's a good idea. For us to be—"

"We're leaving at ten in the morning, through the afternoon. Might even catch a sunset."

"What are you doing?"

"Inviting you to go sailing."

"And?"

"I just want you to come with me. *Te extraño.*"

"Let me think about it."

"That woman is calling you," Tony says, pointing at a gently waving Lee, who is summoning me.

"Those are the Scholtzs," I say. "She told me she might need me to talk about the other piece."

"What other piece?"

"That one, the balloon one," I say, pointing to the center installation.

"The sewn-up shirts? They're gonna buy *that*?"

My father, made up of patches, the pieces of a man about to float above it all. Tony's wearing his old familiar face, a confused grimace that used to hurt me but that I don't care about anymore. He can deal with the two-dimensional surface of *Altar Piece*, but give him more and he drowns, shoves it off.

"They might. I gotta go."

"Okay, *gordita. Suerte. Véndelo.*"

"I know where the Captain's slip is. If I'm not there by ten, leave without me."

When I turn back toward the Scholtzs, who have now wandered toward Leo's piece with Lee as their guide, I see Nina. She's standing inside *Balloon*, Dad's shirts distending above her like the inside of a belly. She has a group of people around her, waiting their turn to walk inside the balloon and look up. But Nina doesn't budge, she just stays there, incubating. Her hands reach up toward the amulets and Dia turns to tell her to be careful, thinking it's just a young woman pulling at the drawings, drawstrings that might bring the whole installation to pieces, but then she sees it's my sister and she lets it be. Mom leaves Vic by the champagne and squiggles through toward Nina, both of us walking across the room from opposite directions toward the center, where we can feel the unseen throb of Nina's sting radiating toward us.

"You didn't tell me you were going to use his shirts," Nina says, her eyes red with a wash of something I can't peel back and read. I can't tell if she's angry at me or whether she just wants to keep this balloon forever, prevent me from selling it to anyone else, fly up and out somewhere she's never been, some shard of sky. I suddenly realize that I've been selfish to do this. She'd seen Dad in every single one of those shirts, some I'd never seen him wear. For Nina, there was a time and place linked to each one, a dinner, a story, Dad's hand brushing his belly, cleaning off breadcrumbs, laughing at his own jokes, charming those around him, pulling them into his orbit. I had missed so many of those times, had pulled away from the particular power of his gravity, and our velocity. To not tell Nina what I was doing with the shirts, to take it upon myself to tear, and thread, puncture, wound, and mend these remains. How could I have been so insulated, so inside myself to not realize or care or understand, when I was building this stupid balloon, that she too was a beneficiary, in every sense of that word? His daughter. She too deserved to be draped in what was left of him and build with it her own particular temple. I had stolen from her.

"Are you angry?" I ask, fearing a lash from her I would deserve. Mom is standing across from me, at Nina's other side, across the hot-air balloon, her hand touching Nina's on the rim of Shell's empty chair. She's just staring at us, like she has no way of telling us that we have no idea, not a clue, what true empathy means, what it means to feel another's pain and mix it with one's own—that we will not know until we have kids, this ache, this extension of heart and self, of feeling reverberating, it's written all over her face.

Dia is keeping the Scholtzs away while we three regroup, the old trinity. Which surprises me, because this scene would turn, after all, to be an excellent selling point if marketed correctly. But Dia is kind above anything else.

"Nina, I'm sorry."

Nina does not respond, she doesn't even look at me. She just stands there. Inside. Me and Mom on the outside. A halo of space around us, Vic nearby but on the periphery watching us, not daring to come over to touch the chair, the shirts. He will hold my mother, after. He will drive them, Nina and Mom, home, and they will all three drink Cuban coffee at the *cafetería* near Mom's. Vic's thoughts are easier to read, they too radiate out instead of in.

Eventually, Nina steps out of *Balloon*'s orb and kisses me on the cheek. "I half expected it to lift off and disappear when I stopped touching it," she says. As if her hand's weight were the only thing anchoring it.

Vic joins us as soon as Nina walks away from the balloon, as if he's been waiting for his cue. Nina couldn't have been there more than five minutes, but it feels as though time has managed the impossible, slowed and wavered through space's structure, like cells under a microscope, an amorphous amoeba.

Mom and Nina and Vic spend almost three hours by my side after that, eyes watering, as I introduce them to all the collectors, artists, dealers, writers. "I'm so proud of you," Mom says before she leaves. "You are a superstar," Vic whispers in my ear. But I still can't tell if that's good thing or a bad thing.

It's one in the morning now and it's just me, Lee, Leo, and a couple of stragglers. Lee's sent Dia to one of the after-parties, to mingle and schmooze, represent the gallery. We're standing at the back of the gallery, looking toward the door, Lee sandwiched between us. *Altar Piece* sold and she has nibbles and a list of possibilities for the other two pieces. She's sure we'll get somewhere with them by the time the fair is over.

"You're a supreme honorable beast, Lee," I tell her, nudging her with my shoulder. "You packed the place."

"*Una bestia*," says Leo, nudging her at the other side.

"I am. That I am. A *bess-tee-a*." Even Lee is a little drunk by now, talking in her thick American accent, tying to invite Spanish to fit in her mouth, roaring. "*Bestia*. Rooaaar!"

"'*Ta loca la americana*."

Lee taps him with her angular hip. "What did you say?"

"Don't worry about it, honey," says Leo, taking her hand and kissing it.

I've never seen Leo be so forward. I wonder also why he's chosen Lee over Dia, who is more familiar, younger—and maybe it is precisely that, this one's a challenge, an adventure, an *americana*. I guess this forwardness, this is the way he is with other women. I get a sharp pang in my stomach—the green-eyed monster lurching with its grizzly bite, surprising me. But no, it's better this way, just friends.

"You honey-ing me?" says Lee, bedroom-eyeing him.

"*Mi miel, mi dulce miel.*"

Jesus.

"So, darling," says Lee, looking at me like she's gonna cum in her pants if I don't give them some time alone. "I'll email you a schedule of the two meetings you have tomorrow and then we'll talk in the afternoon, especially about trying to nail those solos abroad. And you might have to talk to the Scholtzs also a bit more, they're not totally convinced about *Balloon* yet, but they might be swayed, I think, if we hit them up right. Unless someone else bites harder first. Meanwhile, I'll talk to the other collectors interested."

I nod. "Okay, tomorrow night." I know I will have to learn to talk about *Balloon* better. That I will have to catch my sister's image inside that balloon and manage to tell the Scholtzs about it. Because in the end that's the point, isn't it? To make them feel, make time slow down, the way it had for me and Mom and Nina just a few hours ago.

"Meanwhile," Lee says, "I'm taking little Leo home with me."

"Oh really?" I say, forcing a devilish look.

"If that's okay with you, V?" Leo looks at me earnestly, as if asking permission, like if I said no, he'd skip it altogether, stay with me the night.

"No, it's fine. Totally fine." I can hardly keep a straight face as I kiss both of them on the cheek. "Have fun." There's a mix of sting and amusement rolling around inside me.

"You should go to an after-party or two," says Lee. "We're hitting a few before we hit the sack."

"No, I've had enough excitement for one night. There are still two, three more nights of parties. I'll make a lot of them tomorrow."

I start walking toward the door, with this mixture of feelings inside me, all laced with exhaustion. As I step closer to the open door, a cool breeze hits me, Miami in December, seventy degrees. Lee kept complaining about the heat, telling Dia to put the AC the lowest it would go, "coldest it'll go, these people are going to melt." But I thought it was perfect. I always thought walking on a cloud was a cliché because I'd never felt anything like it. But now it's as if I'm drifting. Bounce, bounce, bounce. Soft and mellow and breezy. No rain. A rush of something sacred and quiet running through my veins. I turn around and wave backwards at Lee and Leo—a complete sense of comfort making its way through my body, because, after all, isn't this the life I always wanted? Hadn't I just crossed over? I'd just made my first big sale, and during Basel, no less.

"Hey, *artista*," Leo calls out when I'm at the door. "Congratulations. I'll be home early tomorrow, let's hang out for the whole day, okay? Celebrate? I'm leaving soon and—" His voice is earnest and nervous.

"I'll be there."

WHEN I get home, I plop myself onto the bed. Tony's face is running in my mind in circles. I wish he were here—celebration sex. My hands drift down under my underwear. Should I go tomorrow? Would it be all bad? What does he want? I'm hot and palpitating, rubbing faster. Tony's beard against me, rough. Faster. Arching back. Aching. Tony. Fast. And, release. Why aren't they ever this intense when you're really fucking? Total and complete. The ease through my toes, a fast and electric rush. Lingering. But then no one to touch, no one to cling to or hold or kiss, or rest inside you afterwards. No softness, just the artificial bang. Okay, Veronica: if you wake up on time, you'll decide what to do about sailing. But for now, let this smooth ride drift you into sleep.

I wake up naturally, sun shining through the windows. Rested. I look at my clock: 9:00 a.m. If I go sailing with Tony, I'll miss some of the Basel appointments Lee has set up; I'll miss my last day with Leo. If I don't go, I'll miss Tony and what he might have to say. I feel split apart, like I can't make this simple decision, so I go with impulse, and let myself be driven by the burning in my chest.

AT THE DOCK, there's Tony, thirty feet away by the boat, waiting, pacing, wearing his pink fishing hat (though he's never gone fishing), his red beard flickering like flame. I want to run to him, put out the flame with my saliva. But I don't. I freeze. Instead, Tony begins to walk toward me.

"*Gordita*," Tony says when he reaches me.

Gordita, gordita. Bubi.

Tony extends his hand, intertwines it with mine. Tenderness takes its roots inside me. His chubby hand.

My father's hand. A puffy, waxy thing in his coffin. Even in the coffin, a handsome man. *What a handsome man.* Salt-and-pepper hair. Silver. Temper-less and quiet.

I look out onto the water. The world is vast but my heart feels small and pressed together, constricted and sealed like in a plastic vacuum. Pain returns, and I wonder if it will ever disappear. Mom throwing her body over Dad. *I'm sorry.* Is Tony sorry? For what? What has he done, except stop loving me? And what is this, this now—him standing before me, staring straight into me?

"What are you looking for?" I ask Tony, softly.

"What do you mean?"

"What do you see when you look at me?"

He says nothing.

"What do you want?" I ask again, determined to get an answer from him.

"I just want to go sailing, *gorda*," he says, laughing a little.

"That's it?"

"That's it," he says, as if not knowing what else there could be.

But there's so much more.

I take my hand from his, releasing the pressure point of our shared pulse, until the beat I feel in my fingertips is mine alone. Tony changes the subject. "*Qué día más lindo*," he says, sadness filtering through as he looks straight up at the sky. Behind him, the water is inviting, so inviting, I almost want to undress and jump in. And let go.

Let it all go. But then I remember Hawaii. And I hold back, my feet gripping the dock.

"I'm sorry," I say, "I can't go sailing with you." The heat rising higher in me, singeing, the hole growing bigger.

Tony doesn't respond, he just looks down, surprised, and I realize how compliant I've always been with him, how really he's always gotten what he wanted out of me, but I've gotten very little of what I truly need out of him. "*Gordita,*" he says again. I want to stop hearing him say that.

"I know what I need, Tony."

I give him a kiss on the cheek. I take his body in my arms, hug him, and I turn and walk away.

As I walk, the heat fills my face, agitating every nerve ending. I'm worried I've done the wrong thing. But something tells me to keep walking. And I do. Suddenly, peace enters like I imagine heroin rushing in must feel, straight through the vein. And I'm not quite sure why, it's just there, this sensation of calm.

A text from Leo: *c u soon. On my way back.*

ok, c u.

There's silence, except for the creaking of the dock as the water rocks it lightly, the sound of the waves, carrying me. Like my ear in a shell, my whole body in a shell, Sandra's ear to Fern's secrets.

Shell.

Leo.

Tony.

Dad.

I'll be okay, Dad. Somewhere, always, there will be a cathedral to catch me. A piece of canvas, waiting for me to fill it, a board waiting to be set afloat, an altar piece, our Sainte-Chapelle.

Right in front of me, a glint shines off something like stained glass, a prism somewhere, scattering light—a rainbow. Such a thing. To really look. Red, yellow, green, blue, purple. Like the patches of my father, his shirts, Fern's dresses. White. Blue. So much blue. And

I realize that that's the thing about light, about white light. White only *seems* like a blank canvas, like shock, or a new slate, a void. But it's not. White is just the opposite, it's really all colors locked in one. Separated by a prism, there it is, made visible, every single one, right in front of me. Maybe white is the true color of mourning. And all I have to do is let the colors unfurl as they might, as they want to, and with whatever force, or pain, or joy. This is the process, just like filling the canvas, or the gesso-white board of my *Altar Piece*.

Which means that, also, this thing I thought was a hole in my heart — it may not be a hole at all, but a thing too full. I'll have to take it apart to understand it. Loosen it, let it pulse with a lighter weight. Just like white light scattering and unthreading into strands and bits of color.

My father is gone. And Tony, I don't know what Tony is, but if he's chosen to forever sail away instead of anchor, if he can't figure it out, then I can choose back, and I can move on. That's the difference, isn't it, between me and Dad and Mom and Nina, and Tony. Mom and me and Dad and Nina, we had no choice. We're simply part of each other's rainbows of white light. But Tony's a mixed color, something made, and with him, with him it's a choice. Sometimes it's the mixed colors that make all the difference, but only if the mixture can manage to keep its particular clarity. Like this shade of blue I'm drenched in: translucent. I still love Tony, with all my heart, hole and all, it doesn't fade, not in an instant, and maybe never, nor does the shade of red he leaves behind, imprinted in me, or the pang that remains like a phantom limb. But that doesn't mean I can't keep walking.

Love. What a thing. More than we knew.

Acknowledgments

There are so many people I want and need to thank. This book has been a long time coming, and even writing these notes, I'm so filled with gratitude that I'm brimming.

Here goes: First, I need to thank my mother, whose undying support for her weird little writer has been endless and bountiful, and I know it hasn't been easy all the time. To my stepdad (dad), for his absolute grace and generosity and all-around wonderfulness, you are a massive blessing in our lives. To my grandfather, Severo Rivases, who taught me how to be an artist. To my grandmother, Dulce Rivases, whose endless love has given me an eternal shield. To Caryl Phillips, my true mentor and great friend, thank you for the consistent care, guidance, and abundance of love all of these years. Mary Gordon, who called me into her office one day at Barnard after class and told me, "You can write; come see me every week and bring me something to read." I did, and it meant the world to me (thank you!). To the University of Miami's MFA program (where I wrote the first draft of this book), particularly to A. Manette Ansay and Jane Alison. Manette, especially you—you sat with me on so many days and helped me edit this manuscript down, back in 2008, from a 600-plus-page beast into a book. I often wonder at the absolute gift of that, and count myself exceptionally lucky. To David Horvitz and Francie Bishop Good, I can easily say that your support has changed my life. That is not an overstatement—your belief in the power of art, and your gifts, they leave me in awe. To Mitchell Kaplan, for everything you've done for me, and for Miami; for Books & Books. To Wole Soyinka, for your time in Abeokuta, for all of your astonishing generosity. To Barbara Bell (Mrs. Bell), on whose podium I wrote many, many years ago, "If I ever become a writer, it will have been because of you." To Carrollton School of the Sacred Heart—the bedrock of my education. And finally, to Rosalie Morales Kearns, who said *yes* to this book, who opened her heart to it and brought it into the world.

About the Author

VANESSA GARCIA was born in the Cuban satellite city of Miami, to Cuban-emigré parents. She grew up in the midst of her grandfather's books and watercolors, and her grandmother's lush yard filled with citrus and mango trees. By the time she started school, she was already writing and painting.

Since then she has pursued her love of both art and writing along simultaneous paths, with a BA in English and art history from Barnard College, Columbia University; a creative writing MFA from the University of Miami; paintings and installations exhibited throughout the United States and the Caribbean; and plays produced on stages as far-flung as Edinburgh, Miami, New York, and Los Angeles. Her most recent plays include *The Cuban Spring*; *Grace, Sponsored by Monteverde*; and *The Crocodile's Bite*. As a journalist, feature writer, and essayist, Garcia has published pieces in the *Los Angeles Times*, the *Miami Herald*, the *Washington Post*, and numerous other publications. She's also a *Huffington Post* blogger.

Currently she is writer in residence at the Deering Estate, whose lushness reminds her of her grandmother's backyard. She is also a a Schaeffer Fellow at the University of California, Irvine, where she is at work on a memoir about American-born Cubans titled *Our Cuban Routes*.

White Light is her first novel. For more about Vanessa, please visit her website: www.vanessagarcia.org.

Also from Shade Mountain Press

EGG HEAVEN: STORIES
Robin Parks

Lyrical tales of diner waitresses and their customers, living the un-glamorous life in Southern California.

"Illuminates a world entirely its own" —*Kenyon Review*

"A skilled and elegiac storyteller" —René Steinke

Paperback, 150 pages, $16.95, October 2014

HER OWN VIETNAM (*Novel*)
Lynn Kanter

Decades after serving as a U.S. Army nurse in Vietnam, a woman confronts buried wartime memories and unresolved family issues.

"Compassionate and perceptively told" —*Foreword Reviews*

Silver Award, Indiefab Book of the Year, War & Military Fiction

Paperback, 211 pages, $18.95, November 2014

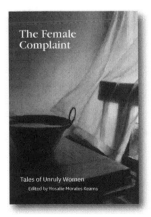

THE FEMALE COMPLAINT (*Anthology*)
Edited by Rosalie Morales Kearns

Short stories by women featuring nonconformists, troublemakers, and other indomitable females.

"Spellbinding…. A vital addition to contemporary literature" —*Kirkus*

"The stories sing off the page" —Rene Denfeld

Paperback, 327 pages, $24.95, November 2015

Shade Mountain Press
www.ShadeMountainPress.com